Murder
Most
Academic

Murder Most Academic

David Stewart

iUniverse, Inc.
New York Lincoln Shanghai

Murder Most Academic

iUniverse books may be ordered through booksellers or by contacting:

iUniverse
2021 Pine Lake Road, Suite 100
Lincoln, NE 68512
www.iuniverse.com
1-800-Authors (1-800-288-4677)

This is a work of fiction. Any resemblance to real persons, locales, or events is unintended and is purely coincidental.

ISBN: 0-595-33334-6 (Pbk)
ISBN: 0-595-66848-8 (Cloth)

Printed in the United States of America

Prologue

JEREMY BRAND'S EARLY-MORNING work habits had started to betray him not long after his 40th birthday, making him drowsy after dinner and ready for bed, especially when he was alone. He'd been up before the sun this day, preparing lecture notes; he thought a little light reading would make a good bedtime counterpoint. He looked through the stack of mail on his desk for the latest issue of *Wine Spectator* but couldn't find it, and then remembered seeing it in the wine cellar earlier. He pulled on a gray cardigan—such an old favorite that his blue oxford-cloth shirt showed through it at the elbows—before descending the basement stairs to the climate-controlled cellar, where the temperature was always a perfect but cool 55°F. As soon as he flipped the light switch, Brand saw the magazine on the tasting table, but the rest of what his eyes took in turned his legs to cement. Hanging from one of the bottle racks were several plastic milk jugs half-filled with clear liquid. A fuse ran from each one to a candle on the floor. The candle's wick ran along its side, not in the middle, and it was burning. It was not difficult for Brand to see that it was an incendiary device rigged to produce a spreading flame. What he could not see was the hand holding the wine bottle that hit him on the head.

The flames cast a reddish glow over the windows. Smoke seeped underneath the door, and the roar of the fire grew louder as the fumes filled the room. He grabbed a sheet from the bed, ran water on it in the bathtub, then threw it around and over his head. He opened the bedroom door but recoiled from the heat that struck him in the face. He turned around and backed crab-like past the flames and down the hallway to his son's room. But his feet were leaden. He could not lift them. He heard the crash of the roof as it gave way directly over the bedroom where his wife and child lay. But he knew it was too late. Too late. Too late.

It had been a while since that dream had haunted Brand, but it always seemed to come at unexpected times. When he regained consciousness he imagined himself in bed, but then he remembered. He thought of the words of

Descartes: "I have often, while dreaming, been deceived." But this was no dream. He was not deceived. Brand blinked sight back into his eyes, and the scene snapped into focus. The plastic milk jugs still hung from the racks. The candle's flame had nearly reached the fuse. Whatever he did, he knew he needed to do it quickly. His only hope, he thought, was to douse the flame somehow. But he couldn't move. He was strapped to a chair with transparent packaging tape that held his arms tight against his torso and his legs firmly to the chair. The chair was taped to one of the floor-to-ceiling wine racks which, because of its valuable contents, was bolted to the wall. The phone on the tasting table was just out of reach, but his mouth was taped shut anyway. Though a pile driver seemed to be drilling inside his head, he summoned all his strength to flex his body against the confining tape. Straining to breathe through his nose, he tensed and released his muscles in a rocking rhythm. The chair conveyed the vibrations to the wine rack, and it began to shake, ever so slightly. Resting among the top rows were some of Brand's most expensive Bordeaux wines—Pomerols, St. Juliens, Margaux—but no thought of their value kept him from his effort.

Flex and release. Flex and release. The minutes seemed like hours but Brand maintained his rhythmic rocking. At last he heard the ring of glass bottles shifting, and that small encouragement gave him the strength to continue. His muscles were sore from the effort and his head burned with pain, but after what seemed like an eternity one of the bottles from the top of the rack crashed to the floor—several feet from the candle. Brand saw that it was a '27 Haut-Brion.

More rocking, and another bottle flew out, a Lafite-Rothschild, but it too fell wide of the candle. This could work, Brand thought. It had to work. Another bottle crashed to the floor, splashing its expensive contents on the cement. But still the candle burned, its flame creeping ever closer to the fuse. Though Brand felt his strength ebbing, he rocked as if in a trance. He thought of his wine as much as of his own safety. If the house burned, his wine would be lost. What bottles were not burst by the heat would be cooked, the wine ruined. He remembered a California wine collector who put all his wine in the swimming pool when his house was threatened by a brush fire fanned by Santa Ana winds. The house was destroyed, but the swimming pool saved the wine while also soaking off all the labels. The collector enjoyed blind tastings for years.

Nausea pulled him out of his reverie, and he worried that he might pass out. The thought of dying in his own cellar sent such a jolt through him that another bottle fell from the rack—a Château d'Yquem, striking the floor just an inch from the fuse. The golden elixir erupted like a fountain and doused the candle. The flame was out. So was Brand.

Chapter 1

"IT IS A MISTAKE," BRAND WROTE, "to think of events in our lives as completely isolated from events in the lives of others." He had open before him the book *Process and Reality*. Always meticulous in the preparation of his lecture notes, he checked a reference and then continued. "The philosopher A. N. Whitehead argued that it is an error to think of any event as completely isolated. 'An isolated event is not an event,' is the way he put it. All events form a system, and whatever happens in one part of that system affects all other parts. The effect may be great or small, but the interconnectedness is there."

While Brand prepared his notes in the pre-dawn darkness, across campus gloved hands were opening the door to a private academic office. A thin beam from the intruder's penlight pointed the way to the only other source of light the visitor dared to turn on. Skillful fingers booted the system and brought the computer screen to life. A short series of keystrokes opened the directory, and then the intruder quickly opened and closed files, directing some of them to the laser printer which, with soft hums and clicks, went about its task.

First known by his footsteps, then glimpsed through the curtained window of the dean's office, a Calloway State security officer made his rounds of the campus. Hoping that the officer would not notice the glow of the thousands of pixels dancing on the monitor, the trespasser moved into the shadows of the office and waited, heart pounding, until the Doppler effect on the guard's footsteps served notice that he had moved on. Moving back to the computer, the intruder continued to open and close files while the laser printer stacked the completed pages in its collection tray. Gloved hands slipped the printed pages into a portfolio and returned the computer and printer to their sleep modes, then the trespasser slipped through a filing room and out the dean's own private doorway to the hall. Soft-soled shoes made no noise as their wearer took the back stairs to the building's side door. The campus was just beginning to be illuminated by the rising sun.

Brand finished his notes and walked into the kitchen for a second cup of coffee just as the sun peeked over the horizon. His large Victorian house was one of three dozen or so built in the late 1800s at the edge of the campus of Calloway State University. Neighborhoods with a campus view were then considered the choicest building spots for private residences. Over the years most of the faculty moved to the suburbs, though the small farms and wooded lots outside the city could hardly be called suburbia. Faculty who came to Calloway State University from New York City saw this as an opportunity for country living denied them during their urban careers. When the nineteenth-century houses close to campus appeared on the real estate market, the university snapped them up and replaced most of them with new academic buildings. The prevailing attitude was to replace old buildings with new ones so that the campus could project a contemporary character. The replacements were the worst examples of misapplied Bauhaus style, drab warehouses propped against the central college green. Some of the grand old houses survived despite the pressures of urban renewal, carved up into offices for various centers and institutes. Only a few remained in private hands. Brand's was one of them.

Brand taught courses in popular culture, a field that includes everything from television to comic books. A culture's ephemeral manifestations, he claimed, show the ever-changing nature of its self-understanding. Popular culture is an interdisciplinary area that cuts across traditional subjects and allowed him to teach courses that attracted large numbers of students, and detective fiction had become a specialty area for him. At first students thought courses like "Literary Themes in Detective Fiction" would be easy, but they soon realized that Professor Brand's standards were high and his assignments demanding.

As Brand walked back to his study, coffee cup in hand, his housekeeper, Hélène Écoles, greeted him with her usual cheerfulness and asked what he wanted for breakfast.

"Good morning, Hélène. Nothing for me, thanks. I'm meeting Sarah Giles for coffee this morning."

Écoles was a woman of a certain age who served as live-in cook and housekeeper, though in the latter role she supervised a local cleaning service more than she had to take to mop and broom herself. She was the widow of a close friend of Brand's father, and her employment in the household provided a welcome supplement to her late husband's pension.

"That's fine, professor. I'll go ahead and just make breakfast for Paul and me."

Paul Ruskin was a household member by default, having ceased his graduate work to take a job as researcher, editor, proofreader, manager of wine cellar records, and general investigator for Brand's various projects. Ruskin had accepted the position with the understanding that his commitment would be temporary, just until a teaching job came along. That was five years ago. The oversupply of literature Ph.D.s made it impossible for Ruskin to find a coveted tenure-track faculty appointment, and rather than accept a string of temporary, one-year jobs, which would make him something of a gypsy scholar traveling from university to university, Ruskin decided to continue working for Brand. The job kept him close to university life and allowed him to teach part-time at Calloway State. The master's degree he held was credential enough for that.

Through the open door of his study Brand saw Ruskin coming down the stairs from the second floor. The two greeted each other, and Brand added, "Paul, I've got some new wine catalogs for you to review. I'll leave them on the table in the cellar, but there's no hurry on them."

"Sure thing, Jeremy," Ruskin responded. "This is my light teaching day, so I should be able to look them over this morning."

Brand gathered his lecture notes and loaded up his briefcase in preparation for a day of professorial duties. At the Daily Grind, the campus coffee shop, he found a table, ordered two cups of Mocha Java, and was scanning the front page of the *New York Times* when Giles pulled out a chair across from him and sat down.

"Sorry I'm late, Jeremy. I hope this meeting won't make you late to class."

"It won't. I went ahead and ordered us some coffee. I hope you like Mocha Java."

"My favorite. Thanks." Giles took a sip of coffee, then put down the cup and pushed her graying pageboy behind her ears and cleared her throat. "You probably wondered why I wanted to meet you like this, Jeremy. My department is so politicized that there are few people I trust enough to confide in. That's why I called you. I need to talk to someone I trust, especially since I may not even have a job in a few months."

Brand guessed the purpose of this breakfast meeting: Sarah wanted to talk about her upcoming review for tenure—the decision making a professor a permanent member of the faculty rather than a probationary employee.

"You're worried about your tenure review."

"And with good reason. I know for sure that Dean McKenzie is going to deny me tenure. He's a sexist pig. His review panel is just a sham. His mind is already made up. My own department's tenure committee split on my case, so anything less than a unanimous recommendation gives him all the room he needs to turn me down."

"To what do you attribute your department's action?"

"Academic prejudice. Research on women in business is new and different from what most of the old guard are used to. They don't understand it. And some of the members of my department just don't like me. They haven't even gotten used to having women in the department."

"Sounds like you're giving up," Brand said.

"Not at all. I'll give it my best shot, of course, but I won't be surprised when Clem turns me down. Disappointed, but not surprised."

"There's not much I can do, Sarah. We're in different colleges of the university, so there's no chance at all that I would be appointed to your tenure review committee."

"I know. That's not the reason I wanted to talk. You're a respected senior faculty member. Everyone trusts you. I just wanted someone to know that there's a lot going on that most people aren't aware of. If something bad should happen, I just wanted someone to know that events might not be what they seem."

"So I'm that 'someone,'" Brand said. "Can you be a little more specific, especially about what you mean by 'something bad'? Just what are you afraid of?"

"Let me just say that I know things that some people wish I didn't know. They want me to go away. Frankly, I sometimes think that tenure is the least of my worries."

"Sounds bad, Sarah. If you think you're in some kind of danger, why not go to the police?"

"They'd dismiss me as a nervous Nellie. Besides, what would I say? Someone in my college doesn't like me? Half the faculty in my department don't like the other half. Disliking your colleagues isn't a crime. If it were, most of the faculty would be in jail."

"You haven't given me much to go on," Brand said. "But if there is anything I can do, you know you can count on me. As for your research, I can appreciate how you feel. Not everyone thinks that popular culture is a legitimate area for scholarship either. Just keep on doing your work, and it will validate itself. Remember that the Harvard faculty didn't think engineering was a legitimate field for university study either, so some of their colleagues left Harvard and founded MIT. Yesterday's discovery has a way of becoming part of today's hot field."

"Maybe, but not if Dean McKenzie has anything to do with it."

"Clem? You think he's opposed to your work?"

"Think? I don't think he's opposed to it. I know he is opposed to it."

Giles delivered a lengthy recital of her recent meeting with the dean. She shared the common faculty dislike of deans, no matter how good or bad they happened to be as administrators. Deans represent power, and Giles, like many professors, held the view that faculty should be the real power in a university, and deans were only to be tolerated, not respected.

"I knew I was in trouble," Giles said, "when I saw the composition of the review committee. The dean chooses the committee, as you know. Even though he asks for my recommendation for one person familiar with my work, he ultimately chooses its membership. He took my recommendation but named three others to the committee, two of whom have made no secret of their dislike of scholarship with a feminist point of view. I'm dead even before the committee meets."

"And who was your choice?"

"Cynthia Lemaster."

The server came and took their orders—a bagel and cream cheese for Brand, dry whole-wheat toast for Giles.

Brand took another sip of coffee. "Who are the ones the dean selected?"

"Shirley Warner, Ray Jones and Archie Scott."

"Tell me about them," Brand said. "What makes you think they'll be a problem for you?"

"Well, let's start with Shirley. She has the classic queen bee complex. Since she's made it as a tenured full professor in the School of Mass Communication, she wants to be the senior female scholar in the college who gets to decide who stays and who goes. She thinks feminist scholarship is an oxymoron."

"And Jones? I don't think I know him."

"The classic male chauvinist. If you looked up the term in the dictionary, you would find his picture there."

"And Scott? What about him?"

"How should I put it—Archie is so weak. He has no backbone at all, a regular Caspar Milquetoast. He'll do whatever he thinks the dean wants."

"Since we're in different colleges, Sarah, why are you talking to me about this? I don't know how I can help."

"The fact that you're not in my college means that I feel I can trust you. Among my colleagues I'm not sure who would run to the dean with what I've just said and who wouldn't."

The bagels and toast arrived. Brand picked up his knife and began spreading the cream cheese.

"I can hear the worry in your voice. I really wish you'd give me more to go on. Can't you at least fill in a few of the details?"

"No, not now," Giles said. "But I have information about several colleagues that they wish I didn't have. What I know is so explosive that…well, it wouldn't surprise me if in a few days the entire academic community of Calloway State University feels like a bomb has gone off."

"Really, Sarah, aren't you being melodramatic?"

"Not at all. You don't know what I know."

Brand took a bite of bagel and tried to sort out the contradictory things he was hearing. Finally he asked, "So, what do you want me to do, Sarah?"

"Nothing, really. I just felt someone should know that strange things and shocking disclosures may take place, and soon. And if anything happens to me, I don't want them to get away with it."

"Them? Who's 'them'?"

"I can't say, Jeremy. Just trust me to know that my concerns are not idle fantasies. And if things happen that make you recall this conversation, remember what I've told you." She looked at her watch, stood up, and grabbed her purse and briefcase off the table. "I've got to get to class. Remember, don't let them get away with it."

Brand finished his coffee and puzzled over his conversation with Sarah Giles. When she said, "Don't let them get away with it," who are "they" and what is "it"? He wished she had been more forthright with him. Her fears seemed to be unformed yet real. He resolved to talk with her again.

Chapter 2

ARCHIBALD SCOTT HAS A DIRTY LITTLE SECRET. He holds full-time teaching positions at two universities. And neither university knows.

He didn't intend to hold down two jobs at the same time; it just sort of happened, an artifact of convenience and administrative negligence. While Scott was on a year's leave from Calloway State University to do research in the Library of Congress on the history of management theory in American business, he thought he would apply for several interesting academic positions just to see what happened. He wasn't looking for a change of position, but with a lot of unstructured time on his hands, he thought he would sort of test the waters. The job search proved to be more successful than he imagined.

When Scott was offered—and found himself accepting—a professorship at Middletown College, he had every intention of resigning from Calloway State. But he delayed telling his dean at Calloway about the Middletown job, and when the head of Calloway's management department agreed to give Scott a three-day-a-week teaching schedule—so he could turn his reading notes into publishable articles, he promised—it occurred to him that he could probably pull off both jobs. He'd give himself a year to decide if he really liked the pace at the smaller college. If he did, then he'd resign from Calloway.

That first year was hell. Scott taught at Calloway Monday through Wednesday, then drove fourteen hours to Middletown, where he then taught Thursday, Friday and Saturday. Sometimes he could get cheap air fares, depending on the season, but usually he drove. Few members of the faculty at Middletown were willing to teach the all-day Saturday seminars for mid-level executives enrolled in the college's executive MBA program. Scott was happy with this unusual schedule. He told his colleagues at Middletown that he was willing to have a killer weekend because it gave him more time the rest of the week to prepare articles for publication based on his research at the Library of

Congress. He wasn't sure how long this deception would work, because he'd produced nothing publishable and wasn't likely to.

He finessed questions about why he hadn't moved to Middletown, pleading the need to delay relocation until his house was sold, and then claiming that the market was saturated and he was unable to sell. He also lied about the days he wasn't at Middletown. He claimed to need to visit various research libraries and to spend a lot of time at the Library of Congress. So far the lies seemed to be working.

Hard as it was, the first year came and went, and the second year seemed easier. Given the geographical distance between Middletown and Calloway, Scott felt that his secret was safe, since the chance of interaction between the two institutions was remote—not impossible, but unlikely.

He developed a smug self-justification for his dual life. He was doing both jobs adequately. He never missed a class. He was known on both campuses as an excellent teacher, attentive to students, careful in marking their papers. He reasoned that Calloway and Middletown were lucky to have a person of his ability, and neither institution had grounds for complaint. Scott convinced himself that what he was doing was not unethical, just shrewd. He was giving Middletown its money's worth. He told himself that without his Ph.D.-endowed presence on campus, Middletown wouldn't have had a chance of accreditation for its executive business degree.

But Scott's professional life at Calloway was beginning to show strains because of his dual loyalties. Since the promised publications had not materialized he knew he would eventually suffer for it. "Publish or perish" was real and not just a slogan at Calloway, especially under Dean McKenzie.

As the dean of the College of Professional Studies, McKenzie blew into town with his independent wealth and spendthrift ways, and at some level of his being Scott delighted at being able to put something over on someone so pompous. McKenzie's luxury cars were bad enough, but what annoyed everyone most was The House. Modeled on the White House, the dean's residence was the source of constant ridicule. Though nowhere near as large as the famous mansion on Pennsylvania Avenue, there was no mistaking its architectural and social design; it even included its own version of the Truman balcony. Such a pretentious construction would look out of place most anywhere, but in College Falls it was ridiculous, and not only because of the presidential aspirations it radiated. Scott believed the rumor that McKenzie had his eye on the university presidency and that The House was part of his scheme to project the image of the rising star.

Scott was nursing his hatred of McKenzie as he walked up the steps of Bucks Hall, named for its donor, Ralph Bucks. The building housed both the dean's office and the department of management. Scott still resented the cracks made by more than one liberal arts faculty, such as, "Aptly named, since the business school's mission is to teach students to chase bucks."

Scott trudged upstairs to his own office first to leave his briefcase and then back downstairs to the administrative offices. He was nervous, given the secret he guarded. A pear-shaped man about 50 pounds overweight for his five-foot, ten-inch frame, Scott was out of breath from negotiating all the stairs when he arrived at the dean's suite of offices. The dean had called yesterday and asked Scott to stop by "for a brief chat about several items."

Sitting there in the waiting room, Scott reflected on just how much he hated the dean. His was an equal-opportunity hatred in that he disliked all deans, but he hated this one with an intensity that bordered on the pathological. Even if Scott were a psychologist, which he was not—his brush with psychology having been limited to a single undergraduate course in the subject—he might not have been able to understand the depth of his loathing for Clement McKenzie. He was convinced that McKenzie had become dean for all the wrong reasons, not that Scott considered the right reasons to be much better than the wrong ones. Some academics become deans because it advances their careers. Others become deans because they enjoy the power of the position, the power to make or break careers, the power to give or withhold largess depending on their whim, or simply the power to say no and enjoy saying it. In Scott's view, McKenzie was that kind of dean.

The last time Scott met with the dean, all his stereotypical views about deans, and this dean in particular, were proved correct once again. In the first place, McKenzie didn't look like he belonged in a university. He dressed in suits that said "expensive" in everything about them, from their cut that shielded his expanding middle to the imported silk and wool worsted that he favored but which gave his clothes a shiny look. Their cut also did not look right to Scott, not that he was a fashion authority himself, since his own appearance made him look even more rumpled than most professors. Scott persisted in purchasing suits one size smaller than his current proportions on the unproved theory that this would encourage him to lose weight. The result was that his suit coats were too tight across the shoulders and so snug in the middle that he rarely could button them. McKenzie's suits, in contrast, fit well, too well. They seemed to Scott's untrained eye to be trendy Italian, better worn, he thought, by a movie producer than an academic dean.

Another thing that Scott could not abide were McKenzie's shirts with their monogrammed initials on the cuffs that extended just far enough from the jacket sleeve to insure their visibility. The shoes were Italian, too, Scott thought: alligator or lizard, maybe snake. The pastel shirts with white collars and cuffs were finished with cuff links set with diamonds or chunks of gold nugget. And why did McKenzie have to wear a Rolex watch with diamonds instead of numerals and a diamond pinkie ring? Though McKenzie was only in his fifties, his expensively cut and blow-dried gray hair was calculated to convey the look of a senior statesman or the CEO of a Fortune 500 company. Scott thought all this just made the dean look…well, old.

His last confrontation with McKenzie had been over the promised but nonexistent publications that were to be the outcome of the sabbatical. The problem with talking with the dean is that you never knew how the conversation would turn out. It usually turned out badly, as that one had. The fact that McKenzie had been an army colonel before entering academic life had something to do with it. The dean was most comfortable dressing down a subordinate like a commanding officer humiliating a new second lieutenant. Such behavior did not go over well in higher education, where interpersonal conflict is much less open and often couched in euphemisms, though nonetheless vicious for all that.

The topic of that meeting was the connection between research and raises. No research, no raise. For McKenzie the formula was as simple as that. He was a believer in the stick over the carrot. The only real motivator at his disposal in dealing with tenured faculty, he thought, was the annual raise. Once you grant tenure you have only one chance a year to shape behavior, and that was the annual compensation determination. The reasons he gave varied but usually had to do with research, or the lack of it. At one level Scott didn't care about the raise; it was only three percent after all, and he had a secret second job. The thing that galled him was the reaction of his colleagues. Such punishment did not remain unknown. Everybody's salary was on file in the library; the state's open records law required it. A zero raise elicited hypocritical expressions of pity from associates and feigned outrage at administration high-handedness. When a pie is to be sliced up, and one person gets no piece at all, the others get larger ones. Scott hated those false expressions of sympathy.

Scott had managed to keep his temper during the salary discussions with McKenzie, but just barely. He knew that the dean enjoyed seeing him squirm, and so he refused to give any overt indication that he was irritated by the dean's decision. Today's conversation would probably be a replay of the same topic, Scott thought, and would likely end in another zero raise this year. Worse things could happen, Scott told himself. It wasn't the prospect of no salary increase that made bile rise up in his stomach but the mere fact of having to talk to the dean at all.

Naomi Beals, the dean's flashy, big-haired secretary, announced that McKenzie was ready to see him, and Scott felt the same nervousness he had the last time he visited his dentist—a good comparison since he was about to undergo the academic equivalent of a root canal.

Scott stepped into McKenzie's office. Small beads of perspiration broke out on his forehead, but the hank of hair drooping onto his eyebrows hid them from view. The dean tried to smile, but Scott could tell by the strained lines at the edge of the dean's lips that the effort was forced.

"Sit down, Archie. Our conversation is not going to be pleasant, so we should start out with both of us sitting down."

Oh shit! Scott thought. He's found out somehow.

"I'll cut to the chase, Archie. I want your letter of resignation on my desk by Monday. Since this is Thursday, that will give you the weekend to focus your thoughts. You can state it however you want and give whatever reasons seem best to you, but the bottom line is that you will leave Calloway State University at the end of this academic year. No additional year's salary, no separation package. We will make the break clean and swift."

Though usually not at a loss for words, Scott said nothing, realizing that McKenzie probably had found him out but still hoping that the reason for the dean's assault was something else.

"Did you hear me, Archie? I want your sorry ass out of this university."

Still uncertain where to go with this, Scott decided to try bluffing. "Why in the world, Clem, would you expect me to agree to something like that?"

"Don't play your bullshit games with me, Archie. I know about your Middletown position. Don't even attempt to deny it. If you don't resign, I'll see that proceedings to strip you of tenure are instituted against you immediately. There will be hearings, all your dirty linen aired in public. If you choose that course of action, you don't stand a chance of avoiding professional disgrace. If you resign, I'll let you go quietly. Maybe you can get another job. I won't tell any future employer about your double-dipping scheme, and I won't blow the whistle on you at Middletown. I just want you out of my college. I don't need to ruin you permanently, at least not if you cooperate."

"You can't do that Clem. I've got tenure and—"

McKenzie cut him off mid-sentence. "I not only can do it, I will do it. There's really no point in discussing it further."

Scott sat in stunned silence. Excuses tumbled over each other in the fog of his consciousness, but he decided there was no point in denying anything. How did the dean know?

"Do you mind if I ask how you found out?"

"Yes, I mind. It's none of your business. The point is, I do know about your little scheme, and I don't intend to tolerate it. Frankly, I would enjoy seeing you become a public spectacle, but it would soak up a lot of time, time that I don't want to waste on you. There would be hearings, lawyers to talk to, maybe depositions, depending on whether you were stupid enough to fight the loss of tenure. I would rather have a clean end to your association with Calloway State. Besides, public disclosure of your dishonesty would hurt the university, and to avoid that I'm willing to let you sneak quietly away. If you refuse, I'll see that no college anywhere will ever hire you."

"Don't you threaten me, you egotistical asshole."

"Archie, please, please. Don't let your emotions overwhelm your good sense. I am not threatening you. I'm offering you a good deal. You'll ignore it at your peril. And, there's another thing we need to discuss."

Scott said nothing, and the dean continued.

"One of the faculty I appointed to Sarah Giles's tenure review committee will be on sick leave the rest of the term, so I'm appointing you to the committee as a replacement. The fact of your dual employment gives me some pause at doing so, but I had already informed the other members of the committee about appointing you before I found out about your scheme. To back out now would raise too many questions, so I've decided to keep you on the committee in spite of your wretched judgment about your own professional life. At least you have an ability to tell the difference between real research and sham efforts that present themselves as 'research.'"

The dean moved two sets of fingers in the air, making the implied quotation marks around the word "research." The dean wants me to vote against Sarah, Scott thought. That's why he's letting me resign instead of firing me.

"Now why should I agree to do that, Clem, after what you've just threatened me with?"

"Threatened? I didn't threaten you, Archie. I gave you a noble alternative, a way out of the mess you have created for yourself that allows you to leave this university with your honor intact. Of course, I expect you to act like an academic while you are here and pull your weight. If you fight me on this, Archie, I can always pull the plug on you and forget that I am trying to help you exit gracefully."

"I get it. You want me to leave Calloway and vote against tenure for Sarah Giles. If I refuse do to either, you'll destroy my career. I recognize blackmail when I see it."

"Really, Archie. 'Blackmail' is such an ugly word. I'm appealing to you as a colleague and a scholar to do the right thing both about your professional situation and your obligation as a scholar to help me keep the standards for scholarship high in this college. But it's your choice. You can do things the easy way or the hard way. Think about it."

Scott sat in silence, not knowing what to say next.

"This conversation is over, Archie. Remember, your letter will be on my desk Monday if you know how to act in your own self-interest. If not…well, you can figure that out for yourself."

His head throbbing from the surge of adrenaline, Scott shuffled like a sleepwalker and slowly climbed the stairs to his own office, which was a mess—not the sort of attractive clutter that faculty offices often exhibit, but a genuine disaster. Scott's two jobs did not allow him time for even scant organizational efforts, but his interests had never run to neatness anyway. Now his professional life was just as disordered as his office.

A pile of old copies of the *Wall Street Journal* littered one corner. The top of the desk wasn't even visible, so covered was it by unopened campus mail, publishers' catalogs, unread journals, and the castoffs of an undisciplined academic life.

Alongside the desk and stacked three and four deep, the boxes containing research notes from his sabbatical remained untouched despite his representations to the dean. Books protruded from the shelves without any regard for order, many of them stacked horizontally instead of vertically. File folders bulging with yellowed notes, clippings from journals, and other evidences of class preparation and past research efforts filled the remaining space atop the books. The crammed shelves forced yet more books to be piled directly on the floor. Unopened boxes containing examination copies of textbooks, sent free by publishers in hopes of a book adoption, formed yet more stacks in front of the bookshelves. Dust overlaid everything, for though Calloway's custodians regularly emptied wastebaskets and vacuumed the floors they did nothing else. Without attention from the occupant of the office, the dust and grime grew like moss on a stone.

The one island of neatness in this sea of disorder was Scott's computer. Like most business schools, Calloway's management department invested heavily in technology on the assumption that computer knowledge was indispensable to a successful career in business. The department networked its computers, making e-mail the dean's favorite mode of communication and an effective mechanism for keeping in touch with faculty who seldom were to be found in their offices.

Scott loved e-mail, finding it a convenient way to communicate with students, who often felt more comfortable asking their professor a question electronically than by raising their hands in class. Class participation always risked the danger of looking stupid. Besides, they could also ask their questions at three o'clock in the morning when they liked to study, or were forced to study because of evenings spent in local bars. Scott also loved e-mail because he could use it to communicate with students when he was away from

Calloway in Middletown, and the students could not tell that he wasn't on the Calloway campus. When he was at Middletown, Scott downloaded his e-mail messages from Calloway's mainframe computer, answered them off line, and then sent his reply back to the mainframe with the same speed that he received them. From the students' vantage point, replies to their queries looked as if they came from Calloway, not from out of state. In one sense they did, because Scott's access was through the Calloway computer, and his long-distance calling was masked by the software protocols. Besides, few students would pore over the jumble of header information that precedes a message even if the codes could give away the fact that Scott was not on campus.

To communicate with his Middletown students, Scott used a laptop that he bought for the purpose and a free e-mail service from an Internet provider that allowed him to change the content of his "From" line to make it look like he was on campus.

Scott had other tricks to hide his double life. On the days he departed Calloway for Middletown he left his office door open so colleagues would think he was in the building, maybe at an important meeting or otherwise temporarily detained. Scott also left his computer on all the time, strengthening the impression that he might return to his office any moment. He protected his screen saver with a password, so no one could get into his computer files.

Scott sat down in his office chair, entered his password, and the monitor attached to his desktop computer came to life. With a couple of clicks of the mouse and one more password, he displayed his e-mail. With a few more keystrokes he deleted all the general announcements from the university news office and then scanned the remaining messages. Most were from students, but the one that got Scott's immediate attention was from Dean McKenzie. He opened the file and began to read.

TO: All Faculty in the College of Professional Studies
FROM: Dean McKenzie
SUBJECT: Travel Funds

Due to a severe budget shortage produced by the decline in enrollment this year, effective immediately all funds supporting faculty travel are frozen. I know that all college faculty will join me in this belt-tightening measure made necessary by the hard times thrust upon us.

Yeah, right, Scott thought. This from a dean who had just returned from an international trip ostensibly to generate new enrollments. He found it interesting that the travel ban—for that was what it effectively was, since few faculty would travel to many professional meetings at their own expense— came *after* the dean's own junket.

Scott realized how cagey McKenzie was and wished there were an easy way out of the professional quandary in which the dean had put him. His choices seemed so unsatisfactory. He searched his mind for ways the dean might have found out about his situation, not that it really mattered. Scott had decided after a year and a half at Middletown that he would rather continue teaching at Calloway State but had delayed acting on that decision. Now McKenzie was going to make it impossible. If he didn't resign as the dean was insisting, he might wind up with no job at all. Middletown would fire him if the college discovered his dual life. So would Calloway. McKenzie was right about that.

Scott felt trapped. His options seemed limited to two: accept the dean's proposal and leave Calloway State, or call the dean's bluff. Scott knew that the dean could not summarily dismiss him. Because of tenure Calloway State would have to go through a lengthy due-process proceeding to fire him, and the university would also have to give him an additional year's salary as severance pay according to the rules of the American Association of University Professors. But that would mean the end of his position at Middletown College unless he could keep his dual employment a secret there. His interior monologue continued. *Will the dean keep his word and not report to Middletown College what he knows? After McKenzie has the letter of resignation in hand, what will prevent him from calling the dean at Middletown and telling all? It's just the kind of thing he would do.*

No, Scott thought. He would not agree to the dean's demand, at least not until there were some assurances that McKenzie wouldn't sabotage the position at Middletown. What guarantee could the dean give that he would honor his promise and not reveal information about Scott's two jobs? And what about McKenzie's source? Could the same guarantee be counted on there? If he pressured Clem to put the offer in writing, maybe that would do the trick. It would be embarrassing to the dean to have to admit later that he allowed Scott's deception to remain unknown to the public.

No, things are not settled yet. Scott knew he needed another conference with the dean and promised himself that it would be different from the meeting he just left. He would be prepared next time, though he had no immediate sense of how he would strengthen his bargaining position. At the moment it appeared that McKenzie had the upper hand, and Scott began to see that his problems all centered on the dean. If something happened to the dean Scott knew he could keep his position at Calloway a bit longer and resign from Middletown in an orderly fashion that would not arouse suspicion. *But what are the chances of the dean's getting hit by a truck or dropping dead from a heart attack?* He could only wish.

He turned slowly away from his desk as if in a trance and began to stuff his briefcase with materials for his classes at Middletown. He was just ready to leave when Ray Jones stuck his head inside the open door.

"Got a minute, Archie? I need some advice."

Scott couldn't believe what he heard. Jones had a reputation in the college of being an opinionated boor who had views on everything and never took advice from anyone.

"Yeah, but make it quick, Ray. I've got an appointment." Scott's "appointment" was for a long drive to Middletown, and he needed to get Jones out of his office as soon as possible. Jones pulled up a chair beside Scott's desk. Not a good sign, Scott thought. He wants to talk.

"Thing is, Archie, Clem appointed me to serve on Sarah Giles's tenure review committee, and I understand you're now on it too."

"Yeah, I guess I am," Scott said.

"Well, I wish I didn't have to vote on Sarah Giles. I figure it's a no-win situation. If I vote for her, I'll be on the dean's shit list." Jones ran his hands through his stringy blond hair. "I think it's clear that he expects me to vote against her. He knows how I feel about so-called feminist scholarship."

"So, vote against her."

"But then I'll have to put up with abuse from all the feminazis in the college. What a great word that is. One thing that Rush Limbaugh got right."

Scott could tell that Jones was not there for advice but to brag about his important committee assignment.

"That's a tough one, Ray. I don't know what to tell you."

"Well, rumor has it that Sarah Giles is professionally dead. There is no way she's going to get tenure. Clem's just going through the motions with the committee. Good thing, too. What this college needs is more real scholars, not women spouting all this feminist stuff passed off as research."

"I'd be careful where you say things like that, Ray. Could get you in trouble if the wrong people heard you."

"Last time I looked, the First Amendment was still in force. Besides, what can they do to me? I've got tenure. They can't fire me—especially for making a controversial statement. After all that's what tenure is all about—protecting our free speech rights and allowing us to make statements about unpopular issues."

Scott's mind was elsewhere. He half-listened to Jones drone on about academic freedom and due process and the demise of scholarly standards now that women are entering the professoriate in great numbers with their demands for day care, maternity leave and changes in the climate they claim is hostile to full equal recognition.

"That's another thing about these women," Jones continued. "They complain that they aren't part of the informal networks in the institution—that they don't get invited out to lunch or for drinks after work by the guys, things like that. But when we do invite them, if one of us tells a joke that they think is off-color or uses profanity, you know, guy-type of talk, they get all upset about that and accuse us of creating a chilly climate or hostile environment. They can't have it both ways. If they want to be treated like one of the boys, then they have to toughen themselves up. Right now there are some women in my department I just won't talk to. I get beat up no matter what I say, so I might as well get beat up for not talking to them."

Scott was still pondering his conversation with the dean. Four days. He only had four days to write his letter of resignation, or Clem would destroy his academic future. Maybe he could think of some alternatives on his way to Middletown. Right now he had to get Jones out of his office.

"That's interesting, Ray, but I've really got to go."

"Yeah, right. Sorry I got carried away. As you can tell, I feel strongly about these things. Before the meeting, let's get together over a cup of coffee and talk about Sarah's 'research,'" he said using his two index fingers to indicate the quotation marks as he turned and left the office.

Scott completed his packing—exchanging his Calloway lecture notes for his Middletown ones—and then picked up his coat from the chair where Jones had been sitting and went into the hallway. He still could not think straight, but he did know one thing: All his problems centered on Clem McKenzie. If somebody else—anybody else—were dean, Scott knew he would have more options. *If only someone would kill the bastard.*

Chapter 3

"Business Sucks! Business Sucks! Business Sucks!" The chanting grew louder as the group of students approached Bucks Hall. Some of them carried crude signs stapled to sticks which bobbed up and down in the air to the rhythm of the chanting and displayed slogans with a common theme: "Down With the Hall of Mammon," "Stop Business Exploitation" and "Students Protesting Inequality."

The students at the front of the procession opened the doors to the building, and the entire horde marched in rhythm with their chants, amplified by the corridor outside the dean's suite. When the dean's secretary, Naomi Beals, opened the door to the hall to see what the ruckus was about, the demonstrators shoved her aside and flowed into the waiting room like water through a break in a dam.

"We want to talk to the dean," the scruffiest-looking one of the bunch said, sharp staccato raps on the desk accompanying his demands.

"He's…he's not, not here—" Beals stammered.

"That's a lie," one of the taller students called out over the group. "We know he always comes to work early."

"He's really not here," Beals said. "I wouldn't lie to you about that. Calm down, young man, and tell me why you want to see the dean."

"We'll tell him ourselves. You just get him in here right away."

Divorced and in her thirties, nothing in her experience prepared her for student demonstrations. This bunch looked frightening with their bodies pierced in various places and earrings more prevalent on the males than on the females, whose jewelry protruded from other pierced parts of their anatomy.

Beals was not afraid of students. The ones in the business program were in and out of the office all the time, but she contrasted those students—always so polite and well mannered—with the ones now occupying her office. They didn't look like the students she knew. And she wondered why they were so angry.

"What do you want?" she tried again.

"We want to talk to the dean. You just tell him to get his ass here right away." As the student said this, there was an accompanying murmur of "yeah," "damn right," and other mumbled assents from the assembled protesters who had positioned themselves on the chairs and overflowed into the floor where they sat, legs crossed, signs held between their knees like the rifles of a platoon of soldiers taking a five-minute break.

Beals, usually fortified by self-discipline and order, felt flustered. Her mind battled conflicting options. Should she call Campus Security? If she ignored the demonstrators would they just go away? Would someone else in the building hear the disturbance and know what to do? She knew that she needed help. She punched an auto-dial button on her phone that connected her to the office of George Helms, associate dean of the college. It was his private number that bypassed the secretaries in his office.

When Helms picked up the phone, Beals felt a surge of relief. "George, this is Naomi. You've got to come quick. We've been invaded!"

George Helms was down the hall and in her office almost before she could hang up the phone. He confronted the demonstrators and yelled in astonishment, "What the hell is going on here?" He grabbed one of the smaller young men by the shirt collar and shoved him out the door.

"All of you can wait in the hall. We won't have this disruption of our office routines."

Like a Sheltie herding a flock of sheep, Helms maneuvered the rest of the demonstrators out into the hall. He slammed the door and locked it. Through the frosted glass window in the door Helms could see silhouettes of the demonstrators in the hall. Their chanting had stopped, but it was clear they weren't going away.

"This has the marks of Lewis Thomas all over it," Helms said.

"You mean the sociology professor?"

"The one and only."

"What interest does he have in disrupting our office?"

"He did his dissertation on the student protest movement and thinks that today's students are too passive. He teaches courses on social protest and stirs up willing students to stage little demonstrations like this one."

"But why?"

"Thomas is pretty convincing," Helms said. "He's made some students believe that business is evil and exploits workers. His current target is international business and its effect on developing countries. He also claims that we are teaching our students to downsize and lay off workers willy nilly and that we are as bad as the businesses who hire our students. He's gotten so obnoxious about it that I refuse to sit at the same table with him at the Faculty Club."

Helms picked up the phone on Naomi's desk. "It's time to put Clem in the picture." He punched her autodialer that connected the office phone to the dean's home phone. After a brief conversation he returned the handset to its cradle.

"Everything is all set. We're going to show these students a thing or two about social protest."

Beals had regained her composure and was puttering around her desk, getting ready for the day's events, whatever they turned out to be.

"So all this is the work of one professor?" she asked.

"More or less. Every once in a while Thomas finds a natural leader among his students who takes a major role in planning the protests. My sources tell me that the current leader is Danny Bennett. He used to be a student in this college—a business major, in fact. His father is a prominent businessman. I've always thought that Danny's radicalism was his way of rebelling against his father's domineering personality. Danny's been an undergraduate student forever. He doesn't seem to want to leave the university."

"Was Danny Bennett here?"

"No, I didn't see him. He's clever about getting others to take the risks during demonstrations. He stays in the background and manipulates things. He gives most of his attention to talking with the media, and he's gotten very good at it, from what I hear. Last month he led an environmental protest against a local mining company that proposed opening a new strip mine on state-owned land."

Helms looked at his watch. "Five more minutes, and then show time."

While the students were laying siege to the dean's office, Danny Bennett was in the Student Union Building meeting with representatives from two local newspapers and three broadcasters, one television and two radio. One of the newspaper reporters was from the campus paper, and the other journalists came from a nearby city. As he looked at the assembled media representatives, Bennett thought about Professor Lewis's description of news media as ravenous beasts in need of constant feeding. Lewis taught that if the media cannot feed on legitimate news, they are more than willing to devour staged events. According to him, reporters were easily manipulated, though they deny it. "Build a demonstration, and they will come," was the slogan Lewis taught his students. Bennett was about to confirm the truth of that claim.

Bennett's organization called itself the SES, Students for an Egalitarian Society. The group found it useful to change its name as needed to fit the current social issue. At its previous demonstration against the mining company it called itself SER, Students for Environmental Responsibility. Today, though, they would be the SES.

At the press briefing Bennett distributed a five-page manifesto from the SES. Quoting liberally from Michael Moore's book, *Downsize This!*, the statement recited a litany of corporate abuses: massive firing of workers at times of record profits, reducing pension funds for corporate purposes, excessive executive salaries, the export of jobs to countries where a worker receives for a day's labor less than the hourly minimum wage in this country and the globalization of business which continues colonial exploitation in a new form.

Reporters from the electronic media thrust their microphones toward Bennett as they asked their questions, and representatives of print media scribbled furiously on their skinny little pads.

"As we speak," Bennett said, "members of the SES are preparing to confront Dean McKenzie with the outrageous fact that this university trains students to continue the exploitation of workers. My organization, Students for an Egalitarian Society, calls for the university to refuse to accept the recent gift from the International Computer Corporation for an endowed chair of management. We must lay an ax at the root. If you will follow me, you can see for yourselves the moral bankruptcy of the educational-industrial complex when it becomes apparent that the leaders of this university have nothing to say in their defense."

Bennett was proud of the phrase "educational-industrial complex." He adapted it from President Eisenhower's references to the "military-industrial complex," though most of the reporters present did not know the source of the phrase. The reporters thought it had a sound-bite ring to it, so it would probably show up on the evening news and in the morning papers.

Bennett led the journalists from the Student Union building to the entrance of Bucks Hall. As the reporters came through the front doors of the building, one member of the video crew aimed the Cyclops-like eye of the camera light right in front of the marching retinue.

Tape rolling, the soft voice of the TV reporter could be heard: "We are entering Bucks Hall where representatives of SES, Students for an Egalitarian Society, are protesting the college's acceptance of a large corporate gift to endow a chair of management studies. The students say this gift will encourage the teaching of how to exploit American workers."

Clem McKenzie came through the front door just as several officers from Campus Security entered Bucks Hall through a side door. Most were in uniform, one was in plain clothes. McKenzie motioned dismissively to Helms, who was standing just beside the door. "I can handle things from here on, George." Helms started to object, then changed his mind and said nothing.

As security officers and students approached each other, the scene began to look like a cinematic confrontation between two rival street gangs.

"What's the meaning of this?" McKenzie asked. The television camera rolled. Strobe lights flashed. Print journalists took hasty notes. The student demonstrators started shouting in unison, "Business Sucks! Business Sucks! Business Sucks!" Their signs moved to the rhythm to the chanting. After twenty seconds or so of noise, Bennett gave the sign for silence from his troops.

We are here protesting the university's complicity in the degradation of American society," he announced. A cheer went up from the demonstrators. Again, Bennett held up his hands for silence. "Business is an evil influence in American life. Especially businesses that fire their workers at will and refuse to pay those remaining a living wage. This university should teach students to resist such business tactics, not train them to perpetuate such outrages against the American worker. The new chair in management is being paid for by a major exploiter of workers. The university should refuse to accept money unfairly taken from exploited laborers." Once more, the students cheered.

At that moment a television reporter thrust a microphone into McKenzie's face. "Dean, what are your thoughts at this moment?" Brushing the microphone aside as he would an annoying fly, McKenzie ignored the question and the questioner.

"Cease this demonstration at once," the dean said. "I will then agree to meet in private with a representative of your group. This is a university committed to rational discussion, not a place for a barroom brawl."

The demonstrators responded with boos and hoots.

"The educational-industrial complex is turning America into a third-world country, with millions of hard-working citizens facing homelessness while the fat cats get fatter," Bennett said, this time almost having to shout to be heard over the background hubbub.

McKenzie was the next to shout. "As I said, I will meet with a representative of your group *after* this demonstration ceases. You are all trespassing. I order you all to leave now. If you fail to do so, you will be forcibly ejected."

The students booed again, then reprised their chant: "Business Sucks, Business Sucks, Business Sucks."

McKenzie turned to the plain clothes security officer—the one clearly in charge—and said, "Get 'em out of here." At this command the campus cop reached into his pocket, pulled out a cell phone, and began speaking softly into it.

Danny Bennett felt good. This was the best demonstration he had yet led. Maybe the press would give him a nickname, maybe even Danny the Rad, or something like that. He had a good idea of what was going to happen next. He had just proved his skill at organizing a demonstration. He now would prove his skill at avoiding arrest.

As the chanting grew louder, Bennett pulled from his notebook a stack of previously prepared documents labeled "Demands to the University" and began distributing them to the media representatives, working his way through them toward the door. He had not yet reached the entrance when the doors to Bucks Hall flew open and more uniformed campus security officers entered the building and headed for the demonstrators. One of the students used his sign to deliver a tomahawk chop to the neck of the nearest officer. She reacted immediately, hitting the student a glancing blow with her night stick that opened a gash over his eye. Blood from the wound ran down the student's face and dripped onto the floor.

The sight of blood angered the rest of the students, and they began pushing and shoving the officers. In their planning sessions Bennett, repeating what he had learned about demonstrations in Professor Thomas's class, warned against giving the police a reason to use violence. He lectured them on passive resistance and how to go limp, forcing the police to drag them away. Never, ever attack the police, he told them, because it gives them a reason to react with violence. He knew from his sociology courses that nonviolent protest took great internal discipline because the natural human instinct is to fight back. To allow oneself to be abused, both verbally and physically, required moral strength that came about through extensive training.

Bennett might as well have lectured on moon exploration for all the good his warnings had. All the students began using their signs as weapons, some swinging them in arcs in front of them, others using them like cattle prods at the approaching officers. Police struck students who had pushed and shoved them. Several participants in the mêlée slipped on the terrazzo floor, slick in spots from blood, most of it from students.

Bennett edged closer to the door, intending to make an escape. He reasoned that he could be more effective by following up with the media and denouncing the panic of the dean and the excessive force used by the police. He wouldn't do the movement much good if arrested. Just as he reached the door, the dean yelled, "Stop him. That's their ringleader." Bennett turned and swung at the nearest policeman.

Two strong hands grabbed Bennett's shoulders, spun him around, and pushed him, face first, up against the wall. Before he had a clear idea of what was happening Bennett heard the click of handcuffs on his wrists and a gruff voice saying, "Come on, let's go. You're under arrest."

Bennett's arrest calmed the demonstrators. They stopped all their activity as though they were an orchestra whose conductor had just laid down his baton. The plainclothes agent said in a calming voice, "OK now, all of you come with us and we'll sort this thing out. We don't want any more of you to get hurt." The campus police herded the student demonstrators to the door, passing the handcuffed Bennett on the way. Bennett looked over his shoulder at the dean and with an expression that was both snarl and sneer said, "You'll be sorry. We'll get you for this.

Chapter 4

ARCHIE SCOTT HATED MONDAYS. They reminded him he wasn't as young as he used to be, that the energy level he used to take for granted wasn't there any more. The trips to and from Middletown, plus the all-day seminars on Saturday, left him exhausted, and the drive back to College Falls on Sunday, with the jostling and uncertainties associated with contemporary air travel, only added to his stress level. He hated having to decline social invitations for the weekend and was afraid that some of his friends would eventually become suspicious about all those nieces and nephews whose weddings he claimed to be attending. Also the ill aunts and uncles, and attendant deaths, if compared, would make his family seem like it was genetically flawed and disposed to patterns of illness worthy of a report to the Centers for Disease Control. It was fortunate that his friends did not compare notes and thereby discover that the reasons for Scott's weekend absences made his family the sickest and most marrying group of humans to inhabit the planet.

Scott awoke late in the morning with a headache and the unhappy realization that he had to go to the dean's tenure review for Sarah Giles. He quickly shaved, put on a shirt that showed wrinkles from having been in a suitcase all weekend, grabbed from the closet a pair of flannel trousers and a tweed jacket. Attired in this standard academic uniform, complete with leather patches on the jacket's elbows, Scott drove into his parking place near Bucks Hall. Realizing that he hadn't eaten any breakfast, he stopped in at the Holy Doughnut Shop, whose logo featured a figure in a bishop's miter whose hands extended over a stylized doughnut as if in the act of blessing it. Looking at the confections in the display cases, Scott chose two sugared cake doughnuts and a glazed one plus the grande latte with extra cream and sugar. All this was stuffed in a bag which he carried out of the shop so he could eat at his desk while trying to decide how he was going to navigate the minefield the dean had prepared for him.

Like many Americans, Scott constantly obsessed about his weight but did little to lose any. He half-heartedly tried one diet, and then another, in hopes of finding the magic formula for weight loss, but with little success. At each annual physical Scott's physician warned him about his weight problem and told him to avoid fats and red meat and to lower his cholesterol, so he found himself eating a lot of chicken and occasionally some vegetables but losing no weight. An objective observer would know why: Scott had a sugar addiction. Sugar in all its forms was his dietary staple: candy bars, sugared soft drinks, sticky buns, Twinkies, pancakes smothered in syrup, cheesecake, pies, ice cream, doughnuts, and in-between-meal snacks heavy on French fries and popcorn and all washed down with ample quantities of beer.

Scott sat at his desk reviewing his notes and brushing from his shirt the sugar that fell from the doughnut like dandruff from dry scalp and didn't hear Sarah Giles enter his office until she spoke his name.

"Archie, I know you're busy, but can I have a minute of your time?"

Her voice exuded a cloying sweetness that made Scott wonder if Sarah was coming on to him. Not that he was particularly interested. She struck him as too prim, and today her gray hair pulled tight in a barrette at the nape of her neck and the stiff, white cotton shirt tucked into her long peasant skirt underscored his opinion. Scott preferred women who were more relaxed and casual. Besides, he was not into dating just now. But if he were, Sarah Giles would not be on his list.

"Yeah, sure Sarah," Scott said, wiping the powdered sugar from his top lip with the back of his hand. "I'm just about ready for class." He extended his almost empty bag to her. "Like a doughnut?"

"No thanks. I've already had breakfast." Then pausing as if to find the right words for her request, she decided on the direct approach. "You probably know what's on my mind, Archie. I'm up for tenure, and you're on the dean's committee. I know that I can count on your support."

Scott plopped the doughnut bag on his desk and directed his eyes away from Giles, focusing them instead on his shoes as though he was inspecting an expensive pair of handmade loafers. As he rubbed his finger along the welt seam, he fumbled for the right words.

"I uh…that is…what I mean is that I just don't know, Sarah. I'll have to wait until the committee meets to really make up my mind." What was really on Scott's mind was dean. McKenzie threat and expectation that he would vote against Giles. Now she was asking him to vote for her. He couldn't do both, but there was no need to give Giles any indication that his objectivity was already compromised.

She continued to press the point. "That sounds pretty lame to me. I've always thought you were a friend and a colleague who supported my work, not one of those anti-female drones that McKenzie attracts to this college like ants to a picnic. What's the problem? Why can't you support me?"

Scott couldn't tell her the real reason for his lack of support, so his mind shifted to overdrive while he fumbled for something that would sound plausible. "I do consider you a friend, Sarah. And I certainly think your work is respectable. It's just that I can't commit myself until I have a chance to read your tenure dossier thoroughly, that's all. I didn't mean to imply that I *wouldn't* support you, it's just that I think it would be inappropriate for me to make an a priori commitment."

With the back of her right hand, Giles cleared a space on Scott's cluttered dusk and put her hands, palms down, on its surface to support her weight as she moved her face to within six inches of Scott's still-sugared lip. "Don't bullshit me, Archie. What's happened? Has McKenzie bought you off? What has he promised you? A teaching reduction for a quarter or two? A raise? What?"

Scott, feeling that Giles had invaded his body space, first pulled his face away from hers and then rose from his chair and positioned himself a good ten feet from her. "Come on, Sarah, don't jump to conclusions. I didn't say I wouldn't support you." Then realizing that the dean never revealed the individual votes of the committee members, Scott decided that he could get away with a lie.

"If it makes you feel better, then of course I'll say now that I'll vote for your tenure." Since the first lie was so easy, Scott decided on a second. "I'm surprised that you ever doubted my intentions. We've been friends and colleagues for a long time. How could you ever think I wouldn't support you?"

"Friends? Colleagues? Oh please, Archie. You don't lie very well. I can tell you're not really my supporter, so I think I should give you some additional motivation. Did I ever tell you that my ex-husband is dean of students at Middletown College in Wisconsin?"

Scott felt as though a knife had been thrust deep into his stomach. His mouth turned dry so quickly that his tongue stuck to the roof of his mouth. The fight-or-flight mechanisms of his body cycled to full alert, but he could neither fight nor flee.

"I didn't know that....I mean I didn't know you had been married....Your ex-husband?" He could not seem to complete a sentence.

"His name isn't Giles. I didn't use his name, even when we were married. Listen to me, Archie. I don't care what people do on their own time. It's no affair of mine. I certainly don't want to ruin anyone's academic career, but I've got to take care of myself, and right now my situation looks pretty bleak. I need all the help I can get, no matter what I have to do to get it. Am I making myself clear, Archie?"

Scott felt lightheaded. He pulled his chair away from the desk and dropped himself into it.

"Archie. Archie." Giles's voice sounded to Scott like it was coming from the end of a tunnel. He looked at her with Little Orphan Annie eyes, round circles that didn't look as if anyone were at home. "Don't zone out on me, Archie. And quit staring. I can see you catch my drift. But don't worry. Your secret is safe with me, so long as you help me. I scratch your back, you scratch mine. Isn't that the standard business principle you management folks teach?"

"I've already said I will support you, Sarah. What more do you want me to say?"

"Just don't forget that promise when you are in the committee meeting this afternoon. There will be people there who will tell me what really goes on, so just remember that when you speak up." Giles looked at her watch. "I've got to go. Just remember our little conversation this afternoon." Scott was not aware of Sarah's departure. He was hardly aware of anything except the terrible pressure he felt in his chest, like iron clamps being tightened across his pectorals. He would have liked to go back home and crawl into bed, but his classroom was full of students expecting to learn from him how to climb the corporate ladder at the top of which would be found money and power. He crumpled the bag containing one uneaten doughnut and threw it toward the trash can, missing it but leaving a trail of powered sugar to mark his failure.

Chapter 5

SCOTT KNEW THE DEAN'S tenure committee meeting could be a disaster for him. The dean and Sarah loomed like Scylla and Charybdis, each threatening to destroy him if he failed to support their incompatible personal agendas. He knew what the dean wanted him to do, yet he hated to become the dean's toady—not that he particularly liked Sarah Giles. Too strident, too cold, too arrogant, too *feminist*. In his heart of hearts he would rejoice if the dean gave Giles the boot, but he knew he had to appear neutral at the very least. Sarah's supporters on the committee would report to her every word he says, and if he appeared to be attacking her...well, the prospects made his head hurt. The dean will expect him to vote against Sarah, but maybe he won't have to speak out much about anything. That would be his strategy.

But it would be tricky.

Scott approached the dean's office and the tenure committee meeting with sweaty palms and a racing heart. Unless he did the dean's bidding, he was history. Yet no matter what he did, Sarah's spy on the committee would report back to her, and no telling what her reaction would be if she thought hs hadn't supported her. To keep his mind from the unpleasant prospects ahead, Scott looked around the room and noticed how much money the dean had spent on decorating his office—a feature that he had ignored on his other visits to the dean's suite. The dean had his own private washroom, and the door to it discreetly blended into the walnut paneling that covered the walls. Expensive brocades covered the windows. The conference table and chairs were all handmade. Although Scott knew that the source of funds for these extravagances came not from university sources but from private gifts, he could not help think how much better the money could have been spent on books. Everyone in the college knew that the private funds came from the dean's cronies who were corporate leaders in their own right and had a vision of the kind of office they thought befitted a dean.

Scott knew that another dean appointee to the committee was Shirley Warner, a professor in the Department of Mass Communication who taught broadcast journalism. She came to an academic career directly from industry and let it be known at every opportunity that she achieved her executive-level position there before the days of quotas and the Equal Employment Opportunities Commission. She was an opponent of affirmative action programs and was outspoken about that opposition. She would be a tough critic in any tenure case, especially for another female.

Then there was Ray Jones. Everyone knew Ray's views on feminism, since he not only failed to keep them secret but discoursed about them at length whenever he had the opportunity, which was just about all the time. When Jones entered the room he gave Scott a conspiratorial wink. One committee member strongly against Sarah, another probably against her, and me, Scott thought. Great. This is just great.

Although Scott did not know who Sarah had recommended for committee membership from her department, he had heard through the grapevine that it was Cynthia Lemaster, a strident and outspoken advocate for women's issues, a rumor confirmed when she entered the office. She strode across the room with arrogant confidence.

The committee is politically correct, Scott thought. Two men and two women.

The dean was the last to enter the room. He took his seat and opened a leather portfolio. "Let me get things started by making a few introductory comments. I assume all of you know each other?" There were affirmative nods all around the table.

"Good. Some of you have served on these committees before, so what I am about to say will be repetitive, but please bear with me. Your role is advisory. You are to give me the best advice you can on the merits of the tenure case you are considering today. However, I want you to understand clearly that the decision is mine and mine alone. I will probably accept your recommendation, especially if you are unanimous in your vote. But again, I may not. I just want to get this out on the table so there will be no hard feelings later. Agreed?"

No one spoke up, so the dean continued. "I will not reveal any of the discussion that takes place in this room, and I ask each of you to do likewise."

He's cagey, Jones thought. That strategy gives him the best of both worlds. If the decision is unpopular, he can imply that he was following the committee's recommendation. If it is an easy decision, he can take all the credit. Since nobody will know what the vote was or what kind of discussion took place, there will be no disputing him.

"The case before us will not be an easy one. Professor Sarah Giles has been here five years, and since this is her sixth year, it is also the mandatory year for the tenure decision. The promotion and tenure committee of her department has not given us a unanimous recommendation. Their vote was three in favor of tenure, two against."

This information elicited murmurs of interest from a couple of the committee members.

"That being the case," the dean continued, "we will need to give her dossier an especially careful look."

"It may be easier than you think, dean," Jones said. "I have always felt that unless a department's promotion and tenure committee was unanimous in its recommendation, it is sending us a warning signal."

"I agree," Shirley Warner said. "I know from personal experience that some departmental committees just don't like to make the tough decisions. After all, it's one of their colleagues they're reviewing. Better to push the decision up a level and let the college committee give the turndown."

"Just a minute," Cynthia Lemaster said. "We're supposed to be here making an independent and objective judgment, and you two have acted as both judge and jury on Sarah. It sounds to me like you made your decision even before you came to this meeting."

"Now, now, Cynthia," Jones said. "Don't get yourself in an uproar. I'm willing to be objective about Sarah. I was just making a generalized statement. There are always exceptions, and I hope that Sarah is one of them."

"Don't you 'now, now' me, Ray. I won't be patronized. It's clear to me that nothing that is said here will have much influence on you. Your mind is already made up."

"No, it isn't. And I resent your insinuation that I can't be objective."

Dean McKenzie rapped on the table with the end of his Montblanc pen. "This discussion is not very productive. Let's get this meeting back on track." At this comment he distributed copies of Sarah Giles's tenure dossier, a document about half an inch thick.

"I have had these materials available to you in the outer office, so I assume that you have all had a chance to read them. Let's now take five minutes to review Professor Giles's file again."

Cynthia Lemaster aimed a withering look at Ray Jones. She opened the dossier's title page with an excessively loud slap on the table and creased its cover back. Everyone was quiet for the few minutes required for the review.

"Now if we're ready to begin, let's discuss Professor Giles's research." The dean distributed another packet to each member of the committee. "I have sent her dossier to several outstanding experts in her field and asked for their comments. These will supplement what you have in front of you."

Scott looked at the additional letters. It was clear that McKenzie was stacking the deck against Giles. None of these letters supported her tenure case. It was all over except for the voting.

Cynthia Lemaster was the first to speak. "Surely you don't expect us to take these letters seriously, Dean. It's obvious that none of these referees has the slightest understanding of Sarah's field of research."

"I disagree," Shirley Warner said. "Every one of these letters comes from a recognized authority in management. I fail to see the problem."

"I'll tell you what the problem is. Sarah is doing cutting-edge research. Because it deals with nontraditional areas, the old-boy network doesn't think the research is valid," Lemaster retorted.

"What you call nontraditional areas are really just women's issues," Jones said.

"That, Ray, is typical of the response I'm talking about. Research of the sort Sarah is doing is just dismissed by your kind as unimportant and not significant."

"I didn't say it was unimportant. My view is that this is not the sort of thing a serious scholar does. Looking into sexual harassment data, promotion patterns for women, things like that, might be an appropriate for a series of newspaper articles, but I fail to see this as real scholarship."

Scott decided he should say something that could cut either way, something that Sarah would not find offensive and the dean would accept as an anti-Giles comment.

"If I may be so bold," Scott began, "the issue seems to me to be how to evaluate a new area of scholarship. There used to be people who thought that the study of management was not appropriate for a university. Some still think that way at Oxford."

"The two are not parallel at all," Warner said. "What we're dealing with here is a very narrow area of research of a broader area. I think Ray is right about this being the topic of an extended series of newspaper stories. It is hardly the stuff of serious scholarship. Not only does it lack rigor, it isn't even interesting. If she wants to be a popularizer, she's failed miserably. If she wants to be a scholar, well, this is Exhibit A that she hasn't succeeded."

"You know the problem with you, Shirley? You have the Queen Bee complex. Since you made it as a tenured full professor, you don't want another woman to give you any competition." As Lemaster made this comment, her face began to redden. If this were a cartoon, Scott thought, smoke would be coming out of her ears.

"Nonsense," Warner responded. "You've just lost your objectivity on the issue because of your friendship with Sarah."

"Please, please," the dean said. "Let's not let the discussion degenerate to an *ad hominem* attack, or perhaps I should say *ad feminam*." He chuckled. Jones smirked.

Emboldened by his previous comment, Scott spoke up again. "The thing that gives Calloway State University our distinctive feature, as it were, and makes us different from other public universities in the state, is our willingness to embrace new areas of study and to break away from the pack." The dean gave Scott a withering look, but he continued in spite of it. "We are the only university in the state that has expanded its business programs into a College of Professional Studies, for example. The question is whether we consider Sarah's kind of research nontraditional scholarship or not."

"What do you mean, nontraditional?" Lemaster said. "That's the trouble with sexism. You don't even know you have it until you make a preposterous statement like that, Archie. You are a prime example for the problem around here. The whole climate has become chilly for women's issues, from hiring, to the lack of day care, to inadequate consideration for research. I could go on and on."

"You misinterpreted what I said, Cynthia. I meant even if it is a new area, like some of the others I mentioned, the study of women's role in business might be a serious area of research. That's really the issue, isn't it. You just have your feelers out too far and distorted what I said. Scott couldn't figure out why Cynthia was attacking him.

"You men can't get off that easily. Your rhetoric betrays you. You think women are second-class citizens of the university to be tolerated but not respected. You don't even have to say it because it sticks out all over."

"But...but—" Scott tried to break in, but Lemaster pressed on.

"There is a ton of research that shows how male faculty like you overlook women in all situations. You don't call on female students in class as much as you do male students. You praise the work of male students more than the work of female students. Sarah is simply applying insights from women's studies literature to business practices. I could cite more research, but it probably wouldn't make any difference. All of you are too far gone."

Ray Jones had a grin on his face as this exchange took place, appearing to enjoy the spectacle of seeing Scott squirm under Lemaster's attack. Never one to avoid fanning the flames of controversy, he couldn't resist jumping in. "Women's studies. Those people need to start with Nietzsche, 'Thou goest to a woman? Forget not thy whip.'"

"Oh pul-*eese*, Ray," Warner said. "Not a quotation from that old misogynist. I remember what Bertrand Russell said about Nietzsche: His attitude toward women was one of fear, and he knew if he had a whip the woman would take it away from him and use it on him."

The dean chuckled. "As long as we are quoting Nietzsche, my favorite aphorism is, 'A woman with a scholarly inclination has a deficiency in her sexual nature,' or something like that."

"I can't believe this," Lemaster said. "This is not a tenure review. This is a professional execution. I refuse to be any part of it." She grabbed her briefcase from the table, draped its strap over her shoulder, and continued, "This is the most outrageous demonstration of male bias and chauvinism masquerading as academic review I have ever seen. I refuse to be a part of this charade any longer."

The dean jumped to his feet and reached out to touch her arm. She jerked it away as though she had been touched with a hot iron.

"Now, now, Cynthia. Let's continue the discussion. Professor Jones and I meant no offense. We were just trying to bring some levity to our discussion."

"Levity, my ass. Ray's biased against female scholarship, and it comes out in everything he says. And when I look at these letters you solicited reviewing Sarah's scholarship, it's clear to me that your mind is made up. You don't need me or this committee, for that matter." With that final declaration, Cynthia Lemaster strode from the room without looking back.

Silence hovered over the room until the dean spoke. "I'm sure we all regret Professor Lemaster's decision to absent herself from this discussion, but we do need to press on. Let's turn now to a discussion of Professor Giles's teaching."

As is usually the case in the aftermath of a public quarrel, everyone was excessively polite for the remaining discussion. Even though everyone was on a first-name basis socially, they reverted to formalities. They became Professor Scott, Professor Jones, and Professor Warner. No one called the dean Clem but always Dean McKenzie. Ray Jones refrained from making any more inflammatory comments. Scott was quiet, still trying to figure out why Lemaster had attacked him. But now that Lemaster was gone, Scott felt in less danger of having his comments reported to Sarah, and he knew that he could vote against her tenure with impunity.

The remaining discussion shifted to an analysis of Giles's teaching. The dean reminded everyone of the college policy he had instituted that required peer review of teaching—fellow faculty visiting each other's classes and writing up reviews of their teaching. "Before I came," the dean said, "the only evaluations we had were student evaluations. It's not that I don't value such instruments, but not all students participate, and they become measurements of the teacher's popularity more than academic ability."

There was considerable discussion of this point. Ray Jones asked why the college should even solicit student evaluations if they are not to be taken seriously. Shirley Warner said that students are in the best position to know if they are learning anything, and after all, it's their money being spent, or the money of their parents. If anything, she insisted, student evaluations should be taken with greater seriousness than peer evaluations because faculty rarely say anything good about each other anyway. The dean insisted that both evaluations were important but that peer evaluations were his contribution to ensuring that teaching was taken seriously at Calloway State. The group finally agreed that the issue was moot in Giles's case since her teaching was ranked "good" both by students and peers.

The third category for review was service. The dean reminded everyone that many professors mistakenly think that "service" refers only to the number of departmental and university committees they serve on, and the chores they do for their professional associations. The dean insisted that while such service could be a component, the term also referred to public service; "letting the taxpayer see some results for all the money they put into higher education," was the way he put it. Even though the service component of the review counted in percentage terms only about twenty percent of the total consideration, the committee managed to spend most of its time discussing what the term "service" ought to include and how much it should count in the total scheme of things, confirming once again the principle of academic committee meetings: Most time in such discussions is spent on the least important issues.

Finally the dean called for a vote of the participants. It was by secret ballot, consisting of nothing more complicated than sheets torn off of a note pad on which committee members were to write either yes or no for tenure. Jones was pretty sure how the vote would turn out, so he was not surprised when the dean announced the results. Archie Scott felt relief, since he was sure Cynthia was Sarah's spy, and her absence meant that Sarah would not know how he voted. He knew he had to vote against Sarah or face the dean's reprisals.

"The vote is three against tenure. We can presume that Professor Lemaster's vote would have been in favor of tenure, but even if we count her vote in absentia, as it were, it is clear that you are not recommending Professor Giles for tenure."

Ray Jones was trying not to smile but was unable to repress a slight upturn at the edges of his lips.

"I would like to thank you all for giving up valuable time from your busy schedule to help me decide this most important matter," the dean said. "Again, I remind you not to discuss the content of our deliberations or the vote itself. I, in turn, will keep your recommendation in confidence and make my own decision. You have given me a difficult one to make, but I assure you I will make the best decision I can for the good of the university."

Chapter 6

THE GUN SHOW took place at the Expositions Building on the county fair grounds. The county was populated by hunters, sporting types and gun fanciers of all descriptions, and The Gun Show—and it had no more formal a name than this—was an annual event just before deer season. Deer season was such an important time in the county that the university administration had learned to allow the custodial and maintenance work force to take a day's vacation on the first day hunting was allowed. Not to do so was to invite widespread "sickness" among the workers of such an extent that nothing got done anyway.

If anything showed the gap between town and gown, or county and gown, it was The Gun Show. Hardly any academics attended, though a few gun collectors among the faculty stopped in to see what was on display. A professor of history bought an Enfield rifle so he could show his class the type of weaponry used in World War I, and the hobbyists who loaded their own cartridges stopped in for a new supply of brass and powder. Other than that, The Gun Show might have been on Mars, for all that the average professor was aware of it.

At the entrance to the show an inspector examined all firearms taken into the building to ensure that they were unloaded. He fitted each with a plastic tie that prevented the trigger from being activated. The same device could be found on all guns on display in the hall itself.

The show featured all major varieties of legal firearms. Gone from the display were the assault rifles that were a staple of the show in past years. While some antique handguns were for sale, most of the firearms available were rifles or shotguns. Anti-government talk was common in the exhibition hall, for most dealers found the government's infringement of their Second Amendment rights unacceptable.

Spread over the numerous tables in the hall were weapons ranging from antique muzzle loaders to inexpensive Chinese imports with open stocks made of plastic. Some dealers offered elaborately engraved shotguns, and others sold shooter supplies of all kinds—gun oil, gunpowder solvents, brass brushes for cleaning barrels, cleaning rods, cotton patches and reloading supplies. On the table of one reloading specialist was a sign proclaiming, "We Buy Your Brass," which the proprietor claimed was an important service since it reduced the cost of ammunition for those who chose not to reload their expended cartridges. Interspersed among the gun dealers, the knife merchants offered an almost bewildering variety of products: switch blades, bayonets, throwing stars, short knives with a 90-degree handle to be held in a fist with the blade sticking out between the user's fingers, throwing knives and collectors-edition knives with engraved blades and carved handles. There was even a seller of blow guns whose projectiles were steel-tipped darts: "great for hunting rabbits and squirrels," the seller told everyone who stopped long enough for her to give a simulated demonstration of her product's capabilities.

In one corner of the hall a lone figure stood beneath a banner that said, "Income Tax is Illegal." On a side table a variety of badly printed pamphlets proclaimed that the "government has no right to your money" and offered advice on how to avoid taxation. The advice was simple and bad: "Don't File a Return," one pamphlet screamed in 72-point type. The text of the pamphlet claimed that the government was powerless in a court of law in its ability to enforce its income tax laws, and if people just refused to pay taxes voluntarily, the whole system would collapse. The looniness of all this was too much for even the most diehard of government haters among the gun dealers, and they shunned the display completely. The anti-tax advocate looked up to see someone he didn't know approach his table.

"Take a pamphlet explaining why income tax is a form of robbery and illegal under our Constitution."

"I'm not really interested in taxes," the visitor stated. "I'm more interested in other capabilities that anti-tax advocates have."

There was something wrong here, the booth-holder thought. The accent was too cultured, not like the drawl of most of his supporters.

"I don't know what you're talking about."

"I understand why you are cautious. For all you know, I might be a government agent. Let me tell you what I want. You don't have to say a thing."

The no-taxer was even more wary. Who was this person?

"I know that anti-government and anti-tax sentiment is sometimes found among militia movements. I want to get in touch with someone who can give me information on incendiary and explosive devices. Preferably made with readily obtainable materials."

The man behind the table shuffled his pamphlets and said nothing.

"I would rather use dynamite," his visitor continued, "except an ordinary citizen like me would have trouble buying it—another example of the government's infringement on our personal liberties."

"You can say that again." The anti-tax advocate warmed to the mention of liberty. "Taxation, gun control, the BATF, the jack-booted FBI, restrictions on your ability to buy dynamite—these are all examples of what my group opposes." Maybe this person is OK, a possible ally, the no-taxer thought.

"Here's what I would like you to do. You don't know me, I don't know you. But here is a phone number. If you know people who can give me the kind of information I need, have them call this number. No names are necessary. All I need is information, and I am willing to pay."

A card exchanged hands. Nothing more was said.

Chapter 7

THE DEAN'S ANNUAL RECEPTION was the social event of the fall. It was not that the dean was a brilliant entertainer; the reception simply provided some members of the academic community an opportunity to inspect The House. The dean invited all the faculty in the College of Professional Studies, along with their guests—a spouse, a significant other, or just a friend. He also sent invitations to a few faculty from other colleges in the university, though the list varied from year to year, depending on the dean's whims and with whom he had experienced a falling out the previous year. Attendance was expected from the faculty in the College of Professional Studies. This year Jeremy Brand was on the invitation list and was one of the few faculty members there from the College of Liberal Arts.

The dean's wife, Tabitha, usually presided over these affairs like a campus Martha Stewart. She supervised every detail: the food, the flowers that decorated the dining room, the service settings, the dress of the servers, the kind and amount of liquor that was served. It was trickier than might be imagined. As the dean of one of several colleges in the University, McKenzie was not too concerned about what the other deans would think of his extravagances, but he had to avoid upstaging the president, whose entertaining set the standard for elegance in the university. It wasn't that the College of Professional Studies was unable to afford lavishness, because it had a hefty endowment from its many business and professional benefactors. It was simply not the thing to do to be perceived as entertaining more elaborately the president, just as the nobility of France had to be sure that their châteaux would not compete with Versailles.

This year, however, Tabitha McKenzie was absent from the annual soirée. One of her three grandsons was in the hospital with a serious staph infection, and her support was needed at his side. "Grandparents are like the National Guard," Mrs. McKenzie told her husband. "We are called in to deal with emergencies." This year the dean was on his own, though his wife, with her usual style, saw to the preparation of everything for the party so that the dean's role was largely schmoozing, participating in what one of his colleagues called S&M, shaking hands and mingling.

Even with self-imposed restraint, the McKenzies' party was still the hottest event in town. Liquor flowed freely and loosened tongues, sometimes to the regret of their possessors the next morning. The dean set up two bars, one in the dining room and another on the terrace so that no glass remained empty for long. Servers in black pants or skirts and white shirts made their way continuously through the house bearing trays of canapés. The heavy hors d'oeuvres that weighed down the buffets crossed the line between finger foods and a full-scale meal so that attendees always ate a light dinner, or skipped it entirely, the better to indulge their appetites at the dean's expense.

Though the exterior of The House copied The White House on Pennsylvania Avenue, the interior rooms were more in scale with what was, after all, a family home. It was in the furnishings that the dean's taste—some said lack of it—became evident. If the exterior, executive-mansion style of the house was not enough to convince the observer of the dean's bad taste, the interior furnishings left no doubt. The decorating style could only be called eclectic-modern-gaudy. The problem was not the decor's cost, for the furnishings reeked of expense, but they still lacked overall harmony, proving the old adage that you can't buy taste. The furniture, window treatments, art works, carpets, table furnishings—everything was wrong. The colors were too bold. The carpets too plush. The art too avant garde or too schmaltzy (both styles found their place on the dean's walls). The table settings were too elaborate, the furniture too heavy.

Many faculty at Calloway State had difficulty making a speedy transition in their careers from their life as graduate students to that of academic professionals. As graduate students they used concrete blocks and pine boards for bookshelves, orange crates for storage, and garage-sale furniture for their apartments. Spending money on houses and furnishings was not a priority then, and it remained during their early professional lives. Comfortable rather than expensive was the norm.

The shock to new professors in the college the first time they entered the dean's home was something to see. Since they were just out of graduate school, the contrast between their current situation and the dean's extravagant lifestyle had a huge and usually negative impact on them. Some of the old hands positioned themselves to they could catch the look on the faces of new assistant professors when they walked into the dean's foyer and first glimpsed his conspicuous consumption.

Faculty members gathered in tight little knots around the house discussing the latest administrative outrage until the dean joined the conversation circle, at which time the conversation turned to sports or the weather. Though most members of the faculty at Calloway State were politically liberal, their attitude toward university administration was that of conservatives toward the government: there was too much of it, and most of it was ineffective. What the university needed was more faculty and fewer administrators. On that all faculty agreed.

The president of the university, Milton Coles, made a brief appearance at the reception, where he glided effortlessly through the crowd. Though professors might criticize him behind his back, the president represented the authority of office and generated polite respect whenever he appeared. At six-foot-five, he was usually the tallest person in the room and fully used the advantage that such height provided. Only his closest friends could bring themselves to call him by his first name, so it was usually "President Coles" whenever faculty addressed him. Coles had a great aptitude for remembering names and prided himself on being able to work a crowd by greeting almost everyone there by name, even though it may have been months since their last meeting.

He saw Jeremy Brand moving across the room and called out toward him. "Jeremy, I just read your article on wine and culture. A splendid piece of work. I especially liked the quotation from Socrates, 'wine delights the soul as well as the body.'"

"Thanks, Milton. The article is a chapter from my book, *Wine Through the Ages*. It's turning out to be a fun project."

The exchange with Coles was brief but pleasant. Many more people needed to be greeted, and the president continued to work the crowd.

Even though the dean spent freely on his party, the wine he served was plonk. It tended to be bottom-of-the-shelf stuff, only a step above jug wines or the cheapest of the imports from Eastern Europe or South America. Brand tried not to be a wine snob, for there were plenty of low-price wines that he enjoyed, but the dean's offering was an offense to his palate. Brand had gently offered to advise McKenzie on wine selection, but the dean ignored such hints, and Brand felt it would be impolite to press the issue. His solution at these occasions was to avoid the wine altogether and drink club soda instead. He moved around the room, inserting himself in this and that conversational group, and it was soon evident that everyone was talking about the confrontation in the dean's office over Sarah Giles's tenure case.

Brand accepted as a matter of fact that there are no secrets in an academic community. Public institutions like Calloway State operated in a climate of sunshine laws and public information statutes such that any taxpayer could get a copy of any document created by the university. As a consequence, many decisions were not reduced to paper, making the grapevine an active source of information. Brand was amazed to hear a blow-by-blow account of the dispute between McKenzie and Cynthia Lemaster. Ray Jones's comments about women's studies became exaggerated as they were retold, much to the delight of the hearers. These discussions occurred only in those conversational groups without women; where female faculty were present, the descriptions were sanitized and dwelt on the unfairness of the dean's requests for outside evaluation of Giles's research.

As Brand moved around the room, his ears tuned to the nuances of the conversations, the general outline of the event became clear: the faculty committee gave the dean a split recommendation, and everyone predicted that he would turn her down for tenure on the grounds of inadequate research accomplishments. Brand overheard one faculty member deliver himself of the following opinion: "Everybody knows that the only thing that counts around here is research. Teaching doesn't amount to shit. Besides, the upper administration always looks for a reason to turn down tenure recommendations, especially when the department gives a split decision."

"I heard that Cynthia pounded the table and walked out of the room, calling the dean a male chauvinist pig as she went out the door." This comment came from a faculty member in another of the male-only conversational groups. "I also heard that Ray Jones said Sarah's problem was that she was sexually biased," another faculty member said. Probably a distortion of what actually happened, Brand thought as he continued his circuit of the room. Taking no pleasure in such gossip, he looked for someone with whom he could have a reasonable conversation.

Sarah Giles came to the reception late, even later than the standard of being fashionably late. The dean greeted her, though there was an edge of correct coolness to his voice and to her response. Her entrance into the room produced a pause in several conversations as their participants became aware of her presence. Giles moved from one group to another, pausing only briefly in each to acknowledge the "hellos" and "good evenings" of her colleagues. She could tell by the looks she generated that her tenure situation was general knowledge, especially when no one spoke to her about it. Even though no letters had gone out from the dean's office, his handling of the tenure review committee was proof enough to almost everyone that he would not be recommending her for tenure. Her colleagues' attitudes were like that of most people to their friends who have cancer: never talk about it, never ask, never probe, never mention the unmentionable.

Giles found herself quickly drinking a vodka tonic. Then another. And another. And still another. She felt a buzz and noticed a thickening of her tongue as she tried to speak. She had come to the reception with a resolve to act normal, as though nothing had happened in her professional life. She would be polite to the dean, cool but polite. She intended to conduct herself as though she had no knowledge of the events in the dean's office, even though she did: Cynthia Lemaster had told all.

As Giles accepted yet another vodka tonic brought to her by one of the servers, someone bumped her, spilling half of the glass on her dress. Looking up, she was horrified to see that the someone was Dean McKenzie.

"I'm sorry, Sarah, terribly sorry," the dean said.

"You're sorry, all right," Giles replied. "You are about the sorriest dean I have ever seen." Giles couldn't believe she was saying the words she heard coming from her mouth, but her anger welled up inside her as though her head was a balloon ready to pop.

"Really now, I don't think—"

"That's right. You don't think. You make up your mind and never consider the evidence put before you. Worse, you contrive the evidence to fit your own preconceived ideas." "Worse" came out "worsh," and "evidence" sounded like "evidensh."

When she first saw what was happening, Lemaster hurried across the room and reached out and touched Sarah's arm. "Let's go. I'll take you home." Sarah pulled her arm away, spilling more of her drink, this time on the dean's Persian carpet.

"Not until I'm finished," she said with her eyes still affixed on the dean. "Do you really think that you can keep secret the hatchet job that goes on behind closed doors in your office? You don't deserve to be dean. In fact, you don't deserve to *be* at all."

The dean was so startled by this outburst that he said nothing in reply. He stood mutely watching as Lemaster succeeded in maneuvering Sarah out of the room and out the front door.

A hush came over the whole room. Rarely was an academic quarrel as public as this one. The exchange between the dean and Sarah would enliven the cocktail party circuit for years.

Chapter 8

WHILE THE DEAN'S PARTY was going full blast, Bennett and his unhappy band of social protesters were having their own affair. Nothing much had come of Bennett's arrest by campus security representatives during the demonstration in Bucks Hall. Most student demonstrations on university campuses are not only tolerated but fully protected by the application of First Amendment guarantees. University codes that regulate "hate speech," the kind of speech filled with racial and sexual slurs, proved to be failures and were falling in courts faster than old-growth forests in the Pacific Northwest. As a result Calloway State had not even adopted one.

Bennett's behavior was rude, but he had done nothing to produce even a charge of disturbing the peace. It would have been hard to convince a local judge that students were trespassing when all they did was sit in a public building on a public university campus, especially since they left the dean's office when told to, so the Office of Campus Security did not even try. Bennett had not assaulted a security officer nor had he directed verbal abuse at him. The head of Campus Security gave Bennett a stern lecture and let him go. The protester who struck the security officer at first thought he would be brought up on disciplinary charges and suspended from the university, but he apologized to the officer, claiming that he didn't mean to hit her and that he was just waving his sign when it struck her. He received a written reprimand that was placed on file with the Office of Student Judiciaries, the effect of which would be to produce an immediate suspension from the university if he had a repeat offense.

The other students were also given warnings but no other punishment. Universities are thoughtful in their reaction to student misconduct, since one of the principal roles is to help civilize the young. Besides, it does a university little good to alienate the very ones it recruits to attend the institution.

The fervor, however, had gone out of the Students for an Egalitarian Society when Bennett called them together. Bennett remained unrepentant. Although he had received an angry phone call from his father, laced with threats of having his college support cut off if there were a recurrence of such behavior, Bennett resolved to continue the good fight. Besides, he liked being a radical, even if it only meant taking on the limited role of a campus gadfly. It reminded him of when, as a boy, he dressed up in costumes and one day played at being a pirate, the next day a bank robber, then a cowboy or explorer or a fighter pilot. Bennett never wanted to be a doctor, a fireman, a policeman or anything conventional; he just enjoyed playing at those roles and was always attracted to the romantic and flamboyant. His current role was that of campus radical.

Bennett's problem now was how to incite enthusiasm among his followers. It was hard enough to convince them to meet again, much less to mount another demonstration. A brush with possible arrest and the challenge of keeping up with studies were enough to cool the enthusiasm of most of the original group. The student who faced disciplinary suspension if he had a repeat offense made it plain to Bennett that he was no longer a member of SES and would not attend any more meetings. The band that faced Bennett was the diehard core of his group.

"We've been marginalized by the educational establishment," Bennett began. "They aren't taking our social protests seriously. We've got to find a way to make a bold statement."

This opening salvo was greeted with some murmurs of agreement, though most of the half-dozen students there seemed disinterested in Bennett's proposal. One student asked what Bennett had in mind.

"Something dramatic. Something that the press will report," Bennett said.

"How about a flaming 'E' planted in the dean's front yard, 'E' for egalitarian," one student suggested. Sneers and laughs greeted the proposal.

"That's too much like the Klan," another student said. "We don't want to be identified with those bigots."

"How about another sit-in demonstration? This time, though, we'll make the police drag us off. We could each dress up and wear letters for IBM, GM, GE and other companies. That would tie our protests to the business interests we oppose." This suggestion came from one of the female students.

"Great! I want to dress up as Mickey Mouse and represent the Disney Company," one of the male students said, to much group laughter.

"I don't know," Bennett said. "It sounds too theatrical. Someone might think we were doing it as a class project or something. Any other ideas?"

The discussion was wide-ranging. Someone suggested that SES organize a massive student letter-writing campaign, but someone else pointed out the cost of postage and the fact that the group had no money. Another suggestion was to do the same thing via the Internet. Since the university provided free and unlimited Internet access, SES could organize a targeted protest aimed at a selected company. The group dropped that idea for fear it would not get media attention.

After about fifteen minutes of suggestions and digressions, and the group was no closer to agreement than when it began, Bennett decided to attempt some closure.

"I know we laughed at the suggestion of a flaming 'E,' but why not? We can prepare a press statement to distribute after the event making clear that we have no connection with the Ku Klux Klan. Besides, it would be easy to do. There are some old two-by-fours in the garage under my apartment. We could nail three short pieces to a long one, wrap it in rags and soak it in gasoline. Wouldn't take us more than an hour to prepare."

"Yeah, yeah," a couple of students said, the rest nodding their agreement.

"Also," Bennett continued, "we could plant the 'E' in the dean's front yard in the middle of the night, say about two o'clock in the morning. I could have the press releases ready to distribute by then so we'll get coverage on the morning news."

With the group seeming to rally around this idea, Bennett started handing out assignments. He told one student to make a list of the local newspapers and television stations so they could be called after the "E" was planted—in time for photos and video tapes to be made while the "E" was still burning. Bennett directed two other students to get the boards from his apartment and begin making the "E." Another student said she had a pick-up truck, and Bennett told her to drive it to his apartment so it could be used to transport the "E" to Dean McKenzie's house. He, being the leader, would write the statement to distribute to the media.

With SES members busily engaged in their various assignments, Bennett's enthusiasm mounted. This is going to be great, Bennett thought. Just great.

While the student members of SES were executing their plan for a demonstration, the dean's reception started to wind down. Brand left about eleven o'clock, and by midnight only a small group of the dean's friends remained. Always the convivial host, McKenzie tended to drink too much at these affairs, and by the time his guests had dwindled down to his old friends Ray Jones and George Helms, it was close to one o'clock. The dean was sitting on the sofa, breathing heavily in what was beginning to sound like a snore. Jones considered it an obligation to an old friend to stick around on such occasions and put the dean to bed, especially since Tabitha McKenzie was out of town. Helms left after having "one more for the road," as he put it, at which point Jones decided it was time to get the dean to bed. He took hold of one of McKenzie's arms and pulled it behind his own neck, holding it fast while he grasped the dean around his waist. Using this classic grip, Jones was able to walk the dean up the stairs toward the master bedroom, though "walk" was scarcely the term for what the dean was doing. When he reached the bedroom, Jones dropped McKenzie on the bed, took off his shoes, and pulled the coverlet up over him. He'll sleep it off tonight but feel like hell tomorrow, Jones thought as he closed the door to the bedroom.

...

Danny Bennett and the SES protesters arrived at The House around one o'clock in the morning. Most students were just ending the evening, but Bennett hoped that no one in the dean's house was still awake. The only lights on in the residence were the porch light and a lamp visible in an upstairs room that Bennett guessed must be the bedroom. Even if the dean was still awake, Bennett reasoned, SES should go ahead with the demonstration. Their target, after all, was not only the dean but also the media. On this front Bennett was less successful than he wished. His attempt to get several journalists to accompany the group failed, and he was left with a single student reporter, though she did have a camera with her, and Bennett was sure there would be photo-worthy events to insure front-page coverage.

The House's landscaping included indirect lighting that bathed the facade with a soft glow and spotlights aimed vertically in various trees and shrubs, adding additional emphasis to the overall ambiance. Bennett picked a spot for the flaming "E" that would give it maximum impact—enough in the darkened areas of the yard to be dramatic, yet not too far away from the front of the dean's house, allowing The House itself to be visible in the photographs he was sure the reporter would want to take. Danny Bennett barked instructions to his fellow protesters like a general preparing for battle. His standard all-black attire, chosen because he thought it made him look radical, tonight convinced him of his commanding presence in the shadows of the dean's front yard. On Bennett's order, four of the students hoisted the giant letter "E" on their shoulders and moved it from the truck to the lawn. It was wrapped in rags but not yet doused with gasoline. With a couple of borrowed shovels, two others dug a hole in the dean's manicured turf and, as silently as the effort allowed, slipped the bottom two feet of the main support into the ground. The upright of the letter was eight feet tall, just the length of a two-by-four they'd scavenged for the job. But at the right proportions, the arms of the letter, made from scrap pieces of two-by-sixes, were too heavy to be supported by the few small nails pounded into the upright. The top piece especially had not been properly attached and was beginning to sag toward the middle one. Because the bottom piece sat squarely on the ground, the construction took on more the appearance of a "P" than an "E." Bennett thought about trying to readjust the top cross piece but decided against it for fear that pounding in more nails would make too much noise and destroy the element of surprise he hoped for. Besides, he reasoned, the news release—already on its way to the local media— would explain what the letter represented. When the whole affair was burning, a little sagging would be the least of anyone's concerns.

Bennett paced around the "E" until he felt satisfied with its placement. He gave the order to douse the cloth-covered framework with gasoline. Two students wielding plastic containers splashed the rags with fuel, starting at the top and working their way downward so as not to spill the volatile liquid on themselves. When he was satisfied that the structure would burn nicely, Bennett took a butane cigarette lighter from the pocket of his black denim jeans and set fire to the bottom of the upright. Flames shot up the structure and onto the cross pieces faster than he'd anticipated, and he had to jump back to keep from setting his own clothes on fire. As the flames licked skyward, lights began appearing in neighboring homes, and Bennett wondered how long it would be before someone in the dean's house awoke to see the display, now clearly visible in the front yard, blazing against the night sky.

Then came a muffled *whump*, accompanied by the nearly simultaneous shatter of breaking glass, as three huge fireballs burst through the windows of the dean's house. The long tendrils of flame extending past the roof line made the diminishing fire of the "E" look pitiful by comparison.

"Let's get the hell out of here!" Bennett tried not to shout when he heard the wail of the sirens. "Everybody get in the truck, right now." With the tires squealing and gravel flying, the students sped off.

Chapter 9

JEREMY BRAND WAS SITTING at his desk working on notes for a lecture when he heard a knock at the door. Still in his pajamas, since it was only six o'clock in the morning, Brand looked through the sidelights of the front door and was surprised to see Police Chief Harriet Strong standing on the porch.

"To what do I owe this pleasure?" Brand said.

"You'll never believe the night I've had, Jeremy." She followed him into his study and poured herself a cup of coffee from the vacuum carafe sitting on the butler's table by his desk. "I'll give you the whole story in a minute, but first let me tell you the bad news. There was a fire at Clem McKenzie's house last night. The dean is dead."

Brand let his cup drop to the desk with a bang. He wished it were Friday afternoon again, and that they were having a relaxing glass of wine instead of the jolt of coffee to accompany such news.

At times like this Harriet Strong was reminded of how interesting her life had become as a local law enforcement official. An undergraduate philosophy major in college, Harriet was both brainy and beautiful, a combination that would have opened a lot of doors had she exploited it. She emphasized the brainy part and downplayed her beauty, adopting the grunge look that female philosophy students seemed to prefer. Tall and thin enough to be a model, she was also a natural athlete and found herself president of the boxing club. Boxing was not a varsity sport but was only given club status at her university, since the athletic association refused to sanction an activity whose only goal was the disabling of the opponent. She defended her choice of boxing to her incredulous mother as causing her less physical damage than her friends experienced from playing field hockey and lacrosse. They always seemed to be nursing bruises and cuts caused by on-field collisions or wayward racquet swings. Harriet's father thought her boxing was impressive but wasn't so sure about philosophy. "What are you going to do with a degree in philosophy?" he asked her at every opportunity. To placate his concerns more than for any other reason, she took the LSAT exam during her senior year, and when the results placed her in the 99th percentile, her academic advisor insisted that she apply to several law schools. It was no surprise to him, though it was to Harriet, that she not only had her choice of schools but was also given generous offers of financial aid.

Law school confirmed for her the old expression that the first year scares you to death, the second works you to death, and the third bores you to death. But boredom took on new meaning when she accepted a lucrative offer as an associate in a large law firm and found herself working long hours researching tiny aspects of big cases. She was on the fast track to a partnership and achieved that goal while also marrying the managing partner, a divorced tort lawyer. Neither partnership—marriage nor professional—proved to be enduring, and when her marriage fell apart Strong decided that the life of a law-firm based attorney was not for her.

The transition from the firm to a different career was made easier for her by the trust fund her grandparents had set up. She had never been motivated by money but was more concerned with finding something interesting to do. The combination of her athletic prowess and law training made the FBI a natural alternative. She discovered that she liked law enforcement but not necessarily in a huge bureaucracy. She placed herself in the hands of an executive search firm and jumped at the opportunity to become chief of police at College Falls. She had grown to like the intellectual milieu of a university community and the more relaxed pace of small-town life.

Strong's separate income stream from the trust gave her more purchasing power than would have been possible on a public servant's salary, but she was careful not to appear extravagant. "The preacher doesn't drive a Cadillac," her father said more than once. Her shoulder-length, light brown hair was always in a simple but fashionable cut, and though her lean frame allowed her to look good in anything, she favored tailored separates and pant suits of good quality. She wore her skirts knee length and always complemented them with dark hose that ended in good shoes, expensive shoes, her one concession to personal style. A belted trench coat and Coach leather brief case completed her signature look.

Brand's friendship with Harriet Strong had two roots: crime and wine. In the process of doing research for his courses and publications on detective fiction, he'd been introduced to the police chief and found her to be an interesting and willing source of information. Conversations with a police official added believability to his analysis of themes in crime novels and kept them from being purely academic exercises. For Harriet, an attorney as well as a law officer, friendship with Brand brought a welcome relief to the humdrum routine of administering a police force. But the thing that bonded their friendship was the discovery of a mutual interest in wine.

They developed a comfortable routine of sharing a bottle of interesting wine a couple of times a week during a late afternoon hour they called "wine time." Being police chief in a small town, Strong had to be careful where and with whom she was seen drinking, and she was scrupulous about not drinking while on duty. Sharing a bottle with Jeremy was both discreet and enjoyable, and Harriet looked forward to these occasional afternoon events as a welcome break from the intensity of her job.

Brand and Strong continued to talk about the death of the dean over a second cup of coffee. Then Strong's cellular phone rang, and her response was terse. "Tell the Lieutenant that I'll be there within ten minutes." She flipped her phone shut and dropped it in her purse.

"Time to go," she said, stretching her long legs before putting her black pumps back on. "The crime scene search unit is already on site, and I'll meet the chief of detectives there. This is going to be a wild day."

"I'm sure your officers will have everything under control."

"Maybe, but remember that we're a small police force in a small town. We rarely have serious crime here, and I'm understaffed. My crime scene unit consists of the two officers I sent to the capital for training by the state police. My chief of detectives is a retired military intelligence officer, and I had to get him out of bed for this." She noted the amusement on Brand's face and rolled her dark eyes in mock disgust. "We know what we're doing, Jeremy, and if I need to I can get backup help from the state Bureau of Criminal Investigation. We'll just have to see what we've got. Why don't you stop by the dean's house later today? You're interested in detective work. You might find it entertaining to see how a small police force deals with a major crime."

"Thanks," Brand said with a smile. "I'll stop by after my eleven o'clock class. And if there's anything I can do to help, let me know."

"There may very well be," Strong admitted as she headed for the door. "I don't know my way around the university. Most of what I know about it I learned from you, Jeremy, so I may need for you to give me some guidance since you know the territory better than I do."

Brand continued his Tuesday morning routine after Harriet left but found it difficult to keep his mind on academic matters. For one thing, he wondered who hated McKenzie enough to murder him—if indeed the fire was arson and the intent was to kill the dean. It was too early to jump to that conclusion, but on the basis of what Harri had said, it did sound like the dean had been murdered.

Arriving at his classroom, Brand was met by a young woman who identified herself as a work-study assistant in the president's office. "President Coles would like to meet with you at three o'clock, Professor Brand. That is, if it's convenient for you. If it isn't, I'm to ask you to please call his office and find a time that works for you." Brand checked his pocket calendar and found that his whole afternoon was free. "Tell Milton I'll be there."

"Thank you, sir. I know the president will be happy." He watched her as she disappeared down the hall, and then hung his tweed jacket on the back of a chair.

What is all this about? he wondered.

When Brand arrived at the dean's house shortly after one o'clock that afternoon, the small crowd of gawkers was kept at bay by yellow crime-scene tape stretched around several trees in the front yard. Strong saw Brand approach and signaled to one of the uniformed officers to let him through. The officer lifted up the tape, and Brand ducked as he walked under the yellow ribbon and onto the dean's front yard. The usually pristine white façade of the home was now scorched and blackened. Half of the roof had collapsed, leaving visible only charred joists and supporting pillars. The few firefighters still present directed small streams of water to various smoldering parts of the building.

"It's arson, all right," Strong said as Brand walked over to where the chief was standing. "My investigators have confirmed our initial suspicions." She explained to Brand that, like most small towns, the local fire department was not staffed or equipped to investigate suspected incidents of arson and left that task to the police and the state fire marshal. "It's our job to determine as much as we can on-site about the causes of the fire and to gather evidence for later analysis by the district fire marshal. He'll be here any minute. Come over here and I'll point out what we think happened."

She led Brand to the front door and pointed to windows on either side of the balcony. "Whenever we find several points of origin for a blaze—and we found three here—that makes us automatically suspect arson. Let's go inside and I'll show you something else."

The professor and the chief entered the hallway and climbed the central staircase, being careful to avoid brushing up against soot-covered walls and sidestepping puddles of water. At the top of the stairs Strong briefly spoke with an officer who was putting various items of physical evidence in metal cans and noting the contents of each on attached labels. "Sergeant Dickinson, this is Professor Jeremy Brand. He was a friend of Dean McKenzie." Brand and

Dickinson shook hands, and Brand asked the sergeant what kinds of things he was looking for.

"Anything that looks unusual. I found traces of a plastic substance, probably from milk jugs if my guess is correct. Also some candle wax. It's funny about fires. They can burn up most everything but still leave traces of the fire's origins."

"So what do you think started the fire?"

"It's still too early to be sure, but it looks to me like gasoline bombs."

"Gasoline bombs?"

"Yeah, similar to what the pyrotechnics people use in the movies to create an explosion. Probably nothing more complicated than plastic jugs partially filled with gasoline tied onto the blind cords and resting on the window sills. The time fuses led to small bags filled with black power stuffed into the tops of the jugs. When the flame hit them, the powder ignited and blew the jugs apart, throwing burning gasoline over everything. You can tell the fire started here."

"How so?"

"Well, there's the "V" pattern of the flames here on the wall. Flames always spread out and upward from the point of origin, and the fact that the jugs were sitting on the windowsill caused this particular pattern. And look at this wall support. It's rounded on the back side. In a fire like this, the flames tend to do that to a beam on the side away from the flame source."

Brand walked around the charred timbers. "How were the jugs of gasoline ignited?"

"It looks like the perp put several of them on the windows and connected them all with the kind of canon fuse you can buy in most any hobby shop. He then tied the ends to a candle. My guess is that the candle had been altered so the wick ran along the outside. He lit the candle and then got out. When the flame reached the fuses, they ignited and burned over to the jugs of gasoline. Then, whoosh-bang. Must have been quite a sight."

"You say 'he' and 'guy.' What makes you think this was done by a man?"

"I don't. I'm just old-fashioned. Haven't gotten into this politically correct stuff. Could be a woman. This wasn't something that took a lot of physical strength, just smarts. We do know for sure that gasoline was used, though."

"How do you know that?" Brand asked.

"The 'sniffer' told us," Strong said, pointing to an instrument lying beside the arson investigation kit. "We use a gas chromatograph to detect the presence of unburned hydrocarbons. The fire department quickly contained the fire, and we were able to detect traces of gasoline. I told you we are just understaffed, but we do know what we're doing."

"There is no doubt in your mind that the object of this was to kill McKenzie?"

"No doubt at all. The fire was started in a way guaranteed to be quick but intense. The curtains on the windows probably generated a lot of smoke in a short time. The object was not to burn down the house, else the first would have been set on the ground floor. The way I see it, the arsonist had one aim in mind—to kill the dean. It doesn't take a lot of smoke to do that. This fire created enough to do the job in short order."

Brand and Strong thanked the sergeant and made their way back down the staircase. "What do you plan to do next, Harri?" Brand asked. Strong explained that she had already assigned officers to interview every guest at the dean's reception, and she told Brand about the protesters that some of the neighbors saw leaving the scene when the fire broke out. She pointed to a pile of burnt two-by-fours lying on the lawn.

"A couple of the neighbors saw this thing burning on the lawn just before the fire broke out in the house. Looks like a 'P.' A student reporter was present and took photographs. We've already talked to her. She gave us a handout from a student organization calling itself 'Students for an Egalitarian Society.' They're the ones apparently responsible for this. Know anything about them, Jeremy?"

"Never heard of them," Brand said. "Could be a group of students influenced by one of our sociology professors who wishes he had been a radical and acts out his fantasies vicariously through student groups. Might be the same bunch that invaded the dean's office but now using a different name."

"Sounds like they're sort of majoring in 'protest,'" Strong said. "Since they were considerate enough to hand out a news release, we shouldn't have any trouble finding them. I don't think they're responsible for the house fire, but if they are, they're the stupidest bunch of students I've ever heard of."

Brand arrived at the office of President Milton Coles a few minutes before three o'clock and helped himself to a cup of coffee from the coffee maker sitting on a table in the waiting room. He wasn't sure why the president wanted him to stop by but suspected it had something to do with Clem McKenzie's death. When the president needed help solving a problem, he often turned to Brand to chair a task force to study it and come up with a solution. He also on occasion asked Brand's advice on various issues of local campus concern. Dean McKenzie's death was now campus concern Number One.

When Brand was ushered into the president's office, Coles rose to his feet and walked over to meet him, hand outstretched. "Thanks for stopping by, Jeremy. And sorry for the short notice."

The office was ample but not extravagant. Its furnishings, in contrast to McKenzie's office, were modest. Coles, as well as previous presidents, felt it would aid the university's public image for the president's office to exude a sense of old elegance rather than look like a new and expensive decorator's project. His desk was a university antique, having served several presidents in the nineteenth century. The walls were lined with bookshelves on one side and paintings from the university's museum collection on two others.

"It's always a pleasure, Milton, to chat with you. And I always enjoy visiting Old Main."

"I like this building, too," Coles said. "And not just because it was one of the original buildings at Calloway State. It's got character, style. Not like some of the tasteless boxes this place built in the '50s. You've been here long enough to remember that my predecessor proposed tearing it down and building a modern building to house the office of the central university administration. Protests from the alumni were so intense that he changed his mind and did a thorough and complete renovation of Old Main, saving it for us."

The president motioned for Brand to take a seat on one of two overstuffed chairs beside the fireplace. "But I didn't invite you here, Jeremy, to talk about architecture. I've always been able to depend on you in times of crisis, so I'm once again coming to you for help in dealing with this McKenzie thing."

"Since it's a case of arson and murder, Milton, I would assume that the police have the investigation well in hand."

"I understand that, but I'm more concerned about how this is perceived by our various publics," the president said. "You know how delicate an institution's reputation is. It doesn't take much more than an event like this—violent death on a campus, I mean—to make a huge dent in our applications rate. I got a call from the governor asking what was going on down here. I don't mean to get in the way of the police at all, but I want all the information I can get. I don't like surprises."

"So, what do you want me to do?"

"I know that Harriet Strong is a good friend of yours, and I hope you can use that friendship to share information. Both ways. But more than that, I want you to conduct your own investigation on campus. Poke around a bit and tell me everything you can about Clem McKenzie—whether he had any enemies, if anyone had threatened him, who might possibly have a motive for this deed—things like that."

"I would be willing to do that, but I need some assurances."

"Anything you want."

"First, I would like it to be clear to the remaining dean's office staff that you have asked me to prepare a report for you. And let's call it a 'report' rather than an 'investigation.' I am referring here to the secretaries, administrative assistants, and the associate and assistant deans. A phone call or two from your office ought to do the trick."

"Agreed."

"Second, I'd like to have carte blanche in the research I do for the report. For starters, that means access to all the dean's records, his office, computer files, correspondence records, phone logs, everything."

"Done."

"I would also propose that I alone have access to the dean's office until my report to you is completed. That may get in the way of the interim dean when you make the appointment, but I would hope that my research won't take too long."

"No problem there," the president said. "I am going to announce either today or tomorrow the appointment of the current associate dean as interim dean. I'm fairly sure he will agree to this. George Helms strikes me as pretty ambitious and will probably jump at the opportunity. Since he has his own office, your use of the dean's office should not cause any difficulty. I'll phone him as soon as we're finished here."

"Finally, I'll need resources, such as secretarial help to set up an interview schedule and possibly to transcribe some of the interviews. I'll need to depend on the University News Services Department for help with the media. There may also be some travel involved. I just don't know at this point all that will be required."

"Those are all reasonable requests. I'll have the university treasurer set up a budget for your use and alert News Services that you'll be calling them. The dean's secretary can supply you the clerical assistance you need. Anything else?"

"At this point I can't think of anything."

"Great. I can't tell you how much I appreciate your taking on this assignment. You're a well-respected faculty member and are known widely in the community. Your leadership on this will be an eloquent statement of the seriousness with which we are taking this tragic event. And be sure to let me know if you need anything else."

Brand wasn't surprised that the meeting was brief. The thing about university presidents is that they don't take a long time to make decisions. The life of a president is a continuous series of decisions, and if a president dallied over each and every one, nothing would ever get done. Yet a university is not a hierarchical place, nor does it function like a military organization. Much depends upon goodwill and cooperation. If a president depending on giving orders, nothing would happen. Brand realized that his role was to be the president's eyes and ears, and only the president's support could get for him complete access to the dean's office files. Beyond that, however, Brand was happy for the assignment for another reason. It was, after all, a mystery. As Brand had told his class earlier in the term, the love of solving mysteries is akin to the love of philosophy, the desire to know, to find out things, and here was a puzzle to be solved. Brand recalled that W.H. Auden claimed that a mystery story had to involve a death to make the stakes high enough. McKenzie's death accomplished that.

Chapter 10

BRAND LEFT THE PRESIDENT'S OFFICE and walked across the quadrangle to Bucks Hall. When he arrived at the dean's office Naomi Beals was just hanging up the phone. George Helms was perched on the corner of her desk holding a paper in his hand. "That was President Coles," she said. "He told me you're going to produce a report for him and asked me to provide assistance for you."

"That's correct. Since I was already on campus, I thought I'd stop by and check in with you, but if this is an inconvenient time," Brand said, glancing at George, "I can come back later."

"This is as good a time as any," Helms said. "Naomi and I were just going over some college business. With Clem's death, she and I are having to pick up some of the slack, but we're about finished." Helms paused and then asked, "Why are you conducting an investigation? Won't the police be doing that?"

Brand explained that he was just producing a report for the president and that his role was in no way to be a substitute for the police's investigation. Anything he discovered pertinent to the case would be turned over immediately to the authorities. Helms expressed the appropriate words of confidence in Brand's ability and then left to return to his own office. When Brand told Beals of his plans for the report, she assured him of her complete cooperation. Her face had the drawn and haggard look of someone who has just come through a serious illness, and it occurred to Brand that Beals had been genuinely fond of the dean. Whatever faults he may have had, Clem McKenzie did not have a reputation for being a bad boss.

"I don't plan to do much right now," Brand said, "but maybe we could get organized. Let's make a list of possible information sources." Brand asked if the dean kept a chronological file, and Beals confirmed that he did. The dean referred to it as his "day file," a calendrical file of memos, letters, forms and other documents created by the office and placed in date order. Beals explained that sometimes it was easier to locate a document by date than by subject. The dean might recall sending a memo a "couple of weeks ago," a rough time frame within which to look. Once found, the document would provide information about where it and accompanying documents were filed in the regular office files.

Brand thought that the date file was the quickest way to see what the dean had been doing the past several months. When Beals asked how far back he wished to go—the office had day files for two years running—Brand replied that he would work backward a month at a time. She brought two large postbinders into the office and set them on the desk.

Brand then asked Beals if she knew the dean's computer password. "These days, more communication occurs via e-mail than regular mail, and I need to inspect his e-mail logs," he explained. She did, and wrote it out for him on a slip of paper. He thanked her and went into the dean's office to compile a list of information sources he would ask her to gather for him.

He took a pad of ruled paper and started listing items he would ask Beals to collect. The first was the dean's appointment book. The next was a printout of all the long-distance phone numbers the dean had called in the past two months. In parenthesis Brand noted that Beals could call the network services department for this information. It's amazing how much information computers have allowed us to accumulate on each other, Brand thought. There is no such thing any more as a private conversation.

Brand knew that he should talk to the faculty leadership in the college, so he wrote down the names of all the department chairs in the college, as well as the associate and assistant deans, with a the request for Beals to set up appointments with each of them. On another sheet he listed the times he was in class each day so that she could schedule the interviews around them.

Since Brand had left the dean's reception before it was over, he knew he should talk with the guests and see if he could determine who were the last to leave. It would help if he could find out who was the last person to see the dean alive. He wrote as the last item on his list a request for the names of those invited to the dean's reception.

He tore off the top sheet of the pad and gave it to Beals along with his class schedule. "Here's a list of. information I'll need to get started. If you could get these things for me by tomorrow, I'd be grateful. In the meantime let's talk about anything unusual that you noticed going on in the dean's life of late."

"Like what?"

"Any altercations with faculty? Any conversations that seemed unusual or out of the ordinary? Anything that you noticed which might shed some light on why somebody would want to kill him?"

"Well, I don't know if its pertinent or not, but last week there was a terrible shouting match in the dean's office between Dean McKenzie and a graduate student."

"Tell me about it." Brand picked up his lined tablet and sat himself in the chair beside the secretary's desk.

"I don't want you to think that I'm a snoop, or anything like that. Besides, the student just barged right past me and into the dean's office, and I followed him in, so I not only heard what he said, I saw his body language."

"Who was the student?"

"His name is Gary Hockney, and he was upset because his fellowship isn't going to be renewed next year. The first words out of his mouth were, "You blankety-blank—I don't really want to repeat the exact words—how dare you cancel my fellowship." I offered to call campus security, but Dean McKenzie told me not to. He said he had everything under control, but given what happened next, I wonder."

"What happened next?"

"I closed the door to the dean's office and went back to my desk, but I could hear almost every word the student said, he was talking so loud. He said that he had no warning he was going to lose his fellowship, and without a fellowship he couldn't stay here at Calloway and that it was too late in the year to apply to another graduate program in business. Later Dr. McKenzie told me his side of the conversation."

"And what was that?"

"That recommendations on fellowships were made by a committee and that he was merely accepting the committee's advice. Every year about this time the committee reviews the records of all scholarship recipients and recommends that some of them not be renewed. We usually have a complaint or two, but nothing as violent as Gary Hockney's."

"You say 'violent.' In what way was he violent?"

"Well, he kept yelling at the dean and saying things like 'You can't hide behind the committee. You made the decision, so don't deny it.' Things like that. He also said that the decision about the fellowship was really a decision to kick him out of the program. The dean denied that he was 'kicking' him out of the program, but Gary said that denying him a fellowship was the same thing as dropping him from the program. Later, when the dean told me about his response, he said he warned Gary that he should learn to control his temper and that there was no place in the graduate program for a person with both mediocre grades and a violent personality. He also told Gary that conduct like he was exhibiting then would get him fired from a job in the business world in a heartbeat."

"A moment ago you said Hockney's response was violent. Did you mean verbally violent or more than that?"

"Both. He was shouting at the dean. I could hear every word. When Dr. McKenzie told Gary that his conduct would get him fired in the business world, that set him off. I heard a piece of furniture fall over, and rushed into the office to see if everything was OK. A table lay on its side with a broken leg. The lamp that was sitting on it was on the floor all in pieces. There were pieces of glass all over the place. It was a Tiffany lamp, quite expensive. But it was a mess. I asked the dean again if everything was all right, and he said, 'Mr. Hockney was just leaving. We had a little accident.' But I know that Gary knocked over that lamp. I call that violent."

"This was not the kind of interchange that goes on in the dean's office every day, we hope."

Beals nervously rearranged some of the items on her desk and continued. "It isn't. I don't recall ever hearing anything like that. But there's one more thing."

"And what is that?"

"Well, when I went into the dean's office and saw the smashed lamp and the broken table and all, Gary was standing up and had his fists clinched. You've heard that old expression, 'if looks could kill.' Well, that's the kind of look Gary had in his eyes. He leaned over the dean's desk with his face about a foot from the dean's and said something like, 'You'll be sorry. You'll regret that you did this to me.' I was about to call Campus Security in spite of what the dean said, but by then Gary was leaving."

"Did anybody else hear this ruckus?"

"No, thank God. I would have been embarrassed if someone else had been waiting here in the office to see the dean."

Brand made additional notes on his pad, tore off a couple of pages, and handed them to Beals. "I would appreciate it if you would type up an account of what you have just told me. Maybe the notes I took while you were talking will be of some help."

Brand walked back into the dean's office. He knew that he should call Harriet Strong and tell her about the president's request for a report. Harri will probably be OK with this, Brand thought, but still it wouldn't be wise for her to hear about this first from somebody else.

He reached across the dean's desk and picked up the phone.

Brand invited Harriet to stop by his house later in the afternoon. Neither wanted the events of the night and day to interfere with their wine time. When they got together for a wine sharing either she or Brand would supply the bottle—nothing rare or expensive, but most times something neither had tasted before. "So much wine, so little time," said the plaque hanging on the wall of Brand's cellar. Being below ground the cellar could maintain the preferred 55 to 60 degrees with occasional help from a supplementary air conditioner.

Brand got his wines from merchants, other collectors, auctions, or by direct shipments from wineries. Whenever parcels arrived Paul Ruskin, brought them into the cellar, unpacked them and set the bottles on the tasting table for Jeremy's later inspection.

Paul still looked like the graduate student he used to be, except that he dressed better now, having exchanged jeans and sneakers for chinos and topsiders. His untamed dark hair pushed its way out from under the baseball cap he usually wore.

Although Ruskin was employed primarily for help with academic research, one of his duties was maintaining the cellar records on a desktop computer equipped with software designed for the purpose. Its special features made it possible for Brand to know the details of any wine he owned, including where it was purchased, its current value, and how many bottles of it he owned.

The cellar furnishings were neat but not overly elaborate. Storage for individual bottles as well as cases was standard-issue racking available by mail order. Along one wall of the main room were racks containing individual bottles of Bordeaux and Burgundies and Sauternes. The racking on the other wall stored California, Washington State and Oregon wines. A smaller room off of the main room contained case lots of wines from Spain, Italy, Chile and Argentina. From that room a rarely used external door led up a short flight of stairs to the back yard.

For this tasting Brand was supplying the wine, a Spanish Tempranillo that enjoyed high ratings from wine critics but was difficult to find because, being inexpensive, it was a great value and flew off wine-shop shelves. Paul Ruskin had been working in the cellar preparing wines for shipment to a future auction when Brand and Strong pulled up chairs to the trestle table that dominated the center of the room. Ruskin uncorked the bottle and poured a small amount into three glasses. Brand swirled the purple liquid in his glass, a motion that formed little eddies to release the wine's aromas. He brought the glass to his nose, sniffed, and then took a sip, chewing the wine to release its flavors onto his palate.

"Very satisfactory," he intoned. "It's young and won't age very well, but a great value. Would go well with paella."

An unspoken rule at these tastings required that no one would talk business, though in a small town the line between community activities and business concerns remained elusive. As the wine level in the bottle decreased, the conversation shifted to recent events.

Strong stared into her glass and said, "I'm concerned about the graffiti on the side of Bucks Hall. I think it must be more than a college prank"

"What graffiti?" Brand asked.

"Someone spray-painted 'Death to the Dean' on the side of the building," Ruskin said. "Nobody saw who did it, but the newspaper received an anonymous call and sent out a photographer to take a picture. I'll look for it in the paper when it comes."

"I wouldn't worry about it," Brand said. "It sounds like a student prank."

Strong shook her head in disagreement. "I'm not so sure. Now that the dean is dead I can't overlook any expression of hostility toward him. I know there's always a certain amount of resentment of deans, but McKenzie seems to have generated more than his share, though I don't pretend to understand all this dislike of deans in the first place."

"It's part of academic culture," Brand said. "You must have encountered the same attitudes in law school, Harri. Most faculty still operate with a medieval notion of the university as a collection of self-governing scholars. Faculty also resent being told what to do and tend to see deans as unnecessary bureaucrats."

"But that's loony. Modern universities are complex organizations with budgets rivaling those of large corporations. So why do faculty resent having a boss?"

"It's part of the academic mindset. Faculty are trained in graduate school to be independent scholars, and they make their reputations for individual work. They also have more loyalty to their academic discipline than to their employer, so they tend to dislike authority figures."

"Believe it or not, I dislike bureaucracy as much as anyone. That's why I left the FBI. But this much venom aimed at administrators doesn't make much sense to me, Jeremy."

"Think of it this way," Brand replied. "There are two organizational structures. First is the official one in which the governor appoints a board of trustees who hire a president who hires vice presidents and deans. Then there are department heads and finally faculty. It looks like the kind of vertical organizational chart you will find in any business textbook. But there is another organizational structure that you won't find in the books. In this one, faculty are at the top of the pyramid. They serve on the presidential search committee, help select the deans, elect their department heads, recruit new faculty for their department, and so on. Trustees are off to the side somewhere, and all the other administrative personnel, from groundskeepers to cafeteria workers to registrars and admissions officers, are relegated to the margins. If you doubt me, ask the next faculty member you see to name the trustees. I bet most professors can't name even one."

"So, which organizational model is correct?" Ruskin asked.

"They both are. And that's what causes the tension. In a real sense the university *is* the faculty. Without faculty there wouldn't be a university. You could have all the deans and vice presidents you want, but without good faculty, students just wouldn't come. No students, no university."

"The attitude you describe may be true of full-time tenured faculty," Ruskin ventured, "but speaking for part-time instructors, I don't think we have a particularly bad attitude toward the dean or other administrators."

Brand took another sip from his wine glass. "That's because tenured faculty have made a career commitment to the university. That gives them a different relationship to the administration than part-time faculty have. They see deans come and go, and after a while faculty become cynical about administrators."

"That's another thing," Harriet said. "Tenure." She reached for the wine bottle and refreshed the glasses all around. "I know the usual rhetoric—tenure protects academic freedom. But tenure has really become a guarantee of lifetime employment."

"In a certain sense that's true," Brand agreed. "But opposition to academic research can come from unexpected sources. Usually people outside the university get riled up over faculty statements about religion or politics, but a few years ago a university in the Midwest was pressured by the state's beef growers association to fire a professor in the School of Agriculture because her research showed that eating beef was unhealthy."

Ruskin sat his glass down and asked, "So what about that group of students that demonstrated in the dean's office? Are they suspects?"

"They are until we have reason to eliminate them," Harriet said. "That stunt with the burning display on the dean's lawn needs to be explained. They had opportunity, means, and perhaps motive. The gasoline they used for the flaming whatever it was makes them look suspicious even if what they were doing was just a student prank that got out of hand."

"It wouldn't be the first time student pranks got out of hand," Brand said. "In spite of laws against hazing, almost every year one of the fraternities gets in trouble for its behavior." He took another sip of wine. This is beginning to sound too much like work, and you know our rules about that. Someone change the subject."

By now the wine bottle was more than half empty. Harriet looked at her watch. "I'd change the subject if I could stay, but I've got to run." As she left the cellar, Harriet turned back toward the table. "I still feel uneasy. Tenure decisions seem to be more than academic exercises. I wouldn't be surprised if a negative tenure decision is at the root of this thing." With that she climbed the stairs to Brand's study and let herself out the front door

Chapter 11

The flames cast a reddish glow over the windows. Smoke seeped underneath the door like a morning fog on the beach. The roar of the fire grew louder as the fumes slowly filled the bedroom. Brand found himself coughing, then choking, then struggling to sit up. He walked, half crawled, to the bedroom door and felt it, noting that its heat indicated a roaring conflagration on the other side. His reason told him not to open the door for fear of spreading the flames, but his empty bed signaled that his wife was not in the room. His son, Willis, often awakened with night terrors, and Brand's wife would go to their son's bed until he quieted. Jumping to the conclusion that this was one of those nights, Brand knew he had to get to his wife and child.

He grabbed a sheet from the bed, splashed water on it in the bathtub, then threw it around him and over his head. He opened the door and recoiled from the heat that struck him in the face like the blast from a blowtorch. He turned his back to the flames and with a crab-like motion tried to move down the hallway to his son's room. His feet were like lead. He could hardly lift them, but he heard the crash of the roof as it gave way directly over the bedroom where his wife and child lay. He knew it was too late. He could not save the two people in his life who mattered most. A firefighter wearing an oxygen tank grabbed Brand by the arm and draped him over his shoulder in the classic fireman's carry. As Brand coughed and struggled for breath, he and the firefighter floated out the window and onto the lawn like a leaf borne by an autumn wind.

Brand sat up in bed, sweating, pulse throbbing. He had not had the dream for months. The tour of McKenzie's fire-blackened house must have brought it back. He got a glass of water and sat down on the overstuffed chair next to his bed. The fire that took his wife and child was accidental, due to faulty electrical wiring. The fire that killed Clem McKenzie was deliberate. Brand wondered how anyone could do such a thing and who would have hatred the dean enough to commit homicide—for homicide it was, if Harri's conclusions were correct. The arsonist had one aim in mind: to kill the dean. The House was damaged, but not destroyed. The fire had been planned for a time when the dean would be there alone, since his wife was out of town. Who would have such knowledge of the dean's household?

Brand turned these thoughts over and over in his mind. Tabitha's departure was not something anyone could have anticipated, since it was occasioned by a sick grandchild. Clem's explanation for Tabitha's absence quickly made its rounds of the attendees, so the arsonist—assuming he or she was at the party—would not have known in advance that the opportunity to kill the dean only, and not his wife too, was at hand. Did the arsonist then hurriedly prepare the makings of the fire? Or was the arsonist always prepared, waiting for a night when the dean was alone? But how would the perpetrator get access to the house on any other night? Maybe the arsonist wouldn't have cared if the dean's wife also died in the fire, and her absence was irrelevant.

By now Brand's mind was in fast-forward, and he knew sleep was an impossibility. He pulled on his bathrobe and went down the stairs to his study. Switching on the light, he pulled a ruled pad in front of him and began to make a list of individuals who, as far he knew, might have reason to kill the dean.

On the tablet he wrote the following names and notes:

Sarah Giles—threatened the dean at his reception.

Brand couldn't bring himself to believe that Sarah Giles was responsible for such a violent act, but she did make a statement that many people would remember as a threat to the dean. She was upset about the dean's handling of her tenure review. Of that there was no doubt, and he could not eliminate her as a suspect yet.

Gary Hockney—angry at the loss of his fellowship.

Brand made a note to ask Paul Ruskin to talk to some of Hockney's friends who might be able to shed some light on his state of mind.

SES—a protest that got out of hand?

It didn't really seem likely that this was a student act, but protests can explode into violence. The police would no doubt talk to Danny Bennett and his student protesters, and Brand was certain that Harriet would share any information she received from those interviews.

Other enemies of the dean???

Here was where Brand was going to need the most help. He knew that McKenzie was not popular among the faculty—few deans are. Sometimes the rhetoric gets strong and tempers flare. But most academic quarrels bear out the truth of the old saying about campus politics: "The fights are so fierce because the stakes are so small." Might have to revise that old saying, Brand told himself. This time the stakes were as high as they get.

Chapter 12

PAUL RUSKIN WONDERED why the people who work in health food stores always look so shabby. Is there some connection in their minds, he wondered, between organic foods, nutritional supplements, whole grain diets and a disdain for personal appearance? He noticed that the clerks were pale and thin, and the women didn't appear to use cosmetics.

When Brand had asked him during breakfast to talk to some of Hockney's friends, Ruskin decided to meet first with Miles Newlin, Hockney's roommate. Ruskin did not want the conversation to seem like a grilling, so he phoned his girlfriend Melanie Carter and asked for her help on the assumption that a three-way conversation would seem less like an interview and more like a casual discussion. Carter was a graduate student and knew her way around grad-student circles better than Ruskin did, and the two of them—after much discussion—determined that a neutral site for the conversation was essential. They decided to invite Newlin to the Nature Grove Cafe.

Locals referred to Nature Grove as the PC Cafe, since it was viewed as the most politically correct place in College Falls to eat. The combination health food store and restaurant was owned by the people who worked there, and it had an ideological commitment to organic vegetables, free-range poultry and hand-made pastas. In addition to offering sandwiches and prepared meals, Nature Grove also stocked a full line of organic foods. Its politically correct image was further enhanced by the store's pledge to sell products from worker-owned farm collectives whenever possible. Its coffee, for example, came only from farmers' cooperatives that avoided pesticides. It didn't taste very good— no comparison to Colombian, Paul thought—but drinking it gave some people a sense of moral superiority.

Many residents of College Falls shopped at Nature Grove even when they did not share the organization's political agenda. It was one of the few places in town offering grains in bulk, unusual ingredients for ethnic foods and freshly baked crusty breads from a local baker. The whole place smelled strongly of curry, and a kind of decrepit dinginess pervaded everything. Still, Nature Grove served good food at its lunch counter—food that most patrons found tasty and hoped was sanitary and healthful.

Ruskin and Carter arrived at Nature Grove before Newlin did, and both ordered smoothies, the specialty fruit drink of the place, while they waited for their guest to arrive.

"I can't understand why a health food place sells so many pills," Ruskin said, his eyes directed toward the shelves behind the cash register. "Look at that wall over there. Looks like a pharmacy. Everything there from ground limestone to ginseng root tablets. If organic food is so good for you, why do you have to take all those pills, too?"

"It's part of the culture of the place," Carter said. "Health food stores and restaurants promote diets that increase one's life span, and certain minerals and substances necessary in those diets are not found in large enough quantities in food, so they provide them in supplements."

Paul rolled his eyes. "I wouldn't be surprised but what it's mostly a scam."

"Maybe. But the people who package this stuff have found a strong niche. Since people are buying it, the marketplace supports it, so what's the problem? It's really Business 101."

"Ever since you started your doctorate in economics, you tend to give economic interpretations to everything, but this is one time when I tend to agree with you that health concerns take second place to economic interests. Besides, I don't think the way of eating they propose is all that healthy."

"I don't think a lot of pills is healthy," Carter said. "Remember when the founder of one of the major health food magazines died on camera right in the middle of the *Dick Cavett Show*?—died!—right there in front of everybody. Cavett figured out instantly what had happened and cut to a commercial. When he came back on the air, he had a different guest sitting there—a live one."

Ruskin laughed. "Yeah, I do remember that. But the guy's magazine is still alive and well."

They saw Miles Newlin come through the door and motioned for him to join them. The three placed their orders. Carter chose the vegetable lasagna, Ruskin the turkey and Havarti cheese sandwich, and Newlin the bean and rice burrito. Ruskin favored the direct approach, but Carter had convinced him that it would be best to engage in small talk first, though Newlin would no doubt wonder why he was being given a free lunch.

Carter and Newlin exchanged queries about how each other's graduate work was going and Ruskin sipped his smoothie.

"I'm glad you're both enjoying your graduate programs," Ruskin said. "I'm certainly enjoying *not* being a graduate student."

Newlin's glass of papaya juice arrived. "Someone told me you used to be in the doctoral program here but dropped out. Why?"

"Lots of reasons. I entered graduate school expecting to have a career as a professor, but I could tell pretty soon that it would be an uphill battle."

"How so?" Newlin asked.

"Everybody was predicting massive retirements, and that would open up slots for people like me. But it didn't happen. Professors continued to teach past 70, since there is no longer a mandatory retirement age, and budget cuts in higher education forced universities to use more part-time faculty and have larger classes. I find that I enjoy teaching part time, and my master's degree was adequate for that. I didn't need a doctorate. Besides, I grew to hate my field."

Newlin looked puzzled. "Hate it? Why?"

"I just couldn't stand all the *theory* that they threw at us. Most of it was imported from French universities. The French approach their academic movements like their clothing styles. They change almost as often as the hemlines in their fashion houses. By the time a movement reaches here, American universities fall over themselves trying to adapt to it, even though the French probably have gone on to something else. Right now the big deal in theory among American universities is postmodernism. I got into literature because I really enjoy talking about what a novel or a what a poem *means*, but around here nobody thinks that's the job of literature professors any more. It's easier to accept the claim of postmodernists that there is no meaning to a work of literature."

"Don't bore Miles with your anti-French diatribe, Paul." Melanie had heard it all before. "Let's change the subject to something more interesting."

"I'm fascinated," Newlin said. "We never talk about stuff like this in the MBA program, and I didn't take all that many literature courses when I was an undergraduate. I always thought that looking for meaning was what the study of literature is all about."

"Not any more. The big debate going on now is whose works we should study. The postmodernists claim that the canon of authors studied in college was chosen not because of the worth of the works themselves but due to the power of the prevailing intellectual class, namely white males, whose choice for great literature included mostly the work of *dead* white males. I'm sure that in another few years another French theory will discredit that view and a new generation of scholars will think the postmodernists are out of it."

"So what? The same sort of thing happens in business. It seems that almost every year there is a new management theory out there. I figure, just learn the stuff and get my degree. Then I'm out of here and can do what I want."

"Not an irrational aim," Ruskin said. "I just got tired of all the literary games. It wasn't that I couldn't play them. In fact, I was rather good at them. But I decided that it was all too boring and that I couldn't keep my enthusiasm up. Besides, I enjoy working for Jeremy Brand. Always something new."

The food arrived, and Newlin picked up his burrito. "By the way, why am I getting a free lunch? I don't suppose you invited me here because of my good looks."

Ruskin laid down his sandwich and swallowed the bite in his mouth. "Everybody has heard about the fight Gary Hockney had with the dean over his fellowship. Professor Brand wanted me to talk to some of Gary's friends, see if he was mad enough to burn down his house."

"So that's what this is about. Brand thinks Newlin is a suspect?"

"I didn't say that. Brand is just gathering information about everybody who was angry with the dean. It looks like a pretty long list."

"Why is Brand interested?"

"A couple of reasons. He was a friend of Dean McKenzie, and President Coles has asked him to put together a report for him. I'm just helping him with some background information. So, how is Gary doing now?"

"OK, I guess," Newlin said. "Gary tends to be a moody guy—a real loner—even in the best of times. He's bummed out about this fellowship thing, and that makes him a little more moody than normal."

"What are Gary's future plans?"

"Don't know. I'm not sure even Gary knows. Ever since he left the Army, Gary hasn't had a good sense of what he wants to do with his life. I never did think he was interested in graduate school. It just sort of happened for him. I think that's why he doesn't know what to do now."

"Gary was in the Army?" Ruskin asked. "I didn't know that. What did he do?"

"I don't know much about Gary's background, except that he was in ROTC when he was an undergraduate. He had to have the ROTC scholarship to get through college. He served two years' active duty then went on reserve status. What with downsizing and all, the Army made it real easy for him to go from active to reserve. He said something once about being in a ranger battalion."

"That must have meant that he had special training in demolition, explosives, things like that? Could he have been upset enough at the dean to burn his house down?"

"Look, you want to know this stuff, ask Gary himself. He's a pretty quiet guy. Pretty nice, usually, except when he goes ape shit like he did with the dean. Keeps to himself mostly, so I really don't know a lot about him. As for burning down the dean's house, I don't think so. Gary's not that kind of person."

Ruskin sensed that Newlin was not going to say much else about Gary Hockney, so the rest of lunch was devoted to small talk and chitchat. Ruskin wondered whether Brand would find the information Newlin provided of interest. He would find out this evening.

While Ruskin, Carter and Newlin were finishing their lunch at Nature Grove, Archie Scott was waiting in another campus eatery, the Golden Dragon, a restaurant typical of those near the campus: inexpensive, not much on decor, but known for good food. Anyone watching Scott could tell he was nervous, betrayed not only by the thumbnail he was chewing on but also by his antsy behavior. His left heel was beating a tattoo on the floor that sounded like a steady drip of water. He was there at the invitation of Sarah Giles, and he did not know why she wanted to see him, though he feared the worst. The restaurant did not provide an intimate ambiance, but it had several booths in the back that offered a limited amount of privacy. Scott situated himself in one of those booths and sat facing the door so he could spot Sarah when she entered.

When she came through the front door, Scott stood up and motioned for her to join him. Sliding into the booth, she laid her bag down beside her and smoothed her hair behind her ears. The decor of the Golden Dragon was standard Chinese restaurant stuff: large murals of imposing mountains, dragon motifs around the doors and windows, red tasseled short curtains separating the dining areas from the cashier. Giles breathed out a long sigh and picked up the menu. "I don't need to look at this," she said. "I know the menu like the back of my hand." Scott ordered the combination plate of Mongolian beef, and Giles the moo goo gai pan.

Scott had decided not to initiate the conversation, though he had a pretty good idea what it was going to be about. What he didn't know was how much Sarah was pissed at him, personally and individually, for the outcome of the dean's tenure review meeting. He knew he couldn't really count on her silence about his Middletown connection, but so far she had said nothing to anyone about it, as far as he knew. Maybe she didn't know the precise vote of the committee; after all, McKenzie died before any letters went out or there was any announcement of the dean's decision. If the other members of the committee kept their mouths shut, then she wouldn't even know the vote, especially since Cynthia Lemaster wasn't there. These thoughts were interrupted by Sarah.

"Archie, have you thought about what a precarious situation I'm in now, with not getting tenure and all? Do you have any idea what it's like to be facing your last paycheck? Or even going on unemployment compensation?"

"I don't know why you think that. I know you're concerned about getting tenure, but with Clem's death and everything, I've heard that no letters have gone out from the dean's office. Who knows. The interim dean—whoever that turns out to be—may give you a fairer hearing."

"Don't be naive, Archie. I'm not going to get tenure. I know it. You know it. Everybody knows it. I know about the travesty of a tenure review hearing that went on in the dean's office—everybody on campus seems to have heard about it. It's just a matter of time until the denial letter comes. I'm thinking about filing an EEOC grievance, but getting some resolution there will take years. In the meantime I need to look for another job. I've already got application letters out to several places. At least I've got a year to find something. Maybe I can find a place where the climate for women is better than it is here. My problem for the short-run is how to support myself while looking for a job elsewhere."

Giles paused and took a sip of tea. Scott was trying to anticipate where she was going with this. He was trying to figure out why she was discussing money in the context of her tenure situation. Then it hit him like a blow to the solar plexus. She was hitting him up for money in exchange for her silence. Better be careful here, Scott thought. Mustn't sound defensive or threatened. Maybe he could take control of the conversation.

"I feel bad about what happened in the committee, I really do. I wish I could have done something about it, but things got out of control, especially when Cynthia went off like a roman candle. I did my best to argue your case, but Clem already seemed to have his mind made up." Scott wondered if the lie would stick. Sarah showed no inclination to disagree, so he surged ahead with what he hoped would be a conciliatory gesture.

"I know the next few months are going to be rough for you, and as one colleague to another, I'd like to help you with your transition, so I'm willing to offer you some financial assistance after your next year's contract is up. Of course, I can only do that if you agree to keep quiet about this Middletown thing. I intend to resign there anyway." Scott wanted to continue at Calloway and resign from Middletown rather than leave Calloway as McKenzie directed him to do. Now that McKenzie was dead, Scott felt that he had more time to work things out. But this wretched women could spoil it all. Public disclosure at this point would be a disaster.

Giles looked squarely at Scott and arched her left eyebrow. "You're trying to bribe me, Archie. You are offering to buy my silence."

"No, no, no," Scott said, enunciating the words in staccato. "Nothing like that at all. I'm just offering to help, one colleague to another. Of course it would be necessary for you to be sensitive to my situation and not speak of it. If you did, the cost to me would be so great that I couldn't carry through on my offer."

"So what did you have in mind?"

"I thought about something in the neighborhood of five hundred dollars a month for the first year following your terminal contract here, for a total of six thousand dollars. That will give you a little cushion for your transition. Again, I don't want to be repetitive, but if my situation became known during that time, I probably couldn't carry through with this."

Giles gave a little laugh that was more snort than chuckle. "You *are* trying to make me into a blackmailer."

"Not at all, Sarah. I am making you an offer, friend to friend."

"Archie, this conversation reminds me of the story about the male professor who, to make a point in class about the power of money, asked a female student if she would sleep with him for ten million dollars. She thought about it for a few seconds and said, 'Yeah, probably.' Then he asked her if she would sleep with him for ten dollars. The student was horrified and said, 'What do you think I am?' The professor replied, 'We know what you are; we're just haggling about the price.' If I'm going to be a blackmailer, Archie, we need to haggle about the price."

This conversation was not going at all as Scott thought it would. "Please don't use the term 'blackmailer,' Sarah. I want to make this gesture as a friend. Maybe I was too low. I could probably make that $750 per month for a year, again beginning a year from now."

This time her laugh was a low-throated chuckle. "I've thought about this too, Archie, and I have a very different sum and different timetable in mind. Let's say two thousand dollars a month starting now."

Scott nearly choked on the tea he was sipping. He coughed, spewing some tea onto the table, and then sat the cup down. "*Two thousand* dollars a month? Really, Sarah, I don't have that kind of money."

"Of course you do. You have two jobs, remember?"

"But I have expenses. Besides, I'll be quitting my second position at the end of this year. I've already written the letter." Another lie, but she seemed to accept it. "Be reasonable, Sarah. I've made you a reasonable offer, and you need to be reasonable about all this too."

"Be reasonable? How reasonable has everyone been to me? Was Dean McKenzie reasonable to me? Has this university been reasonable? I think my demand to you is very reasonable after all I've been through."

"Let's say—just for the purpose of discussion–that I was able to provide the sum you are mentioning. How long would you expect me to do this?" Scott asked.

"For at least two years. Maybe longer, depending on whether I get relocated by then. We'll just have to wait and see."

Scott now knew what the phrase about one's blood running cold meant. This conversation was not going well at all.

He did not say a word but stared straight ahead as the server put two plates of food on the table. Giles picked up her purse and slid out from behind the table. "I'm sure I'll be hearing from you, Archie. Enjoy your lunch." She turned and walked toward the door.

Scott could not bring himself even to pick up his chopsticks. He had lost his appetite.

Chapter 13

WHEN BRAND ENTERED HIS HOUSE he could smell the aroma of fresh baking emanating from the kitchen. His housekeeper had settled down to a routine for the household, and today was her baking day. The aroma was either deep-dish apple pie or strudel, Brand thought.

Brand's Victorian house contained many details typical of expensive houses of the period, such as the cherry woodwork and circular stairs and banister that led to the second floor. The house featured an entry foyer separated from the rest of the house by another door. Immediately past the door on the left was the stairway to the second floor. To the right was the living room, the "parlor" of the nineteenth century. Behind it was the dining room, which had doors leading to the kitchen in the back of the house. Across the hall from the dining room was Brand's study. The door to the wine cellar was under the circular staircase.

The house was large, but not ostentatious. The rooms were spacious, and with twelve-foot ceilings, the sense of expanse increased. The hardwood floors throughout were covered with rugs, mostly Oriental, of varying sizes and provenance.

Dinner was often an occasion or entertaining friends, and tonight the meal included Paul and Melanie who announced that after dinner they were going to see a French film at the local art-film theater. "It will probably turn out to be a moody drama so typical of the French where everybody dies in the last reel," Paul said. "But at least Melanie and I know there won't be any car chases or explosions."

"I find it interesting that the French feel threatened by American films," Brand said. "They have even passed a law requiring French exhibitors to show a certain percentage of French films. If it weren't required by law, few cinema houses in France would show French films because American films are more popular. But this may not be an especially good thing, since so much of American culture glorifies violence and mayhem."

Melanie nodded her head in agreement. "Last year on my trip to Spain I met a Dutch woman who said she was afraid to visit the United States because of all the violence she saw in American films. I tried to assure her that Hollywood trades in make-believe, not reality, but she said she would rather spend her vacation in Spain, just to be safe."

"But French films are so predictable," Paul said. "In an article I read the author proposed to a French director a different ending for his film, and the director replied, "but that would have been a happy ending, and there aren't happy endings in real life.' When the author argued that there are indeed *some* happy endings, the director replied that nobody would believe such a film ending, that it was a matter of *vérité*."

"That's much like the French attitude toward their language," Brand added. "The French Academy thinks it can control the evolution of French by passing laws against *Franglais*, that mixture of French and English that crops up everywhere in France—quick lunch, le weekend, le sex shop, things like that. Languages evolve just as species do. It's impossible to stop either."

The rest of the dinner period devoted itself to a further dissection of French culture. After they all took their dirty dishes to the kitchen, Paul and Melanie excused themselves, leaving Brand to the solitude of his house. The housekeeper would return later after seeing to her father's needs, but for the meantime the house was quiet. Tonight promised to be a time for some quiet hours with a book and a review of the cellar records Ruskin had updated.

Brand's early-morning habits led him to go to bed early, especially when he was alone. He looked around for the latest issue of *Wine Spectator* to provide bedtime reading but couldn't see it anywhere in the office. Then he remembered that he had seen in his wine cellar earlier in the day. He opened the door to the cellar, turned on the lights, and descended the stairs. Brand saw the *Spectator* on the tasting table, but as he walked toward it, he saw a sight that made him stop as though his legs had turned to cement. Hanging from three of the racks were plastic milk bottles half filled with clear liquid. All three were connected with fuses that ran to a candle burning on the floor. The candle's wick ran along its side, not in the middle. Wrapped around it were the fuses leading to the plastic jugs. So unexpected was the scene that that it took a few seconds for the sight to register itself fully on his consciousness. He was looking at the same kind of incendiary device that set fire to Clem McKenzie's house. What he did not see was the hand holding the wine bottle that hit him on the head....

When Brand regained consciousness he was strapped to a gurney inside an emergency medical vehicle bouncing along one of the brick streets of College Falls while a paramedic made sure the intravenous drip in his arm stayed put. With his free hand he reached up and touched his head, which felt like a boulder had dropped on it. What his fingers discovered there was a thick strip of gauze wrapping. His fingers explored further and discovered that the wrapping encircled his head. Brand looked down at his sweater and saw that it was covered with his blood, as was his shirt, which started out the day blue and now looked like something he had used for an oil change on his car.

The police chief was already at the hospital emergency room when the ambulance arrived. She showed her badge to the paramedics and walked alongside her friend as the orderlies wheeled him into the emergency room.

"Can't even trust you to keep out of trouble when you are home by yourself. You must be getting close to something."

Brand started to speak, but his speech was slurred, and he found that he had difficulty articulating the words.

"Don't try to talk now, Jeremy. We'll sort it out later. In the meanwhile we'll let these folks take care of you."

A physician was shining a light into Brand's eyes while the nurses were taking his blood pressure and monitoring his other vital signs. Brand felt sleepy and wondered when they would leave him alone so he could get some rest.

In the morning Brand awoke with a splitting headache. That phrase was the first that came to his mind, but "roaring" also seemed appropriate, for it felt to him as though a hundred surfs were pounding inside his skull. His physician, Abe Cohen, stopped by shortly after the nurses' assistants delivered breakfast.

"Well, Jeremy, I see you got yourself in a bit of trouble last night. But you're going to be fine. There's a slight concussion but no permanent damage. You may have quite a headache for a few days, though."

Brand asked for more details about his injury and was told he had a cut on his head that required twelve stitches. It might leave a scar, but even that was doubtful. In a couple of days he would feel his normal self again, the doctor told him.

"How did I get to the hospital?" Brand asked.

Your housekeeper came home and found you in the cellar unconscious and tied to a chair, broken bottles and wine everywhere. Blood too. That's the way it is with head injuries; they bleed like the devil, even when the injury is rather small. She called 911 and the paramedics brought you here. Lucky for you that you have such a hard head." Cohen chuckled and Brand responded in kind.

"A hard head; another interesting metaphor for stubbornness," Brand said. "It seems that this blow stirred up the metaphor-awareness of my brain. I'm beginning to see the metaphorical significance of everything."

"I'll write out instructions for your release this afternoon. No need for you to spend any more time in the hospital than necessary. Make an appointment with my office for a couple of days from now and we'll give you another check-up to make sure everything's fine."

The doctor had no sooner left the room than Harriet entered.

"Glad to see you looking so good. I just saw your doctor, and he says you're going home this afternoon." She pulled up a chair. "You were attacked because of something that you know, or something that the killer thinks you know. Have any idea what it is?"

"I don't have a clue. I wish I did."

"Well, when you're feeling better, we'll review everything and see if we can figure out what it is. Meanwhile, take care of yourself. And, by the way, be careful from now on. Our killer is getting bolder."

By the time Brand woke up the next morning in his own bed, he felt more like his normal self, except for the headache. A bandage covered the stitches on his head, though it was small enough to be covered by a hat. Today, he hoped, would be a normal day.

The police had made an investigation of the cellar and found that Brand's attacker had forced entry through the door that led to the back yard. The attempt by the police to find fingerprints yielded nothing. Most people have seen enough television programs involving police investigations to know that they should wipe off their fingerprints from potentially incriminating objects. Even if fingerprints from people not in the Brand household had been found on the wine bottle, that would not help much to identify the attacker, unless the person were a criminal with a police record. Brand knew that most people have never been fingerprinted, so their prints are not on file anywhere. If his attacker were, as Brand supposed, someone within the academic community, the chances that the person's fingerprints were on file with some law enforcement agency were minimal. The only exception to that would be if a faculty member needed a security clearance to do research sponsored by certain agencies of the federal government, but few at Calloway did such research.

After three days Brand felt well enough to get back into his usual schedule. The classes he had missed were covered by his teaching assistant, who gave additional reading assignments and conducted study sessions. When Brand returned home from his first class meeting since the attack, he was beginning to feel more normal. As he walked onto his front porch, the familiar unmarked police car driven by Harriet Strong pulled alongside the curb. Brand waited while Strong got out of her car and joined him on the porch.

"Glad to see that you're back to work, Jeremy. How was your class?"

"Fine. Everybody seems to know about my mishap, and that's all the students wanted to talk about for the first ten minutes. I finally got them back to the syllabus."

"That's understandable. Nothing happens in a small town without everybody knowing about it, and following on the dean's death…well, you can see why everybody's concerned. Until we find out who's setting these incendiary devices, the whole town's going to be jumpy."

"So you don't have anything new to report?"

Strong brushed back the lock of hair that had fallen over her forehead. "I wish I did. Right now you're my best hope. Let's go inside and see if we can figure out why somebody wants to kill you."

The professor and police chief stopped in the hallway long enough to deposit their coats on the hall tree. As they entered Brand's office, Strong deposited her briefcase at the end of the sofa under the bay window and sat down on the leather cushions. "The way I see it, the murderer thinks you may know something that would be threatening. We've just got to find out what that is."

"Don't think I haven't racked my brain, at least that part still functioning after the attack, to figure out what. I haven't come up with an answer, though."

"Let's review your movements the day of the attack. That might tell us what the murderer thinks you discovered."

Brand took his appointment book out of his shirt pocket and thumbed through it. "Most of Thursday was routine—classes, one committee meeting, lunch at the Faculty Club. The only unusual thing I did was spend some time in the dean's office looking through his computer files. Didn't find a thing."

"But maybe the killer thinks you did, or is afraid that you did. Maybe the information isn't on the computer but is somewhere else in the office—in the files, notes in the desk, scribbles on the appointment book."

"I'll go back this afternoon and take another look. Could be that I overlooked something obvious." Brand picked up the short report that Paul left on the desk about his meeting with Miles Newlin. "We do have another person who hated the dean."

"The list seems to be getting longer every day. Who's the latest addition?"

"This one is a graduate student, Gary Hockney." Brand told Strong about Hockney's outburst in the dean's office and his threats to the dean. "Paul is a friend of Hockney's roommate, Miles Newlin. I asked Paul to see what Newlin knows about Hockney. Here's his report." As Brand read each page of the three-page document, he passed it on to Strong.

"I don't see much here, Jeremy," Harriet concluded. "Apart from his time in the military, where he might have gained knowledge of explosives and such, Hockney seems to be just another angry graduate student."

"I agree," Brand said. "Occasionally you read stories about a graduate student who becomes violent. The most recent one I remember is the California student who shot three professors who failed him on his thesis defense. Hockney's nonrenewed fellowship might have given him a motive, but I can't see how he had the means or opportunity."

"I agree. But we'll keep him on our list just in case." Strong reached over the end of the couch and retrieved her briefcase. "Gotta run, but I'll let you know if anything else turns up. And I want to be the first to know if you find anything else in the dean's office."

Chapter 14

IT WAS AFTER LUNCH before Brand made his way back to Buck's Hall and the dean's office. He looked around the now-familiar surroundings and wondered where he should begin to search. He opened all the desk drawers and found nothing that looked like a repository for incriminating evidence. Next he examined all the bookshelves, looking behind all of them to see if the dean had put something there out of sight. Nothing. All of the books were real, and none was hollowed out in the fashion of hiding places in bad spy movies. The only files in the office were a few the dean kept in the drawer of a credenza behind his desk. The official documents were kept in the filing room, and the only records McKenzie had in his office were largely personal—payroll records, receipts for 403(b) annuity deposits, a few country club bills, some credit card receipts. Brand looked through all this, finding nothing that would explain the attack on him in the wine cellar. It has to be the computer, Brand reasoned.

Like many executives McKenzie had excellent keyboarding skills and wrote almost nothing by hand—even though a Montblanc fountain pen and ball-point lay on his desk. Beals said the dean used these only for signing documents and letters. Brand had looked over the dean's day files for the past two months and found nothing of particular interest. Although he had looked at the computer files during his previous visit, he must have missed something.

Brand used his own computer extensively both in preparing presentations for class and writing his books and articles and therefore knew his way around most of the major software programs. He was also familiar with communication software and didn't feel the need to call in expert help—at least not yet. Even different programs have enough in common with each other to allow someone familiar with one to make the transition to a different one quickly. The communications program the dean used kept three sets of files: messages received, messages sent and messages deleted. The user could delete both messages received and messages sent, and they would then be saved in the messages deleted file. The writers of software come to the task with the assumption that users will make every mistake possible, so they build into their products ample safeguards from the most common faults.

Brand brought up first the deleted files in order to get a sense of the dean's computer discipline. He knew that most users of e-mail programs simply delete a file they no longer need and never give it another thought. Rarely do they bother to inspect the deleted file set, so that it continues to grow larger. To clear out the deleted files requires another action. Only then do the deleted files disappear.

The dean's e-mail software allowed the sorting of files by date, sender or receiver, with date order being the default position. Brand moved to the top of the list and discovered that McKenzie had files from the past six months. Didn't bother to delete his deletes, Brand thought. Next he sorted the files by sender. Most of the messages were to and from department chairs, the next largest category was communication with faculty, and there were numerous communications from persons with names Brand did not recognize. Probably students, he thought. He scrolled up to Danny Bennett's name and found there only a brief note written before the confrontation in Bucks Hall, the content of which was Danny's complaint to the dean about being closed out of a class he needed. The dean had replied that he would have someone look into it. Since there was no further exchange on the issue, Brand concluded that the dean's office must have been successful in dealing with the problem.

Brand next scrolled to Gary Hockney's name. There he found the following message:

You are utterly insensitive to the needs of graduate students. Withdrawing my fellowship will destroy my life. I could only wish that you will experience something that is as devastating to you as this is to me.

The message was unsigned, but the software labels a message from its sender, so there would have been no doubt in the dean's mind as to the source of the e-mail. Did Hockney think he was sending an anonymous note? He would be foolish if he thought he had, but it was obvious that the note was written in anger, and maybe Hockney just didn't care.

Next, Brand scrolled to the place in the alphabet where Sarah Giles's name appeared. There he found only one message:

Dean McKenzie, your handling of my tenure review is the worst I have ever heard about at Calloway State and a perfect example of the arrogance of power. You are a disgrace to your profession. You have absolutely no awareness of the need for diversity on the faculty, and you have no sensitivity whatsoever to the need for affirmative action. I realize that by writing this to you I am destroying any chance that you will reconsider your obviously biased decision, but I just could not let you get away with this without telling you that I know what you are doing. Someday somebody is going to pull you down from that patriarchal perch on which you are sitting so smugly. You will deserve whatever happens to you. S. Giles

Brand checked the sent messages and saw that the dean had not replied to Giles, and concluded that he probably thought that any reply would be wasted or maybe even trigger another outburst. Brand clicked on the "print" command and removed a hard copy of the message from the printer. He made a note to ask Giles about her final comment, which could be interpreted as a sort of threat.

Brand closed the e-mail program and opened the word processing software. Beals had told Brand that the dean prepared rough drafts of many of his memos and saved them on the shared drive in their network, which then allowed her to format the letter or memo and prepare it for his signature. Brand brought up the "S" drive first and quickly scanned its directory. Nothing there jumped out at him, so he next shifted to the dean's own directory on the computer's hard drive.

Brand first called up the directory and found a "folder" labeled "reports" which contained a variety of documents, probably drafts for subsequent review. It was a source of amusement to Brand that the writers of software, in an effort to make their product user-friendly, used terminology that applied to the older print media, such as "files" and "folders" and "erasing" a file. The intent was to give the computer novice some assurance that the new technology was only a new way of using the old technology. Must remember this as an example of metaphor for a lecture on metaphor as the frontier of language that gives rise to new ways of talking, Brand thought.

What particularly caught Brand's attention, though, was another "folder" labeled NTF. He opened it and saw many files with names beginning with NTF and having an abbreviated name or topic following the "F." Brand had previously seen printed documents in the day files marked NTF and asked Beals what it meant, and she told him that it meant "note to file." It was the dean's practice to make notes of phone conversations or meetings in his office immediately following them and file the documents in the appropriate file as a reminder to him later of what took place at the meeting or what the topic of the phone conversation was. He printed them out at the end of each day in the office for Beals to file later.

The file names contained many abbreviations, since DOS—the Disk Operating System—limited the file name to eight characters or numbers, a fact which Brand knew but resented at the moment, since he could not decipher all their meanings. Must ask Beals to go through this list and translate the abbreviations for me, he thought, the better to survey these files without having to read every one. Even without knowing all the abbreviations he recognized the importance of one file with the following name, NTFGiles—eight characters, a perfect DOS file title leaving no doubt whom this file was about. Brand opened the file and read it.

Sarah Giles called today with a complaint about my review of her tenure case. I told her that I had received and read her e-mail to me on the same topic.

That was it. Two sentences. The date was a week ago, but the file contained no specifics. Brand clicked on the print icon and waited for the hard copy to emerge from the laser printer. He picked it up and read it again, puzzled as to its brevity. He turned in his chair and depressed the intercom button, asking Beals to come into the dean's office.

"Have you seen this memo, Ms. Beals?" he asked.

"It doesn't ring any bells immediately, but I probably did. The dean always printed out his notes to file every evening, and I filed them first thing in the morning. Let me go check the filing cabinets to see if there is a copy there."

Two minutes later she was back in the dean's office with a copy of the memo. "I found this in the files, so he must have printed it out in the regular fashion."

Brand compared the two pages. Both contained the same two sentences.

"Did the dean make many notes to file like this—this short, I mean?"

"His notes to file vary in length. Some were long, others were short. This is obviously one of the short ones."

"So a memo to himself this short was not unusual?" Brand asked.

"Well…it is sort of unusual. Most of his notes to file would be a couple of paragraphs. I guess this one is rather short."

"I just can't figure out why he would even bother with a note this short," Brand said. "It doesn't contain any information except to say that Sarah Giles called. Don't you keep a phone log of all calls this office receives, and wouldn't her call be recorded there?"

"It would," Beals said. "I keep a log listing the caller and the number from which the call was made—we added that feature to our phones last year. I can check the log if you want me to and see if I noted Professor Giles's call, but I'm fairly sure I would have."

"No, that won't be necessary at this point. Since the dean knew that you kept a phone log and would assume that you noted her call there, what reason would he have for writing such a brief note to himself?"

"I really can't say, Professor Brand."

"Oh, sorry. I wasn't really asking you, just thinking out loud, a bad habit of mine. You'll have to overlook that little idiosyncrasy."

They both laughed, and Brand turned back to the computer as Beals left the office for her own desk.

Why the devil would Clem have written this note to file? Brand asked himself. It just doesn't make sense. He looked over the e-mail message from Giles again and began to run the fingers of his left hand through his beard as though he were scratching some insect bite underneath, a nervous habit that was a sign of being completely absorbed in the intellectual puzzle that faced him. Brand looked back over the directory of files with NTF in their label and opened several and printed them. They were of varying lengths, but none was as short as the NTF about Sarah Giles.

He laid all the documents out on the desk in front of him and began to compare them. In the lower left-hand copy of the NTF about Sarah Giles, McKenzie had printed CM and the date. On others there was only the date, no "CM." The initials must have meant that Clem typed these notes himself, Brand thought, remembering that Beals said that the dean prepared the notes and she printed them out and filed them as a future reminder of the conversations they recorded.

Brand remembered from looking through the day files that many of the memos contained CM/nb in the lower left hand corner, which indicated that Beals prepared the document from dictation, so the notes with only the dean's initials would be documents he had prepared himself. The addition of the date was a reasonable way to record when the note was prepared. Not all notes to file contained the dean's initials, though all contained the date.

Nobody's consistent, Brand reminded himself, but Clem was methodical, some would even say compulsive, about details. Still there was Emerson's comment about consistency being the hobgoblin of small minds, so the dean's lack of consistency could merely indicate that there was a lot going on in the office at the time or a lot on his mind. Or did it?

Then the answer hit Brand like the proverbial flash of lightning. Given the state's open-records statute, any person could request any document created by the university, including personnel files and the day-to-day documents created by a dean's office, or any university office. Student records were protected by federal law, as were medical records and certain legal documents, but everything else was fair game.

Brand knew that some administrators tried to get around the open records statute by taking sensitive materials home with them, thereby making them unavailable for public inspection in their offices. It was illegal, and were they to be caught at it, they were liable to a fine. Some people didn't know that computer files were included in the public records statue, which came as a shock to those university officials who used e-mail to express particularly outrageous thoughts under the erroneous assumption that only printed documents were covered by the law. The first time a reporter turned up in an office and asked for a copy of all the files on a particular administrator's hard drive, the word got around quickly that computer records were as open as documents written on paper.

Brand brought the document labeled NTFGILES back up on the screen and then clicked on the "View" button. When the dialog box opened, he saw that one of the options was "annotations." He clicked on it, and the computer screen immediately split. Below the horizontal line that defined the split additional text became visible, though only two lines of it could be read at a time. Brand moved the cursor to the "File" button and clicked on it, then on the "print" option from the dialogue box. The print menu offered several additional choices, one of which was "options." When Brand clicked on that, a whole new menu appeared giving a variety of choices for the printing of the document. Casting his eyes down the menu of choices, Brand saw that two options were "hidden text" and "annotations." Choosing both options with a click of the mouse, he then gave the computer a command to print the document and watched with fascination as a document began to emerge from the printer.

When Brand picked up the document from the receiving tray and looked at it, he was disappointed to see the same message he had read before: "Sarah Giles called today with a complaint about my review of her tenure case. I told her that I had received and read her e-mail to me on the same topic." At first Brand was afraid that he had entered an incorrect command or had misread the "View" option, but the thought had no sooner entered his head than the printer ejected another sheet into the collection tray. Brand picked it up and read it.

When Sarah called, she was almost hysterical (I now know why Freud said that hysteria was a particularly female problem). She said that I was unfit to be dean and that if she didn't get tenure there were going to be some dead administrators. I asked her if she was threatening me, and she said I could take it any way I liked. Then she slammed the phone in my ear. I considered calling Campus Security but decided not to unless she does something else that seems threatening. At this point I am willing to chalk this up to the ranting of an unbalanced personality. Maybe she can get some professional help.

So that is what Clem's codes meant, Brand thought. The documents with "CM" and the date were ones in which he had embedded annotations. Those with only the date had no annotations. Brand checked his hypothesis against several of the files and was pleased to see it confirmed. McKenzie made private notes to himself in the only place he felt would not be read by others. There was a remote chance that someone looking at the file on a computer would do what Brand had just done and discover the hidden text, but no one could do it on the dean's computer without his permission, since it was password-protected. The dean was also counting on the fact that most people scarcely get beyond the superficial capabilities of computer programs and never learn their more intricate features. Besides, Brand reasoned, Clem probably thought that he could respond to a document request for records on his computer by simply printing copies of all his files, and then none of the annotations would be available for inspection. No one reading the notes to file would have the slightest sense that some files contained additional, but hidden, text in their computerized forms—unless they puzzled it out as Brand did. The chances of that were slim, Brand thought; he had almost missed it.

Brand picked up the phone and dialed a number he knew from memory. When the police chief answered, Brand said, "Harri, I've found something interesting."

Chapter 15

BRAND HAD AGREED to meet Strong at her office in City Hall and was sitting in a chair beside her desk when he handed her the two documents from the NTFGILES file.

"I found these on Clem's computer. He routinely made notes of phone conversations and meetings and had his secretary, Naomi Beals, place them in the files under the appropriate heading to jog his memory later. His note about a phone conversation with Sarah contained hidden annotations, which I printed out on the second sheet." Brand explained in detail how the procedure was done on the dean's computer.

Strong read both documents twice. "What do you think, Jeremy?"

"I'm of two minds about the document. On the one hand, I don't really think Sarah Giles is capable of murder, even though the dean's note indicates she was extremely angry about what she assumed would be his negative tenure decision. She was still angry when she attended the dean's reception, but arson doesn't strike me as something Sarah would do. On the other hand, the conversation seems incriminating—assuming it occurred, and given where I found the record, I have no reason to doubt that it did."

"So you think she was upset, but not enough to burn down the dean's house."

"More or less. When she told me that she knew things that some people wish she didn't, I wondered what that meant." Brand told the chief about his conversation with Sarah in The Daily Grind. "Something big was on her mind. What wouldn't she tell me?"

"You saw her at the dean's reception. Did she seem to you then as though she hated the dean enough to do something drastic?"

"I couldn't say. She'd been drinking too much, and that loosened her tongue in a way that she probably regretted the next morning. Cynthia Lemaster took charge of her and got her out of there before the confrontation became worse."

"Could she have come back later and rigged the fires? Maybe she hadn't drunk as much as she pretended. I can see a possible scenario in which Giles leaves the reception, comes back later as the party is winding down, sneaks into the house after everyone has left and the dean was asleep, rigs the fires, and then leaves a second time."

"An interesting plot line. Would be good for a detective story, but as I see it we can't prove any of it."

"I agree there's no proof, but right now Sarah Giles is the only person I know about who had a strong motive to kill the dean. She could have had opportunity; that's all I am saying. As for means, well…the fire bombs were not complicated and required no great strength. They would have been well within the capability of a woman."

"So what are you going to do?"

"The dean's note to file about her phone call to him shows a highly agitated state of mind. Do you think the conversation took place?"

Brand paused. "The fact that it was hidden in the dean's computer files indicates to me that he wrote the note for his eyes only. I don't see any reason to doubt its authenticity."

"And that makes Giles a prime suspect. Let's go talk to her. I'll meet you at her house in an hour."

When Brand and Strong met at Sarah Giles's house, the chief said that the document Brand discovered on the dean's computer had not provided enough probable cause to get a judge to approve a search warrant. "In asking for a warrant I'd also have to say specifically what we are searching for, and at this point I don't know what that would be. We'll just have to see if she is willing to talk to us. If she isn't, we'll have to leave."

Brand knew that Harriet was being sensitive to town-gown relationships by coming to Giles's home rather than to her university office. Rarely did the police have any direct contact with university faculty. The county's criminal class usually did not include the faculty, and barring the occasional DWI charge, university professors—except for those who taught in criminal justice courses and were aware of the police as an extension of their academic interests—knew of police matters only through accounts in the local newspaper. From some of his friends who were local attorneys Brand knew that they did not even like to have professors on juries. They talk too much, dominate jury deliberations and exert undue influence on other jurors. Lawyers use their preemptory challenges as much as possible to keep professors off of juries.

Strong knew that if she had chosen to interview Giles in her office, that would have been on the campus grapevine in a nanosecond, regardless of how the conversation turned out. There is no tradition in American universities, as there is in European ones, that the police do not come onto a university campus. In practice, though, rarely did the local police confront either students or faculty on the university grounds—at least that was Strong's operating procedure. When they had to do so, the police worked through Campus Security and were always accompanied by a university security officer. All the local police forces—county, city and university—cooperated with each other and had a formal agreement that stipulated the rights of each force to enter the territory of the others in doing their duty. Such cooperation was enhanced by the fact that all the police officers, though not their commanders, were members of the same union.

Brand and Strong rang the doorbell and waited for Giles to answer. When she opened the door a crack, Strong showed her police badge and introduced herself.

"I'm Chief Harriet Strong of the College Falls Police. I'd like to talk with you, if you have time. I think you know Professor Brand."

"Oh, of course. Hi, Jeremy. Come in, both of you."

She motioned for her visitors to sit down. "What can I do for you?"

Brand was the first to speak. "I'm looking into Dean McKenzie's death at the request of President Coles. In the process of reviewing the dean's files, I found a document on the dean's computer that I felt needed to be turned over to the police."

Harriet handed Sarah a copy of the note to file and a copy of the separate sheet of annotations. "This is the document Professor Brand mentioned. Would you please look it over and tell me if it is correct?"

Giles read both documents and then looked directly at Chief Strong. "What are you suggesting? Am I some kind of suspect here? Do I need to call my lawyer?"

"You may certainly call a lawyer if you wish," Strong said, "but at this point I'm not charging you with anything. I just want to know if you made a call to Dean McKenzie of the sort he described in this document."

Giles read the document again. "I did call the dean and protested what I knew was going on in his office. He had no use for me or my scholarship. There was no secret about that. I just felt someone should tell him that he wasn't as clever as he thought he was. Maybe I came on a little too strong, but I certainly didn't threaten him. Why are there two documents, by the way?"

Brand explained to her the annotations feature of the dean's word processing software and how he used it to make notes to himself that would not be apparent to the casual reader. Sarah read the annotation again.

"That sounds like something Clem would say: 'hysteria was a particularly female problem.' A statement like that shows just how biased he was against anything he thought related to what he called 'women's issues.' But I certainly didn't threaten him. He was paranoid, and I mean that in a clinical sense."

"Did you say that he was unfit to be dean and if he denied you tenure there were going to be some dead administrators?" Strong asked.

"I might have said that he was unfit to be dean since he was unfit to be any kind of administrator. I don't recall saying that part about dead administrators."

"Then you're saying that he just made that part up? Why would he do that?"

"I told you, he was paranoid. I may have made some comments about his being a dead hand on the throttle or something like that, but I didn't say that part about dead administrators."

"So you did use the word 'dead.'"

"I may have. I just don't remember the conversation he records here at all. I think he made it all up."

"Would you tell me what happened after you confronted the dean at his reception? Where did you go? And who saw you?"

"I knew you were going to mention that," Giles said. "I had drunk too much too fast. That's all there was to that. I know I embarrassed myself, but when Cynthia Lemaster took me home, I went straight to bed and immediately to sleep. All that alcohol, you know."

"Did Professor Lemaster stay there with you?" Strong asked.

"No. She dropped me off here, made sure I opened the door and turned on the light. Then she went home; at least I presume that's where she went."

"In other words, no one can corroborate your account of your activities after leaving the dean's reception."

At this point Giles stood up. "I don't like this conversation at all. Am I a suspect? Are you here to arrest me?"

"No, but you have acted unwisely, Professor. Some people took your comments to the dean at his reception as a threat. It's been reported that you said that someone ought to kill the dean and put him out of everyone's misery. Then there is this angry e-mail message you sent to him and his account of a phone conversation in which he says you threatened him. If things are as you say, would you mind if I looked around some? Perhaps even took a peek in your garage?"

"I have nothing to hide," Giles said. "Be my guest."

Strong excused herself and entered the garage through the door that connected it to the kitchen.

While Strong was looking in the garage, Brand got up and walked over to Giles.

"Sarah, I'm sorry that things are turning out like this. When I found the document I had to turn it over to the police. I know you were upset with the dean, but if you didn't threaten him, you have nothing to worry about."

"I may have talked tough. Sometimes I drink too much and say things I shouldn't. You saw me at the reception. But even if I did say something about dead administrators, I didn't *mean* anything by it. You believe me, don't you?"

"So Clem may have accurately described his conversation with you?"

"Maybe. Oh, I don't know. I can't remember everything I said. Can you recall every detail of the last conversation you had when you were really, really angry?"

Chief Strong opened the door. "Professor, would you please come with me?" She held the door open for her and asked Giles to walk to the garage. The rear door of her sport utility vehicle stood open.

"Are these two empty gasoline containers in the back of your vehicle yours?"

"Yes, but I can explain."

"Go ahead."

"Well, this car uses a lot more gas than I'm used to. I've run out of gasoline twice, so I always carry a can of gas in the back in case that happens."

"That's not smart, Professor," Strong said. "Gasoline is a powerful explosive. It's dangerous to have a can of it inside your vehicle."

"Any more dangerous than running out of gas on a deserted street at night? I teach one of my courses in the evening. I don't want to get stranded without gas."

"Why *two* cans of gas?" Strong asked.

"I provide the mower and gasoline for the boy who cuts my lawn. He ran out last time, and I intended to get more."

"Isn't it a little late in the season to be buying a full can of gasoline for a mower?"

"I don't know about that," Giles said. "The lawn boy asked me to get him some more gas. I just haven't gotten around to it yet."

"Why are both cans empty?" If you needed more gasoline for your mower, why not just use the spare can of gas you so unwisely carry around in your car?"

"I can explain that," Giles said. "I ran out of gas last week and had to use the can I carry around with me to get to the filling station. I couldn't use that can for the mower because it was empty."

"But you said you used the gas from that can to get to the filling station. Why didn't you refill it then?"

"I don't know," Giles said, with a whiny tone creeping into her voice. "It was late, I was tired. I wanted to get home. I don't have to answer these questions."

The chief pointed to a corner of the garage. "How do you explain those empty milk cartons over there?"

"I recycle, Chief. Every environmentally conscious person does. I save my newspapers, plastic bottles, cans, even cardboard and take them to the recycling center once a month. That's not against the law!"

"Let's review where things stand. Someone put gasoline bombs in Dean McKenzie's house. You have two empty gasoline cans in your car and a supply of empty milk jugs in your garage. You have no proof of where you were after the dean's reception. You made threatening statements to the dean, statements which half of the college heard. All this puts you in a highly ambiguous situation."

"So, are you going to arrest me for having empty milk jugs and empty gasoline cans in my garage? That's pretty lame. Besides, this conversation has come to an end. If you have anything else to say to me, you can say it through my lawyer."

"By all means, but tell your lawyer to meet you at the police station, because that's where you and I are going to continue this conversation."

Chapter 16

LIKE MOST SUCH PROGRAMS, the College of Professional Studies was staffed by some faculty with academic backgrounds and some who came from the professions for which the college prepared its students. This pattern was especially evident in the Department of Business Communication, where about half of the professors came from business and industry backgrounds, and half from academic career paths.

The practitioners and theorists generally worked together in an uneasy alliance, but their fundamental approach to the teaching of communication differed. The academics prepared students for teaching careers and stressed statistical research, critical analyses of media content and poll-based investigation. The practitioners emphasized the art and craft of writing and speaking and felt their job was to prepare graduates for work in the real world, as they put it. In the academic pecking order, the academics looked down on the practitioners as mere wordsmiths who were not interested in knowledge-building research.

Harvey Glock was one of the practitioners. Though a journalism major in college, Glock was never a working reporter. After several years in the corporate communications departments of several companies, he accepted a position on the faculty in the Department of Business Communication. Not being research-trained or having a Ph.D., Glock did no serious research and suffered something of an inferiority feeling as a result. Instead, he threw himself into teaching and counseling students, and liked to represent himself as a former journalist to students who wrote for the campus paper, *The Mirror*. They always found him a ready source for story leads, and they flocked to his office like moths to a flame.

Glock retrieved his morning mail from the departmental mail boxes and returned to his office. He hung up his coat on the hall tree standing in the corner, laid his briefcase on the desk, and began sorting through the accumulation of memos, publishers catalogs, notices of various meetings and printed flyers that constituted an average day's mail. He noticed that one business-size envelope carried the return address of the president's office and opened it first. It contained a single sheet of paper bearing the woodcut logo of the university that the president alone used.

TO: The College of Professional Studies
FROM: Milton Coles, President

We are all saddened by the tragic death of Dean Clement McKenzie, and our sympathies go out to his wife and family during this time of loss. I know that Dean McKenzie would want us to honor his life and work by continuing the mission of this college in the same fine manner that he would do were he still with us.

Accordingly, I am announcing the appointment of Associate Dean George Helms as Interim Dean while the search for a permanent dean gets under way. Dr. Helms has served this college for several years in an administrative role and will provide the kind of leadership we need during this difficult time. I know that all the faculty, staff, and students of the College of Professional Studies will rally behind his leadership.

Glock wadded the president's memo into a ball and threw it toward the trash can in the corner of the room. He missed, and the wad joined several others around the wastebasket. "What a crock," he muttered under his breath. "We get rid of one asshole only to have him replaced by another one." Never one to be realistic about his own situation, Glock had harbored administrative ambitions. He kept applying for chairmanships and deanships at various other universities but could not even get invited for an interview.

Glock's administrative ambitions were well known around the college and became the source of many jokes in the coffee lounge and at cocktail parties. But his search for administrative jobs was no joke to Glock. When the vacancy occurred in the college leadership, he assumed that the president would call on him to be interim dean. Now that it was clear this was not to be, the resentment that already scarred Glock's soul burned even hotter. At a level so deep in his psyche that it did not even give rise to conscious expression, he knew that his new task was to undercut Helms's effectiveness.

Glock usually left his door ajar during office hours, and Sally Turner, a student reporter and journalism major, stuck her head in. "Professor Glock, I need your help."

Glock motioned for her to come in and waved her toward a seat beside his desk. "I write for *The Mirror*, as you know, and I've got to come up with twelve inches of copy by tomorrow noon, and I just don't know what to report on."

"I've said this to you before, Sally, but I'll say it again: You won't have a chance at a job in this industry unless you develop a solid file of serious news stories while you're still a student. The student newspaper gives you a great opportunity to do that. Never, *ever* pass up a chance to build that portfolio. Write twelve inches of something that will knock their socks off."

"I'm trying, really I am. But at the moment I just don't have any serious leads."

"Have you thought about following up on the death of Dean McKenzie?" Glock asked. He was beginning to form an idea. "I've heard on the grapevine that President Coles has asked Jeremy Brand to do a report for him. My guess is that Coles wants a cover-up."

"A cover-up? Of what?"

"I don't know what he's trying to cover up. That's for you to find out. But I know Coles well enough to believe that he wouldn't put Brand onto this thing if he didn't think there was something there potentially embarrassing to the university. It's your job as a good reporter to answer your own question."

"But I can't just confront the president and ask him what he's trying to cover up," Sally said.

"Of course not. I'm not suggesting an interview strategy here, just the assumption you bring to the interview. I know you're young and idealistic, Sally, but you've really got to accept the fact that people in authority are *always* trying to cover things up. It's just a matter of finding out what they're trying to hide. Take this dean thing, for example. McKenzie was a terrible dean. Everybody knew that. But would the administration do anything about it? Not on your life! Why? Because they protect each other, that's why. My guess is that Coles wants to find out who killed the dean before anyone else does so he can hush it up."

"Why would he want to do that?"

"Image. Image pure and simple. Suppose McKenzie was killed by another administrator or by a member of the faculty. Coles wouldn't want that to get out, now would he? Or if it did, he would want to put some kind of spin on it that would protect the university's image."

"But how could I go about getting at that story?"

"Pose a hypothetical. Say something like, 'a source within the university has said that Interim Dean George Helms was involved in the dean's death,' and then ask the president to comment on that."

"But nobody has told me that."

"Sure they have. I just did. I'm 'a source within the university.'"

"But you're just making that up, Professor Glock. What you said isn't true."

"You don't have to claim that it is true. You're just asking questions. The more provocative the questions, the better. The point is to get the president talking. The more he talks, the more copy for your story."

"I don't know. Is it right to lie like that?"

"You won't be *lying*, Sally, for God's sake. You're asking questions. Call them hypotheticals if that makes you feel better. A hypothetical doesn't have to be true, just provocative. Think of what it will do for your career if you could write this story, Sally. You could have your pick of internships, and a good internship leads to a good job. You know how that works."

"How can I get an interview with President Coles? Do you think he would even talk to me?"

"He'll talk to you. Just tell his office you're writing a story on the death of the dean and would like the president's comments. If his secretary refuses to make an appointment for you, tell her to inform the president that you will have to report that his office stonewalled your attempt to get the facts. That will smoke him out."

"OK, I'll do it. But before I leave, please give me some suggestions for interview questions."

"No problem with that." Glock reached into the drawer of his desk for a pad and pencil.

Sally Turner had no problem getting on the president's schedule. She didn't even have to use her threat. The president set aside half an hour each week to take student reporters' questions, but no one else had asked for an appointment, so the time slot was open. Turner felt a little let down that she hadn't had to bluster her way in but decided that the interview would get off to a better start on a friendly basis anyway.

Since Glock had told her that the president would be hostile, she was unprepared for his warm smile and extended hand when he opened the door.

"Good afternoon, Sally. I understand that you have some questions for a story you're working on."

"Yes, sir. And thanks for finding time to meet with me." Mustn't sound too submissive, she thought. Glock had warned her about that, but Turner was a southern girl, and "yes, sir" and "yes, ma'am" came as naturally to her as breathing.

"Fire away, then," Coles said.

"Well, I was wondering why you felt it necessary to ask Professor Brand to conduct an investigation of Dean McKenzie's death. Won't the police be doing their own investigation?"

"They certainly will, and we don't intend to get in the way of that at all. And I wouldn't call what Professor Brand is doing an 'investigation.' What I need is a report that will be useful in helping the university community deal with this tragic event."

"I don't understand."

"From your viewpoint, Sally, the university is just a place you go to school. From my viewpoint the university is more like a small city. If I were the mayor of a small city and one of my chief administrators was killed, I would need to have all the information about that I could find. We've had a tragic event in our midst, and I need to know why it happened."

"What do you mean the university is like a small city?"

"Look at it like this, Sally. I'm responsible for the management of thirty-five hotels. That's really what dormitories are—small hotels. I also run nine restaurants—five residence-hall dining rooms, three snack shops and a faculty club. Add to that two radio stations, one television station, one cable provider for the dorms, and you have a pretty good start on a city."

"I can see what you mean."

"I've just started, Sally. We operate a vehicle rental service for departments, a police force, a printing plant, a book publishing operation, a telephone company that provides phone and network services to all campus buildings, a small fleet of aircraft used for instruction and transportation, a repair service that features all the skilled crafts—plumbers, bricklayers, carpenters, electricians, carpet layers, mechanics, tile cutters, painters, plasterers and equipment operators. I am also responsible for entertainment—music and drama and dance. We run two theaters and an art gallery. I could go on, because I haven't even begun to talk about our educational and research infrastructure, but I wanted to give you an idea of the complexity of the place."

"I still don't understand why you need your own report. Are you afraid that the police will discover something before you do? Do you want to know first so you can cover it up?" That was a question Glock wrote for her, and hearing herself ask it made it sound much less reasonable than when he jotted it down.

"Not at all. I don't know who put that thought in your mind, but there's nothing to cover up. As I just explained, a university is a complex place. It is also a fragile place depending on mutual trust and good will. When something like the death of a dean occurs, we risk the undermining of that confidence and good will. My job is to see that this doesn't happen, and to do this I need information. Anything I find out will become public knowledge. There may be a killer on the loose in our midst, and I want to be sure that we do everything we can to find out who it is. We are working closely with the city police. As you know, the university has its own security force, and they have a responsibility to insure a crime-free environment on campus. Any information we can get about the dean's death will help with that mission."

A killer on the loose in our midst. That would make a good headline, Turner thought. There might be a story here after all.

"Why did you ask Professor Brand to get involved?"

"Professor Brand is a respected senior faculty member. He's not a member of the faculty of the College of Professional Studies, but is well known there. I want to send a message to the faculty that we still believe in faculty governance and that faculty should be involved in all important issues on campus."

Turner now thought it was time to drop the bomb.

"A source within the university told *The Mirror* that Associate Dean Helms was involved in Dean McKenzie's death. Would you care to comment on that."

"Who said that?"

"I can't reveal my sources."

"Whoever told you that is guilty of the worst sort of rumor-mongering. Right now the police are still investigating the dean's death, and to my knowledge have released no information on the status of that investigation. Until they do, you would be well-advised to refrain from publishing any statement like that."

President Coles denies that the associate dean had any involvement in Dean McKenzie's death. That should be worth at least a paragraph in the story. Turner knew that she also should talk to Brand but decided to interview him later. She realized she did not have enough for a long piece. At the most this story would get only about ten inches in the paper, even with the "killer in our midst" lead. Better than nothing, she thought, but not much help in building her portfolio. She thanked the president and left his office with mixed feelings. It was not much of a story, but at least it was a start.

Chapter 17

ARCHIE SCOT TRANSFERRED TWO THOUSAND dollars from his savings account to his checking account so he could make the first payment to Sarah Giles. He considered mailing the check to her but decided a face-to-face meeting was in order. It would allow him again to appeal to her to change her demands. Maybe he could offer a one-time lump-sum payment that would satisfy her for the present, with another lump-sum payment a year from now. It was important to Scott to buy a several months' silence from her so he could disengage from Middletown in an orderly fashion. Now that McKenzie was out of the way, all his concerns for the future focused on Giles. If the woman would only see reason.

Giles was back at home, though she had not met her classes in two days. The evidence that led Chief Strong to take her to the police station was circumstantial, and she was not charged with the crime. Giles's lawyer refused to let her answer any more questions. Strong had not arrested her, even though to be safe she had informed Sarah of her Miranda rights. Though Giles was free, the stigma of being taken to the police station was an embarrassment, and she did not want to see any of her friends for a few days. She was not surprised, though, to hear from Scott when he called. Yes, he could come by her house. And yes, she was still expecting the first payment as per their agreement. The word "agreement" struck Scott as strange since it implied mutual satisfaction, and there was nothing mutual about this. Giles was blackmailing him pure and simple.

Giles opened the door and asked Scott in. She hung up his coat but with no pretense of pleasantries asked, "Did you bring the money?"

"Of course I did, Sarah. But let's talk about this a bit."

"What's there to talk about? We have an understanding. I expect you to live up to it. End of discussion."

"I wouldn't exactly call it an 'understanding,' You're blackmailing me. I *understand* perfectly what you are doing."

"Now, now, Archie, don't get testy with me. By the way, did you know that testy comes from the word 'testicles.' It's a particularly male problem. Women may be hysterical, but men are testy. I kind of like that."

"That's a bogus derivation, Sarah, and you know it. Besides, I'm not *testy*, as you put it. I just want to talk some more."

She laughed, a low, sneering laugh. "You say it's a bogus derivation, but you're not sure, are you? What do you want to talk about?"

"Our last conversation. We didn't really get to finish it."

"So, talk."

"I have another proposition to make."

"Proposition, Archie? As in seduction? Are you trying to seduce me?"

"Get serious, Sarah." She's the last person he would want to seduce, Archie thought. Why do the ugly ones always put a sexual turn on things? "I have another offer to make. How about my giving you ten thousand dollars now and ten thousand dollars a year from now. I would expect you to sign an agreement in writing to the effect that you will make no disclosures about my private life."

"I am perfectly happy with our present arrangement, Archie. I see no reason to change it. What would I possibly have to gain from accepting your offer? Two thousand a month for two years is more than ten now, ten later."

"I can't pay you for two years like you asked. I am willing to make an alternative offer. Two payments: ten thousand each. An agreement signed by you to that you will make no statements about me. I am trying to be reasonable."

"I am touched by your thoughtfulness," Giles said, with a mocking tone to her voice. "Thanks but no thanks, Archie. And of course you can pay me. You have two jobs, remember?"

"Do you know what you are doing to me?"

"Of course I do, Archie. I'm screwing you. Metaphorically speaking, of course. But then that's all you men have wanted to do to us for years. And by the way, I'm not signing any agreement."

A wave of heat rushed to Scott's head, and he could see only a red blur in front of his eyes. His arm seemed to be moving of its own accord as he formed a fist and drew it back in preparation to hit Giles in the face. Then his reason took over and he stopped, with fist still clenched.

"Oh, all right, Sarah. Here's the damn check."

"Check, Archie? Get serious. I won't take a check. I want cash."

"I don't have that kind of cash with me. I'll have to come back."

"So come back, then. But not without the cash."

Scott grabbed his coat and opened the door. "I'll be back, but if you know what's good for you, you'll think about my offer." With that he left, slamming the door behind him, hard. Scott felt a sense of panic that his own timetable was now in disarray. If only he had resigned from Middletown after one year, none of this would be happening. But as he continued to stew about his situation, Scott ceased blaming himself for getting in such a vulnerable position and directed his anger to Giles for what she was doing to him. His anger morphed into intense hatred. That wretched woman is going to bleed me to death, he thought. Something really needs to be done about her.

Chapter 18

BRAND KNEW THAT HE SHOULD talk to people who were guests at the dean's reception before their memories of the evening faded. It is hard enough to get coherent and consistent stories from eyewitnesses to an event immediately afterward and harder a week later. The difficulty would only increase with the elapse of more time.

In preparation for the meetings, Beals and Brand reviewed the guest list to select the names of those to interview. Since Brand had himself been at the reception, he could remember most of the people who were there, but the list helped him decide on those best qualified to review for him the events of the evening. He started with the names of several of the department chairs in the college. They could help reconstruct the events of the evening and would also know of any undercurrents in the college that might have bearing on the dean's death.

Brand decided that he would talk to people in their offices rather than call them to the dean's office because he found people more forthcoming in their own offices than when summoned to a place that reeks of authority. Brand asked Beals to schedule all the meetings. The associate dean would be his first one.

Brand reviewed the interview schedule and his list of questions for a final time before he left his office in the Lester Rhodes Humanities Building. As he came down the steps and started across the quadrangle, he turned when he heard someone calling his name and saw Sally Turner running toward him.

"Glad I ran into you, Professor Brand. I was intending to talk with you anyway, and running into you like this will keep me from having to play phone tag with you. Mind if I ask you a couple of questions?"

"I'm on my way to a class, but we can talk while we walk, if that's OK with you."

"Great. I'm doing a follow-up story on the death of the dean, and I just got through talking with President Coles. He said that you're doing an on-campus investigation...."

Brand broke in. "Not an investigation, Sally. That implies something that is much more formal than what I'm doing. I agreed to write a report for the president just to keep him informed."

"Will your report be a public document?"

"Of course. You know the laws governing such things. All documents created by this institution are public documents. You will see the document in its entirety in due course."

"Great. For now, though, I need to ask you about a couple of things. First, do you have any leads as to who killed the dean?"

"Again, Sally, the term 'leads' has too formal a ring to it. The police are doing the investigation. I am not."

"OK. So how about the assistant dean, George Helms. A source inside the university told *The Mirror* that George Helms was involved in the dean's death."

Brand stopped and looked squarely at Turner. "Who told you that, Sally?"

"I can't reveal my sources, Professor Brand. You know that."

"That is a terribly pernicious thing to say about Dean Helms. Unless you have solid evidence for it you'd better be careful using a statement like that. If you discover evidence for it, you have an obligation to inform the police."

"So I can quote you as saying that you have found no evidence that Dr. Helms has any involvement with the dean's death."

"Sally, I don't even want my name associated with such a scurrilous statement as that. I don't want you to quote me at all."

"But you are denying any knowledge of Dr. Helms's involvement?"

"Absolutely. And, again, I advise you not to name names like that. I can tell you of a certainty that if you print that rumor, you'll be talking to the police before the ink is dry on *The Mirror*."

"Thanks, Professor, for talking with me. I've got to run." Turner stuffed her narrow note pad into her shoulder bag as she turned and walked away.

After his class Brand turned to his interview schedule and decided to talk first to the associate, now interim, dean. George Helms had an office on the same floor as the dean, though a few doors down the hall. Brand knew that the associate dean would be familiar with the day-to-day affairs of the college, more so than would the dean. Deans deal with the big picture—and think big thoughts—and have to contend with many off-campus groups. Everyone wants to see the dean: alumni, donors, legislators, parents, and in the case of the College of Professional Studies, representatives of businesses and the professions.

Associate deans come to their posts directly from the faculty after serving as chair of a department or having had some other major administrative assignment. Service as associate dean can be a boost for anyone seeking a deanship. Search committees look for someone who is a scholar (like them) but also has demonstrable administrative experience at the college level. An associate deanship provides the requisite qualifications.

Brand first met Helms at a cocktail party when he was new on campus. Helms had been a member of the Calloway State management faculty for five years before accepting the appointment as associate dean. A successful teacher and scholar, he rose through the ranks quickly and demonstrated along the way his ability to handle administrative tasks. As he put it, he answered his mail and returned phone calls.

Brand knew that Helms was ambitious. It was an open secret in the college that several headhunters had his name in their files and that it was only a matter of time before the right fit for him came along and the college would lose an able administrator to a dean position elsewhere. The puzzle was why it had not happened already. The popular take on his being appointed interim dean by President Coles was that Helms desperately wanted the appointment—and wanted to be named the permanent dean too—but he was projecting an aloof attitude that fooled no one.

"Congratulations on being named interim dean, George," Brand said. "It's a tough job in the best of circumstances, and these times hardly qualify for that."

"Thanks, Jeremy. It was a tough decision for me. As you probably know, I'm looking around for a possible deanship somewhere, and I don't know whether accepting this interim appointment will help or hurt me. I haven't decided on whether I'll be a candidate for the permanent position here, but if I do, the interim appointment probably won't help me too much. The insider candidate always is at a disadvantage. You can't do a job like this very long without generating some baggage, and the outsider comes in with a clean slate. Besides if I were appointed permanent dean, I would get no honeymoon at all. Everyone would expect me to hit the ground running. But I have great respect for President Coles, and when he asked me to step in, I agreed. I always want to do what is in the best interest of the college. I will worry about the consequences of that decision for my dean aspirations later."

Helms had a reputation for being loquacious but Brand had forgotten how wordy he could be. Brand told himself that he had better focus the conversation or he would be here all day. Helms just seemed to be one of those people who cannot talk in short sentences.

"Well, I'm glad you accepted the appointment," Brand said. Then changing to the topic that brought him here, he added, "I'm here to find out what you might know about the dean's death."

Brand explained his strategy for carrying out the president's assignment and that he would be talking to several people in the college over the next couple of days.

"Do you know anyone who might wish to do harm to the dean?"

"No more than usual. Sometimes professors get upset over a dean's decisions and talk tough, but nothing comes of it. Most times it's work load, office space and annual raises. I don't think we do anything around here that creates as much resentment as annual merit raises. Those who get low raises are offended, and those who get high ones think they should get more. I remember three years ago when the legislature mandated no raises at all. It was the quietest spring in anybody's memory. But I'm digressing. To answer your question, nobody in the college I know of has threatened the dean with bodily harm."

"What about graduate students?" Brand asked Helms if he knew about the confrontation between the dean and Gary Hockney.

"I heard something about it. I know Hockney from other events. He is a so-so student. He shouldn't have been surprised to learn that his fellowship isn't going to be renewed. I suspect that his main concern is that the loss of his fellowship will force him to make a decision about his future. He strikes me as pretty aimless right now."

"What do you know about Gary's background?"

"He came to the university after a brief military career. He is pretty much a loner, as I understand it. Doesn't socialize much with the other students. About the only time I have seen him is when he came in to complain about something or other."

"Do you think Gary would be capable of taking some kind of direct action against the dean?"

"Don't know," Helms said. "Where is this leading, Jeremy? Do you suspect Gary of being responsible for the fire at Clem's house?" Helms raised his eyebrows in an unusual expression of interest.

"I'm not suspecting anybody. It's just that I don't want to overlook any possibility at this point."

"Well, let me talk to a few people in the college and see if anybody has a reason to think that Gary might have a violent streak. I'll let you know if I discover anything."

Brand's next stop was the office of the chair of the Department of Business Communication. One of the largest departments in the college, Bus Com, as everyone called it, was in one of the oldest buildings on campus. It had been on the renovations list for years, but lack of state funding and the absence of an external donor prevented much being done to the building except for repairs required for health and safety reasons. The floor tile showed wear and, in places, was cracked. The elevators were always breaking down, and the walls were painted institutional green.

Within the classrooms, however, the department's priorities were evident. The department had two sorts of classrooms: low-tech and high-tech. The low-tech classrooms were equipped with the usual kinds of audio-visual accessories: VCRs and video projectors, Elmo units and overhead projectors. The high-tech classrooms, of which the department had four, offered all the equipment found in low-tech rooms plus computer-driven audio and video capabilities. Large computer monitors mounted at several places in the classroom allowed the instructor to bring in CD-ROM disks to aid classroom presentations or receive direct feeds from the Media Distribution Center of materials kept there in digitized formats. The computers also were networked both within the department and with the university's mainframes so that a variety of materials could be made available to classes. Teleconferencing from both inside and outside the university featured compressed video technology that brought talking heads into the classroom in something less than broadcast quality but still good enough for most purposes.

The head of the department was Robert Elliot, who came to the position after serving as communications director of a Fortune 500 corporation. He claimed that Calloway needed to find a niche for students trained in communication other than the traditional ones of journalism or radio/TV production, since too many universities already had such programs and were flooding the market. In his previous job Elliot planned daily teleconferences with company executives at the corporation's many dispersed plants, oversaw both the internal and external communications programs of the company, and in general used all forms of communications technology to add value to the corporation. Some graduates of his program found jobs in traditional media, print, broadcast and cable, but most went on to careers in corporate communications.

He ran the department in much the same fashion as he had run his corporate operation, and his faculty let him get by with it because the department enjoyed a national reputation, and Elliot was known for fairness, even when not all of the faculty agreed with his decisions. His report to Brand was consistent with what Helms had said. Except for the usual and expected faculty hostility toward the dean, no one seemed angry enough to take violent action against him.

"Is there any friction within the college that an outsider wouldn't know about?" Brand asked.

"Some. Several of the chairs always think they can do the dean's job better than he does and make no secret about that. And everybody knows that George Helms is terribly ambitious and would like a dean's job somewhere. For my part it's a job I wouldn't have for any amount of money."

"Speaking of George, I was just confronted by Sally Turner in the quadrangle on my way over here. Someone is spreading the rumor that George is involved in the dean's death. I warned her not to print anything like that without solid proof."

"She asked me about the same thing," Elliot said. "I also told her in no uncertain terms that it was irresponsible to ask questions like that."

"Did she tell you who her source was? She refused to give me that information."

"No, but there was no need. I know who set her up. Harvey Glock. George hasn't even been associate dean a full day, and already Harvey is trying to undercut him."

"You don't think *The Mirror* will use Sally's piece?"

"They probably will use something under her byline, but the editor is much too savvy to give innuendo and unsubstantiated rumors a place in the story. He's a senior journalism student and knows what's proper and what isn't."

"What makes you think Harvey Glock was Sally's source?"

"It's the kind of thing he does. He thinks nobody knows that he's behind a lot of the stuff going on around here, but everybody knows and recognizes that he's a bitter man."

"Why?" Brand asked. "Why is he bitter?"

"I think I have it pretty well figured out. Glock was something of a troublemaker in his previous job, but we didn't know that when we hired him. His academic career has been mediocre. He published a book on the history of American journalism, his only book. That got him promoted to associate professor with tenure, but since then he hasn't done anything. He can't seem to produce anything else worth publishing. He will probably retire from academic life as an associate professor, and that thought just kills him. Harvey's current mission in life seems to be to bedevil the administration. He uses student reporters as guided missiles. He gives them leads, suggests their interviewing strategies, even helps write their stories. When the editorial page writers are unable to come up with a topic for the day's editorial—and the student editors feel they should editorialize every day—they turn to Glock, who never fails to have something for them. More often than not it's an attack on the administration."

"How many people in the department know this?"

"Most everybody. The senior faculty hate it, of course. But Glock is tenured, so what are you going to do? Glock is popular with students, though. He helps them get internships, shows them how to build portfolios, prepare for job interviews. They love him."

"How about his colleagues?"

"It's mixed. Some faculty, as I said, avoid him. Others like the fact that he craps on the administration. When the dean's death became known, Glock assembled a group of cronies in the basement and opened a bottle of champagne. Pretty petty stuff, but, then, that's Glock."

Brand had heard enough about Glock and decided to shift to a new topic. "I'm also trying to discover who might be the last person to see Clem alive. Can you give me any help there?"

"Well, I wasn't the last person to leave but close to it. Most of the department chairs stayed around almost to the end—sort of our duty, you know. When I left the crowd had dwindled down to three or four, not counting Clem. Ray Jones was still there, as was George Helms and another chair or two."

"George Helms stayed that long? Funny, he didn't mention that to me, and I just finished talking with him."

"I think I'm correct in that...I'm sure I am. Yep, George was still there when I left."

"So you think it likely that George or Ray may have been the last person to see Clem alive," Brand asked.

"Yeah, I think so."

"That's good, Bob. I'll follow up with both of them. Strange that George didn't mention that to me, but I really didn't explore that line of questioning with him. I'll give him a call later."

Brand's next stop was the Department of Accounting. His conversation with Hillary Pierce about college politics proceeded much as had his previous interviews with George Helms and Robert Elliot. Brand directed the subject around to the dean's party.

"How about the dean's reception, Hillary? Did you pick up on anything there that might be relevant to my investigation?"

"You were there most of the evening, Jeremy, and probably saw everything I did. Except for Sarah's unfortunate display, everybody was on their good behavior."

"About Sarah. Is this the first time she's done anything like this?"

"It's the first time I've seen her make such a public fuss, but it was well known around the college that she hated the dean."

"Was it because of her tenure case?" Brand asked. "No notification has yet gone out from the dean's office, but I hear that she's convinced the dean's decision was going to be negative about her tenure."

"It wasn't just about tenure," Pierce said. "Sarah isn't a member of my department, but I had heard that she was vocal about her displeasure with the dean. She felt he was too judgmental about her scholarship and that he was insensitive in general to anything that seemed to be feminist in orientation. You will find that view shared by a lot of people in the college."

"Bob Elliot told me that he was among the last to leave the reception, and there were only two or three others still there."

"Yeah, we chairs are expected to stay around as long as possible, like oil for the social machinery. I left about the same time Bob Elliot did but a little before he did. I remember seeing him come out the door when I got in my car, which was parked in Clem's driveway."

Pierce also confirmed that Ray Jones and George Helms were still at the party when she left.

When Brand got back to Bucks Hall, Beals handed him two phone messages: one from Ray Jones asking Brand to conduct the interview by phone rather than in person, and the other from Wilbur Knox, head of the management department. Brand picked up the phone and dialed Ray's number.

"Thanks for calling, Jeremy. I had something come up and needed to come back to my house. Sorry to have to change the schedule."

"No problem, Ray. I'm trying to find out who the last person was to see Clement McKenzie alive. From what I've found out, that person may be you."

"It is me," Jones said, "unless someone stayed in the house I don't know about. Clem and I were old friends, and more than once I have had to put him to bed after he's had too much to drink. Tabitha usually did that, but she wasn't there, as you know."

"Did Clem overindulge in alcohol often?"

"I wouldn't say often. Once in a while, though, he would get two sheets to the wind, and if we were out somewhere I'd drive him home. He'd go back the next day for his car."

"Was he an alcoholic?"

"I wouldn't go that far, but he was a problem drinker. I was worried about him and even confronted him about his drinking. But like many people who abuse alcohol, he denied that he had a problem. Usually Tabitha kept him in control, but she wasn't at the reception, so he kind of lost it that night."

"Tell me in as much detail as you can exactly what happened before you left Clem's house."

Jones recounted all the events of the evening, including the difficulty he had putting the dean to bed. "There really isn't much more to tell, Jeremy. I turned off the light and shut the front door. I knew that Clem would sleep it off and be OK in the morning. Of course, I didn't know an arsonist would show up, or that those crazy kids would pull their stunt either."

"So you didn't see the student demonstrators there when you left."

"They weren't there, or I would have seen them. As I understand it, they didn't arrive until later. Clem probably didn't have any idea of what was going on in his front yard. It's ironic. They came to demonstrate in front of his house, but he was too drunk to notice."

Brand thanked Jones and hung up the phone. Not much here, he thought. Everybody he talked to had pretty much told the same story.

Wilbur Knox was in his office when Brand called, and since it was a call back, Brand let him direct the conversation.

"The reason I called, Jeremy, is that I know you're doing a report about Clem's death, and I wanted you to have all the facts."

"Such as?"

"Well, you probably wouldn't know this, but behind that calm and urbane exterior, Clem had a nasty streak. He could be mean and vindictive."

"I know that he wasn't liked by all the faculty, but few deans are."

"It was more than that," Knox said. "Clem had his own private enemies list. It maybe wasn't written down or as explicit as Richard Nixon's, but he definitely had an enemies list. If you got on it, Clem would undermine you any way he could. Outwardly he was all sweetness and light, but he inwardly he was a mean-spirited man."

"So you think someone on his 'list,' as you put it, might be responsible for the fire at his house?"

"I'm suggesting that it's possible, and I'm not surprised that his house was the target. It was such a monstrosity, an embarrassment to the college. It was so typical of his showy ways. Maybe whoever set the fire didn't intend to kill the dean but just get back at him by attacking the thing that he valued the most."

"So far I haven't found any evidence of what you're telling me."

"You probably won't," Knox said. "He was much too careful to leave a written trail. But his vindictiveness was real. I just thought you ought to know."

Chapter 19

THE DAY AFETER AN AUCTION was almost as hectic as the auction itself. After his lectures and other university commitments, Brand managed to shoehorn into his afternoon schedule a period of time in the cellar. Ruskin did much of the data entry required to keep cellar records up to date, but decisions about future needs and overall cellar management was Brand's responsibility alone. He also found that immersing himself in the details involved in managing his wine holdings was a form of relaxation, and he preferred not to be disturbed. When working in the cellar Brand turned off the telephone ringer on the extension phone and let his housekeeper screen the calls. She rarely allowed him to be interrupted, so he was surprised when the intercom buzzed. He picked up the phone and found Écoles on the other end of the line.

"Professor, you just got a call from the police chief. She said to call her back on her cell phone." Brand called the number Écoles gave him, and Strong answered almost immediately.

"Jeremy, I'm at Professor Giles's house. Come over here as soon as you can. I think you will want to see this."

When Brand pulled up at Sarah Giles's house, he saw two police cruisers and an ambulance with lights and strobes flashing. A band of yellow police tape stretched across the driveway between two trees in the front yard. He coasted to a stop behind one of the cruisers and got out of his car. As Brand walked toward the police tape, Harriet saw him and gave a signal to one of the uniformed officers who lifted the yellow tape so Brand could pass through.

"Is this what it looks like, Harri?" Brand asked.

"I'm afraid so. We got a call about an hour ago from a neighbor who saw exhaust smoke coming out from under the garage door. The neighbor called us, and when we arrived we found this unpleasant scene."

As Brand walked toward the house, paramedics were loading a blanket-wrapped bundle into the ambulance. Brand and Strong entered the garage where a uniformed officer, hands encased in latex gloves, was coating glass, metal and plastic surfaces in the car with black fingerprint power. The rear window was opened enough to allow the insertion of a vacuum cleaner hose. The other end of the hose was pressed over the exhaust pipe of the car, making for an effective killing machine. Brand walked around it and looked at it from all angles.

"She must have had a central vacuum system," Brand noted. "That hose is much longer than one from an ordinary vacuum cleaner."

"Right. And look at the way the nozzle end was attached to the exhaust pipe—with duct tape. This was not a snap decision but a carefully planned act. We'll know more after the coroner's report, but it looks like death by asphyxiation. It was made to look like suicide."

"You say 'made to look like suicide.' What leads you to think it might not be suicide?"

"Nothing I can point to," Strong said. "At least not yet. But it doesn't feel right to me. Let me show you what else we found."

Brand followed the chief into the house and into the study. She pointed to a piece of paper lying on her desk which contained a message printed on a laser printer sitting beside the computer. "Don't touch the note, Jeremy. My officers have yet to dust the surfaces in here for finger prints."

Brand shoved his hands into his pockets and bent over the desk to read the note.

> I can't live with the guilt any longer. I killed the dean but didn't mean
> to. I only intended to burn down his house. I hope everyone will
> forgive me.

"Looks pretty straight forward," Brand said. "You must have your reasons for dismissing it as suicide so quickly. What are they?"

"Everything is too pat, too contrived. I suppose in theory a person who uses a computer for all her daily work could write out a suicide note on a computer, but this one seems phony. Say it's woman's intuition if you must, but it doesn't feel right."

"Did you detect any sense of remorse when you had her in for questioning earlier?"

"None at all. If she was the arsonist, she had nerves of steel. Over the years I've developed a pretty good sense of when people are lying to me, and I don't think she was. Besides, amateur criminals crack pretty easily when confronted with their crimes. She showed no evidence at all of hiding something."

"So if this wasn't a suicide, you need to find someone who had a reason to kill her."

"Right, and I don't know where to start. After we search her house, we'll start interviewing her neighbors to find out if anybody saw anything."

"I'm sure you'll also want to talk to her colleagues and to the chair of her department, but I'll poke around some too and see if I can learn anything. I'll let you know if I turn up anything."

"I'm glad there's someone like you inside the university I can talk to," Strong said. "This will be a high-profile case—a second murder within two weeks, more than we have had in the previous two years. I plan to call in the BCI boys for help with this."

"BCI?" Brand asked.

"Bureau of Criminal Investigation, a state agency designed to help out small-town police forces like ours with additional forensics analysis. We'll bag and label all the evidence we find here. We'll pick up any fibers we can with our vacuum from the seat cushions and send that along. You'd be amazed at what the forensics experts can do. When I get the report I'll let you know if it tells us anything helpful."

Brand thanked Harriet for calling and letting him visit the scene—Brand was not sure whether it should yet be called a crime scene. As he was driving back home, he decided to stop by his office at his university office. On his voice mail he found a message from President Coles.

"Jeremy, Milton Coles here. Campus Security just called and told me that Sarah Giles has been found dead at her home. That's two members of our faculty dead in less than a week. I'm worried about the effects of this negative publicity on the university. I'm off to Washington today, but when I return early next week I'd like you to brief me on where things stand with your report. Maybe by then we will know more about Sarah's death. Thanks."

Dinner at the Brand household was usually a small, relaxed affair. The housekeeper prepared dinner, though she rarely stayed to enjoy the fruits of her labors. She looked in on her aging father every evening, fixed his supper and generally saw to his welfare. Melanie Carter joined Brand and Ruskin for dinner two or three times a week, depending on her schedule and sometimes on what Écoles prepared. Carter always made it a point to dine at the Brand house when the menu included lasagna, one of the best dishes to come from the Écoles kitchen. That was tonight's menu, and Brand chose a California Zinfandel "to wash down the pasta," as he put it. Brand had a firm policy against letting dinner conversation deal with work or work-related issues, but over coffee talk turned to the day's unpleasant events.

"I understand that you were at Professor Giles's house this afternoon while the police were still there," Carter said. "Any idea of what actually happened?"

"Harri thinks Sarah's death was made to look like a suicide, that it may be murder. There was nothing about the crime scene to suggest that it wasn't suicide; she just thinks everything looks just a little too contrived. Until she gets the autopsy from the coroner and the report from the forensics team, though, there's no reason to think that it wasn't a suicide."

"Everybody on campus was talking about it and wondering why she killed herself," Carter said. "I ran into a couple of graduate students in the management department, and they said nobody had noticed anything out of the ordinary about her activities. They were as surprised as anyone to hear the news."

"But that's the way it is with suicides," Brand said. "People who've decided to kill themselves can become quite calm after making the decision. It's as though intending to end their life gives them a purpose they'd been lacking."

"Did you see anything at Professor Giles's house that made you agree with the chief?" Ruskin asked.

"No, but I didn't get to look around much. We'll know if there's anything to Harri's intuitions when she gets reports from the coroner and forensics people. Until then everything is pure speculation."

Carter announced that she had a term paper to complete, and left after helping carry dirty dishes into the kitchen. Ruskin helped the clean-up process and then opened the door to the cellar. "I'm going to finish up recording the results from the auction. Anything else you want me to do?"

"The annotations will be fine," Brand said. We're getting close to the publisher's deadline for the book, and I need to spend some time making selections from these photos of Greek kraters and rhytons for the chapter on wine-drinking vessels."

Brand was so deeply involved in writing that all thoughts of Sarah Giles's death had faded from his consciousness until the phone rang. It was past ten o'clock, and Brand wondered who would be calling at that hour. Though unprepared for it, Brand was not totally surprised to find Harri on the line.

"Jeremy, we discovered the damnedest thing, and I knew you would want to know."

"Surely you don't have the forensics report back already."

"No, this isn't something from BCI. We were doing a routine crime-scene investigation, and we checked Professor Giles's computer. All her e-mail files are gone."

"They might not be gone for good, Harri. There are several software packages on the market that can retrieve deleted files unless they've been overwritten with new text."

"That's just it. These files were not deleted in the customary way. All her e-mail files were deleted, and then her hard drive reformatted. That means they really are gone."

"Uh-oh," Brand said. "But so what? It could have been that this was another way Sarah had of preparing for her death–wiping the slate clean, as it were. I admit that it's a stretch, but suicides have done stranger things."

"Could be, but this is one more detail I don't like."

"Another thing," Brand continued. "Sarah was a methodical person. Very precise in everything she did. I can imagine her setting the stage for her own death. I wouldn't be surprised if she even emptied her trash baskets."

"As a matter of fact, she did. But we'll go through her garbage cans. The pickup isn't until tomorrow, so nothing she threw away has been hauled off yet."

"So, erasing all her e-mail files seems comparable to emptying her trash. It all seems in character to me. Maybe there were things there she didn't want anybody to read. If you were going to kill yourself, would you want people rummaging through all your old letters and files after you're dead?"

"I don't have a real argument against what you're saying, Jeremy, but I'm still bothered about the entire scene, which doesn't feel right to me. There also is one little detail that seems completely out of character."

"Which is?"

"I know I sound like Columbo when I tell you this, but here it is. If Professor Giles was as methodical as you say she was—and I accept your views about that—picture the scene: She prepares her car as a death machine by fastening a vacuum cleaner hose to the tail pipe. Just to make sure it doesn't come off or doesn't fail to send enough exhaust into the car to do the job, she fastens it in place with duct tape. Duct tape! How many people would do that? She empties her trash baskets. She's all ready for the 'big sleep,' as Raymond Chandler called it. She writes the suicide note and then erases all her e-mail files. After that she turns off her computer. Then, presumably, she goes to the garage, gets in the car and starts the engine. But there's one detail she forgot. The printer."

"The printer?"

"Yeah, the printer. She leaves it turned on. Why would a person who goes to all the trouble she did do a thing like that? Why didn't she turn off the printer?"

Chapter 20

BRAND KEPT THINKING ABOUT STRONG'S analysis of Sarah Giles's death and formed a plan of what might be done to move the investigation of her death forward. He proposed the plan to Harri, who agreed that it was a good idea. They'd go public with the chief's suspicions and see what happened.

Central to the plan was Brand's standing commitment to host once each month an episode of a locally produced radio show called "Eavesdropping." The director liked to describe the content of the show as like overhearing an interesting conversation from the people sitting behind you on an airplane, hence the name. Sometimes the director served as the host, but there were guest hosts as well, scattered throughout the month. The guest hosts–and today that would be Brand—could choose their own topic, and when Brand had told Gerald Snow, the head of Broadcast Center, what his chosen topic would be, Snow said the promos for "Eavesdropping" would be doubled over the weekend, thus insuring a larger than usual broadcast audience. Snow put his own spin on the proposed topic and entitled the program "Death on Campus: Conversations with Police Chief Harriet Strong." He could already see his audience expanding.

Snow met Brand and Strong in his office in Broadcast Center, and when Harriet said this was her first time to visit the Center, the Director launched into a description of the Center's functions. It was obvious that he had given this speech a thousand times. "As you can see, Chief, the Center is quite complex. It houses the university's FM station, its sister AM station, and the university's television studios. We're also responsible for the university's media distribution system."

"What's that?" the chief asked.

"It's a system for sending digitized instructional materials to fifty of the university's classrooms—things like prerecorded videotapes, multimedia programs, any visual information a professor wants. Instead of having fifty videotape machines in the classrooms, we have this central distribution center that allows us to send anything a professor needs directly to the classroom."

As the trio walked down the hall to the broadcast studio where Brand's program took place, Snow continued his spiel. "Calloway's development of broadcast capabilities happened in the same way as it did at many other institutions around the country. Campus radio began in the '50s as a carrier signal distributed through the electric wiring of the dorms. It soon graduated to a small-wattage AM station, and then to a fifty-thousand-watt FM transmitter. Television came along later."

"Do you get most of your programs from national sources?" Strong asked.

"Yes and no. The AM station caters to the tastes of students, so we program mostly pop music. We do purchase most of the programs for the FM station from public broadcasting sources, but some local programming originates from campus. "Eavesdropping" is one of those. Needless to say, we're delighted to have you here today, Chief. I know this edition of the program will have a huge audience."

When they entered the production studio, Strong looked around at the racks of tape decks and control equipment and expressed admiration for the complexity of the place. Snow shrugged his shoulders. "The equipment was state-of-the art when installed, but technology has improved faster than our funding sources have. The university provides about half our budget, but we use those funds for the salaries of permanent staff. There just isn't enough left for upgrading our equipment, especially with cutbacks in federal funding. This is unfortunate for students, since they don't have exposure to state-of-the art equipment. Calloway State allows—even encourages—students to work in the broadcasting operation. They're glad for this kind of experience before they go out on the job market."

Snow showed them into the small booth where the interview took place and left them in the hands of a student engineer who was at the control panel. He directed Brand's attention to the clock that would indicate they were on-air. When the sweep second hand reached twelve, a student-announcer introduced the program.

"You are tuned to 'Eavesdropping,' a conversation you want to hear, taking place in the Broadcast Center of Calloway State University. Today's host is Professor Jeremy Brand."

Brand noted the cue indicated by the pointed index finger of the announcer and began.

"Good morning. Welcome to 'Eavesdropping.' Today my guest is Harriet Strong, Chief of Police of College Falls. Chief, welcome to "Eavesdropping."

"Thank you, Jeremy. I'm happy to be here."

"I'm glad we can have this conversation, because I know there are lots of rumors flying around about the two recent deaths here in College Falls of university personnel. Do you have any comments you'd like to make?"

"As you know, I can't make many public statements about ongoing investigations, but I will say this: At this point we have no conclusive evidence that the two deaths are related. We do know that Dean McKenzie died in a fire that was deliberately set. We are still investigating Professor Giles's death, for which she apparently claimed responsibility. However, we have reason to doubt that her death was a suicide."

"Really? On what do you base that?"

"At this point in our investigation I'm not prepared to say. Let me just note that our investigation is ongoing, and we are leaving open the possibility that her death was a homicide."

"Are you anticipating making an arrest soon regarding the dean's death?"

"Not at the moment, though the evidence that Giles was murdered and didn't take her own life is getting stronger by the day. We have every reason to assume that our investigation will produce results shortly."

"Are you getting good cooperation from the university in your investigation?"

"Splendid cooperation. I have appreciated the university's full disclosure on anything we need to know. We also enjoy good relations with the university's Campus Security division and have their full cooperation in this inquiry."

"Let's talk about how your department interacts with Campus Security. Many people may not be aware of the mutual assistance agreement that the two departments have signed."

In preparing for the program, Brand and Strong agreed that they would reveal few details of the investigation. The main purpose of their discussion was to unsettle the nerves of the murderer so he—or she—might do something that would confirm the chief's suspicions. Most of the conversation centered on the more general topic of how the university's police and the city's police forces worked with each other. Such cooperation was essential for those big weekends when College Falls was packed with visitors—homecoming, commencement, and much to the displeasure of the university, Saint Patrick's Day, when hordes of students from around the state descended on the town and campus for a spring fling, a street party that sometimes turned rowdy. Strong also talked about the department's initiatives in public schools in the area, especially its drug education programs. Toward the end of the half-hour broadcast, Brand brought the conversation back to the two recent deaths.

"Living in a small community gives us a sense of isolation from the problems of urban centers, so it is upsetting to our community when violent death interrupts the peaceful nature of our town. If anyone listening to this program today has any information that would help Chief Strong's investigation, please get in touch with her office, or call my office and I'll see that the information is forwarded on to her. I know all of us would like to see this matter cleared up as soon as possible."

Brand then recited phone numbers and concluded the program. The student announcer immediately took over the airwaves. "This is WCSU, your quality programming source in College Falls. Stay tuned for 'Afternoon Concert,' which immediately follows. Then at four o'clock, 'Evening Edition' comes your way."

When they left Broadcast Center, Strong and Brand lingered on the street corner to continue their conversation.

"I'll have the coroner's report this afternoon, Jeremy. I'll drop by your house after I get it."

When Strong arrived at Brand's house in the late afternoon, Brand had set up the essentials for another wine chat. Brand had the bottle and wine glasses on a tray sitting on his desk in the study, instead of the cellar, where they usually uncorked the selection of the day. For the occasion Brand provided a bottle of California Chardonnay. He told Strong that the wine had been chosen Wine of the Year by a national wine publication, yet it cost only $20 due to the large production from the vintner. "The three wonders of this," Brand continued, "are that the Wine of the Year was a Chardonnay, the winery made a lot of it and that its price was modest."

"Where did you get a bottle?" Strong asked.

"Finding one wasn't easy. The distributors allocated most to their restaurant accounts, but a friend of mind in the restaurant business, whom I've helped from time to time with his wine list, sent me three bottles." As Brand and Strong sniffed and sipped the wine, they talked briefly about the wine's overtones of fruit and nut flavors.

Strong reached into her briefcase and pulled out a stapled document. "I've got the autopsy report on Sarah Giles. But first let me tell you about her alibi. My investigators have checked it out, and it stands up. It appears she was telling us the truth about the gasoline cans in her car."

"Then she did need gas for her mower," Brand said.

"Yes, We talked to the young man who regularly does her lawn, and he confirmed that he'd asked her to buy some more gasoline for the mower. She has a mulching blade on her mower, so he continued to mow her grass well into the fall and mulched a lot of leaves."

"What about the other can?"

"A clerk at the combination filling station and convenience store where Professor Giles bought her gas remembered her coming in for a fill-up after running out of gas on her way home from class. She was berating herself for letting it happen, and the clerk remembers that Professor Giles said she'd come back later and refill the can."

"Since she had a full tank of gas and the hour was late, filling the empty can was something she could do later. Is that how you read it?"

"Right. None of what we've found rules her out as a suspect in the dean's death, but I still don't think she did it. Now that we have checked out her story, and combined with my skepticism about the suicide note, I think she was murdered, and the murder was made to look like a suicide. Then there's the autopsy report. She died from carbon monoxide poisoning, just as we suspected. But there was a large quantity of barbiturates in her blood. That's puzzling because we found a bottle of the stuff in her medicine cabinet but in a bottle without a label. It looked like someone had given her some of the medicine from a prescription and put it in another bottle, an aspirin bottle."

"So you think someone drugged her?"

"Maybe," Strong said. "I know that people share prescription medicines all the time, in spite of warnings from physicians not to. You have trouble sleeping. A friend says he has some sleeping tablets his doctor gave him and offers you some. You take them, maybe more out of politeness than anything else. Then some night you have trouble falling asleep and you remember the sleeping pills."

"You said the pills were in an aspirin bottle. Maybe Sarah intended to take an aspirin and got hold of the wrong bottle."

"Possibly, but someone had taken a felt-tipped pen and marked through the aspirin label. Of course it still looked like an aspirin bottle and would have felt like the typical shape of one, too."

"The more troubling question is why someone who's going to kill herself would take a sleeping pill first."

"Exactly," Strong said. "That's one thing that bothers me. I am also bothered by the suicide note."

"Because it was written on a computer?"

"That and the fact that forensics found no fingerprints on the note. Professor Giles's fingerprints are all over the computer, but there are none on the note itself."

"Isn't it possible that she just moved the note from the laser printer to her desk without actually picking it up? It isn't like the old days of pin-fed printers where you had to grasp the printed sheet to tear it off of a continuous roll of computer paper. A laser printer prints a full page at a time, and you could just sort of slide it out of the tray."

"It's possible. But there are other things that seem out of the ordinary, too."

"Such as?" Brand asked.

"The printer. Let's say the note was printed by Professor Giles. I've already mentioned that we found the printer still turned on, so that means she would have turned off the computer but left the printer on. Here's another reason I think that the setup is phony. She had her computer and peripherals plugged into a surge protector like most people do so they have some defense from power surges. A single switch turns off the whole thing."

"Are you saying that the switch on the surge protector was turned off?"

"Not only that, all the sockets were used up. The computer itself, the monitor, a scanner, external speakers attached to the computer and the light on her desk filled up the surge protector. Five plugs. All used."

"So the printer was plugged into another outlet."

"Exactly. When you turn off the switch on the surge protector, it turns off everything *but* the printer. Professor Giles would have known that. A stranger wouldn't. If Giles turned off her computer and other things by using the switch on the surge protector, why didn't she also turn off the printer?"

"That's something of a stretch, Harri. Maybe you're putting too much weight on the fact that the computer was turned off. She could just as well have left it on and you'd have no suspicions at all."

"I agree with you that people who commit suicide are often methodical and the act is planned out in great detail. Besides, from the looks of things in her study, Professor Giles was neat to a fault. Leaving a computer on wouldn't look right. At least that's what the murderer thought. The murderer probably thought that the switch on the surge protector controlled everything and just didn't know that the printer was plugged in somewhere else. Professor Giles would have known that, though.."

"So you're absolutely convinced that Sarah was murdered."

"Not 'absolutely.' But there are too many things that don't add up. I've mentioned the lack of fingerprints on the suicide note and the fact that the printer was left on while everything else was turned off. But there's another thing. She was found on the passenger side of the car."

"So?"

"Well, think about it, Jeremy. You live alone. You're the sole driver of your car. You never ride on the passenger side. But you decide to kill yourself and do so by sitting on the passenger side? I don't think so. And then there are the barbiturates. She had double the amount in her bloodstream necessary for sleep. She was drugged. All that adds up to a probable murder."

"So, let me see if I can sketch out the scenario you have in mind," Brand said. "Someone drugs Sarah. After she is out that someone prints out a suicide note on her computer, mistakenly leaving the printer on. He—and it is probably a he since it would take a great deal of strength to do what I am describing—*he* carries Sarah to her car and places her on the passenger side. Then he rigs up the vacuum hose, starts the engine and Sarah dies from carbon monoxide poisoning."

"That's the way I read it."

"But aren't you making a bit much out of her being on the passenger side?"

"I don't think so," Strong said. "Remember how her place is laid out. The garage is on the left-hand side of the house, which means that the door from the house to the garage would always open onto the passenger side of the car—unless you backed your car into the garage, and who does that? So the murderer carried Sarah into the garage and opened the most convenient car door, on the passenger side. Besides, it is difficult to move an unconscious person. Getting her behind the steering wheel would have been much harder."

"What about fingerprints on the car? Any help there?"

"All hers. The perpetrator probably used gloves, so no other fingerprints are on anything."

"So, someone went to a great deal of trouble to make it look like Sarah Giles killed the dean. I just don't buy it."

"I realize that leaves me with a problem. So far I've been better at ruling out suspects than finding them. At this point I have no viable leads. I don't even know if we're looking for one murderer or two. Maybe your radio program this morning will stir things up a bit."

Brand walked over to his bookcase and pulled out a book. He laid it on the desk. "This book contains a mystery story Harry Kemelman wrote entitled "The Nine Mile Walk," in which someone applies deductive skills to an overheard snatch of conversation to infer that a crime had been committed and to discover the perpetrator. We can't do that in real life as neatly as the author of this story did, but we can see where the logic leads us for both a single killer and for two killers."

Harriet stretched her legs and kicked off her shoes. "OK. Let's assume that Sarah Giles didn't kill the dean and that we're looking for a single killer."

"In that case," Brand said, "we'll start first with the assumption that the two deaths are related, though not in the way the suicide note said. The killer of the dean had some reason also to kill Sarah Giles. One motive for killing her might be that she saw the killer start the fire. But we know that's unlikely since Sarah had too much to drink and had to be taken home and put to bed."

"I agree," Strong said. "I don't think she was an eyewitness to the crime, but it might be that she found out later, somehow or other, who was responsible for killing the dean, and the killer murdered her to keep her from revealing what she knew."

"Those are about the only two possibilities, assuming that the crimes are related. Let's look at the possibility of two separate crimes. It could be that the dean's killer had a totally unrelated reason for killing Sarah, and when she first appeared to be a suspect in the dean's death, he thought he could kill her and tie her death to the dean's death, making it look like a suicide."

"That's plausible," Strong said. "It might have worked, too, if we hadn't been able to check out her story and also if there weren't so many things to arouse my suspicion."

"So let's pursue the possibility that these were two separate crimes. Here again we have two options: a single murderer or two murderers. If we're dealing with a single murderer, we need to find a motive someone might have for killing both the dean and Sarah. Thus far we haven't identified anyone with such a motive."

"And if we have two murderers, we need two motives. So far we don't have even one, so that pretty much leaves us where we started," Strong said.

"We can narrow the possibilities down somewhat. If we have two crimes and two murderers, then why did Sarah's killer try to get us to *think* she killed the dean? It wouldn't be necessary. In fact, no suicide note would have been necessary. She could have just gone out to the garage and gassed herself to death, leaving you to determine it was suicide. But the suicide note raised your suspicions."

"What you're implying is that the murderer wrote the note hoping it would give us a convenient solution to the dean's murder so we'd quit looking for the real killer."

"Precisely. The killer would have been smart not to attempt to tie the two deaths together, because that's what aroused your suspicions. If the killer had just rigged up the car to look like a suicide and left it at that, you would have assumed that Sarah was depressed over the pending negative tenure decision she expected and took her life as a result."

Brand got up and put the volume back on the shelf. He then paced back and forth in front of the sofa on which Strong was sitting. Finally Harriet interrupted. "You've something else on your mind, Jeremy. What?"

"Well, I think the scenario we have outlined is plausible. Killing Sarah would have been a credible way for the murderer to misdirect us—by giving us the dean's killer. But we can't rule out the possibility that there were two murderers. Consider this: Someone else other than the dean's murderer kills

Sarah, for whatever reason, and at the moment we have no idea what that reason might be. Again I will use 'he' to refer to the murderer. He knows that Sarah was a suspect in the dean's death. It was in the local paper, so there is no secret there. What he doesn't know is that her alibi stood up and that she would no longer be a suspect if she were still alive. Right?"

"That's right," Strong said. "Given what we now know, we wouldn't be able to charge her with anything. Having empty gasoline cans in your car is not a crime."

"OK. But the murderer doesn't know that her alibi checked out. He thinks she's still a suspect in the death of the dean. He kills her and makes us think she took her own life in an act of remorse. If he succeeds, you attribute her death to suicide. You have also solved the murder of the dean. The murderer is off the hook."

"But we don't have enough information to know whether there was one killer or two. If there was only one, we need to look for one person who was tied in some way both to the dean and to Giles," Strong said.

"That could include half the faculty in her college. But if there were two murderers, we need to find out why someone wanted to kill Sarah. We simply need to know more. Maybe my radio program this morning will, as you put it, 'stir things up.' In the meantime, have some more Chardonnay."

Chapter 21

His conversation with Harriet convinced Brand of the need for more information about the death of Sarah Giles. Over the weekend he continued to look through the Dean's day files but found nothing relating to Giles. Except for his notes to file and the E-mail exchanges the Dean had with her, nothing in the dean's office provided any motive that would lead someone to want to kill her.

On his way to campus Brand decided to stop by the office of Bob Elliot. As chair of the Department of Business Communication, he would be able to let Brand into Giles's office. Elliot said he was happy to help in any way and used his master key to open the door to her office. "Just shut the door when you're finished, Jeremy. The door will lock automatically."

Brand looked around the office and noted how death serves as the great interrupter. A stack of unopened mail lay on the corner of the desk. In an in-box sitting to the right of her computer keyboard was a pile of correspondence on which Giles had scribbled notes outlining her reply. A notebook containing class lectures sat next to a pile of textbooks sent by hopeful publishers angling for an adoption. Brand flipped through the correspondence stack and saw the usual stuff in an academic's office: requests for reprints of a recent article, a letter attacking the central premise of the same article, forms for recommending students to graduate school, an inquiry from an editor of a Festschrift about an overdue paper, an invitation to present a paper at a forthcoming conference, announcements of the program of the regional professional society meeting and inquiries from prospective students about Calloway's program in mass communications. He thought about the neatness of Sarah's home office where all the loose ends seemed to be tidied up. Her university office was full of uncompleted projects.

He started looking through the drawers of her desk and found nothing that looked in any way personal, except for her appointment calendar, and it contained only the kind of things one would expect of such a document. The usual array of committee meetings and appointment with students and an occasional dinner reservation provided only a brief insight into Giles's personal and professional life. On the date of the Dean's reception Giles had written, "Dean's Orgy! (Ugh)." Some resentment there, but nothing that looked criminal.

Brand then switched on the computer. The diagnostics ran, checking the system configuration and the CPU memory. Brand waited for the familiar screen-full of icons to appear, but because the hard drive had been reformatted, there was nothing.

Brand turned off the computer and left Giles's office as he had found it, shutting the door behind him as Elliot has requested. He stopped by the Chair's office and told him about the status of Giles's computer.

"That's news to me," Elliot said. "I haven't been into Sarah's office since her death, and no one in the department has asked me for the key. As far as I know you are the first one to enter that office since she died. Of course, if someone took Sarah's key, they could get into the office and erase the files."

"What about others in the college? Who else has a key?"

"The janitor, of course. I assume that the dean's office has a master key to all the offices in the building, but I don't know that for a fact." Brand made a note to ask the Dean's secretary about a master key and also to ask Strong if the police found a key in their search of her house.

When Brand got back to his office he checked his voice mail. There was a message from a graduate student requesting that his appointment to discuss the second chapter of his thesis be rescheduled. Another message was from an undergraduate who had been ill and missed an exam. Brand made a note to ask his teaching assistant to schedule a makeup test for her. The third message seemed at first like a hang-up. It was a source of constant amazement to Brand how many people didn't like to talk to an answering machine, and when they called and heard a recorded message chose to hang up rather than state their business. But after about five seconds, a muffled voice came on the line: "*I heard your radio program. Sarah didn't kill the dean. If you want to know who did, find out who has been reading books on bombs in the library.*"

Brand reached into his desk for a small recorder that he kept there, turned it on and tapped in the code on his phone to replay the last message so he could record it. On second hearing it was clear that the caller had taken some pains to disguise his or her voice. It sounded as though the caller was speaking through a handkerchief and using the lowest vocal range possible and speaking slowly. The effect was like playing an LP record at slow speed. Brand's voice mail date- and time-stamped every message, and this one came in on Saturday.

He slipped the tape recorder in his briefcase, picked up his lecture notes and went off to class.

Brand felt his lecture had gone well. A half-dozen or so students lingered after class, talking to him about the change of view from the medieval world to that of The Enlightenment, a shift that Brand both admired and criticized in his presentation. He wandered back to the departmental office, checked his mail and then returned to his office to deal with the memos and other paperwork that seemed to be an inevitable part of academic life. He had gotten through about half the accumulated stack of publishers' catalogs, announcements of fellowship opportunities for students at other institutions and routine announcements from the registrar about scheduling for the spring semester, when his phone rang. The caller was the now interim dean, George Helms.

"Jeremy, when we talked a couple of days ago I promised to do a little checking on Gary Hockney. Sorry it has taken me so long, but you know how busy things get. And with the appointment as interim dean and all, my work load has just gone into orbit. But I didn't want you to think that I had forgotten my commitment to you to do some investigation. I just regret that it has taken me so long, but better late than never, right?"

Hope he gets to the point soon, Brand thought to himself.

"Now I don't want you to think that I am stirring up trouble for the young man. It's just that I feel a sense of duty to help anyway I can with your investigation, and I want you to know that I'm willing to do anything I can to help clear up this dreadful situation. Anyway, I've asked around, and just about everybody I talk to says that they think the man is dangerous."

"Dangerous? In what way?"

"Well, I wouldn't exactly say psychotic or anything like that—I'm not a psychologist, you know, and I would hate to throw around a clinical term like that without knowing whether or not it really fit—but his teachers tell me Gary is moody and sometimes given to outbursts of temper. One of his professors—I won't say exactly who, just because he asked me not to—said that Gary really lost it in class a couple of weeks ago. Apparently another student made a comment about Gary's seminar report that Gary took offense at. I guess he thought the other student was making fun of him or something like that, and he actually got on his feet and made a move toward the other student as though he was going to hit him or shove him, or do some kind of bodily harm. The professor had to impose himself physically between the two students to prevent an incident."

"Was this the only case of that kind you discovered?"

"Well, yes and no. Apparently Gary is quite argumentative in class, sometimes even to the point of calling his fellow students names. I know that Dean McKenzie had talked to Gary about his behavior in the past, but it apparently didn't do any good. This latest report is the only incident I know of where he started to get physical, but it's consistent with his somewhat irascible personality. And there's another thing. Tabitha McKenzie told me that Gary sometimes called the dean at home and that she heard him shouting over the phone at Clem."

"Sounds like Hockney cuts a pretty wide swath."

"That's putting it mildly," Helms said. "Hockney has an intimidating presence, kind of like the schoolyard bully, if you know what I mean. He seems to think that if he just keeps arguing and talking loud enough to people, he'll get his way. I think that's why the loss of his fellowship was such a shattering blow. It was the first thing that happened to him here that he couldn't talk his way out of. But I think having him out of here is the right thing to do. Good riddance, I say."

"So you don't plan to reconsider his fellowship status."

"Not in the least. I would have made the same decision as Clem made. In fact, I would have made it sooner. The man is just not cut out for a career in management. The last thing we should do is foist off on business another psycho boss—not that I really should use the term, since I'm not a psychologist, and I don't want it to be thought that I throw such terms around carelessly."

Brand wondered how any man could use so many words to say so little. No wonder Helms had not succeeded in snagging a deanship in spite of his many job interviews. Brand had seen candidates talk themselves out of a job more often than not. It was probably a combination of inexperience, lack of confidence and uncertainty, but someone on a search committee would ask a question and the candidate would talk for fifteen minutes.

"Anyway, Jeremy, I don't know if this will be helpful to you or not, but I thought I should pass this information on to you. I definitely think you should look into that young man's situation more. I'm not leveling a charge against him, you understand, but I do know that he was very angry at the dean's office, and given his unpredictable temper, I wouldn't put anything past him."

Brand decided he would bring the conversation to a close. By now he had heard everything that George had to contribute, and it wasn't much. "Thanks, George. I appreciate your call. I know you've got lots to do, so I'll let you go."

After he hung up the phone Brand reviewed the list of original suspects he had made early in the investigation. Sarah's death/suicide removed her from the list, and Gary Hockney, while still a possibility, didn't seem to Brand to be a compelling candidate for murderer–in spite of what Helms had just said. If the deaths of McKenzie and Giles were related, and he couldn't rule out that possibility, no evidence linked Giles and Hockney in any way. While there might have been opportunity, no one had yet found a motive for him to be involved in her death.

The undergraduate students calling themselves SES were hardly suspects. They seemed to be playing at the role of campus radicals, and after their latest incident at the dean's home they had ceased to exist as a distinctive group. The police were conducting interviews of neighbors of both Giles and McKenzie, hoping to find someone, somewhere who saw something that might aid their investigation. But so far, nothing.

Paul Ruskin, at Brand's direction, had begun files on both Giles and McKenzie. Brand picked them up on his way out of the house and was now able to spend some time with them before his next appointment. The files included all kinds of stuff: Brand's notes on conversations with various people, news accounts of the deaths, programs from the memorial services for both Giles and McKenzie, obituary notices, even copies of their *curriculum vitae.* Hoping that reviewing these materials again would point him toward some new line of inquiry, Brand first opened the file for Clem McKenzie. The record of his academic career reflected in his CV was impressive: A young assistant professor rises rapidly through the ranks and is promoted to full professor within eight years of receipt of his doctorate. He serves on several important committees, is made head of his department. He takes an associate deanship at another university. Calloway hires him from that position to be dean of the College of Professional Studies. The obituary notice listed all these accomplishments and described his surviving family: one brother, an older sister, his wife Tabitha, two daughters, three grandchildren.

Sarah's CV also revealed a young academic of promise. A doctorate at a good graduate school. Publications in several journals prominent in their field. A book-length manuscript submitted but not yet accepted for publication. Anyone familiar with tenure rules could tell that this was the year for her tenure decision, an event that occupied so much of her energy the last months of her life.

Brand then looked at the program of her memorial service and the obituary from the local newspaper. As he read the newspaper account he noticed a detail that had escaped him earlier: her surviving family was listed as her mother, two sisters—all of whose names and addresses were listed—and "her former husband, Dr. Lester Forrest, who is Dean of Students at Middletown College, Middletown, Wisconsin." Brand remembered speaking briefly to Sarah's mother and sisters at the memorial service but had no recollection of meeting her former husband on that occasion. He decided that it might not hurt to have a talk with Dr. Lester Forrest.

Brand looked up the area code for Middletown and dialed the information operator for the college's number. Even the smallest of institutions and businesses now have call director answering systems that require the caller to route the call using appropriate numbers entered from a touch-tone phone. No, Brand was not interested in application information, did not know the extension of the party he was calling, and yes, he did want to talk to an operator. After navigating through the various options the call director system gave him, he finally was connected to a receptionist who gave him Dr. Forrest's extension. He entered the three-digit number and was soon talking to Giles's ex-husband.

Brand extended condolences. "I'm sorry to be unable to extend my sympathy in person, but I do not recall our meeting at the memorial service."

"Unfortunately, I was unable to attend the service. I was laid up with pneumonia, and my doctor wouldn't let me travel. Even though we had been divorced for several years, Sarah and I remained friends, and I consider her death a great loss."

"Indeed, her death is a loss to all of us," Brand said. "When did you last see her?"

"During the summer, in August. I made a trip to College Falls and spent several days there. I always have had hopes of reconciliation with Sarah, but last summer she decided that we should continue in our separate paths. I never really gave up the possibility of our getting back together, though."

Forrest explained that early in their marriage they had accepted academic appointments at different institutions. They solemnly promised to each other that they would not let the distance that separated them destroy their relationship, but like many academic couples whose separate jobs strain their marriages, they found themselves drifting apart. Ratifying the realities of the situation by divorce seemed the only honest response, though Forrest again said it was always his hope that they would get back together.

"I know the tenure decision was much on her mind, so I tried to convince her that there was life after a denial of tenure and that she should move to Middletown and live with me until she decided on her future. I even brought along Chamber of Commerce literature about the area and recruitment brochures from the College, which are full of color photos showing how beautiful the place is."

"What about Sarah's state of mind just before her death?" Brand asked. Forrest said that although she was clearly worried about the tenure decision, her general outlook was positive. He had never seen anything suggesting that she might commit suicide. When Brand told him that the local police were leaving open the possibility that she was murdered, Forrest stated how shocked he was and asked whether there were any suspects. Brand told him that the police investigation was still underway, though there had been no arrests. Forrest promised to call Brand if he thought of anything that might help the police.

Brand hung up the phone and then heard knocking on the door. The visitor was Harriet Strong.

"I was on campus meeting with the head of Campus Security," Strong said. "I thought I might catch you in."

"Our minds were on the same channel, because I was just getting ready to call you." Brand said. He then told Strong about the conversation he just had with Sarah's ex-husband.

"Did he say anything about giving her money?"

"No, the subject of money never came up. Why?"

"As part of our investigation into her death we looked at Professor Giles's financial records. Nothing unusual about them. The university's direct deposit of her monthly salary is the biggest item in her checking account. She had a modest savings account, but there we found a deposit of two thousand dollars made just a few days before her death. It couldn't have been a supplementary payment from the university, because the deposit slip indicates it was a cash deposit. It may be unrelated to her death, but it does need explaining."

"A cash deposit of two thousand dollars? Forrest made no mention of money even though he was candid about details of their relationship. You could call him and ask if he gave her the money; but the fact that it was in cash makes it unlikely, unless he wired it to her and she requested the funds in cash. But why would she do that?"

"I agree," Strong said, as she jotted down a reminder in her notebook. "But I'll still phone him, just the same. Now, what were you going to call me about?"

Brand told her about finding the computer in Sarah Giles's office completely erased. "It bothers me that her computer was erased while the in-box on her desk was filled with correspondence it appeared she was preparing to answer. Except for the computer, nothing in her office looked like she was trying to clear the deck or erase the board in preparation for taking her own life. I just find an erased computer puzzling."

"All this just fuels my suspicion that her death was not suicide," Strong said. "She had no financial troubles that we can discover, and except for her concern about tenure, her professional life was OK. Now you tell me she had an ex-husband who was apparently still in love with her and who offered her a place to recover from professional disappointment. None of this adds up to suicide."

"What I'm about to share with you will confuse things even more." Brand placed the tape recorder on his desk and turned it on. *"I heard your radio program. Sarah didn't kill the dean. If you want to know who did, find out who has been reading books on bombs in the library."*

"Play it again," Strong said. She listened to the message once more and then added. "I guess it's time to go to the library."

Chapter 22

BRAND HAD AT HIS DISPOSAL instant access to the library's database. Using a modem it was possible for him to interrogate the library's central catalog from a personal computer either in his university office or at home. Gone were the days when a library's card catalog was the only access to its holdings, and this was true of Calloway State's library. Since Strong was there in his office, Brand thought it might be useful for both of them to visit the library in person.

Strong said this was her first visit to the library. "The public library serves most of my needs, and this is the first time any local crime has involved the university library in any way at all."

As the pair entered the revolving doors that marked the entrance to the library, Brand pointed out the darker rectangle of carpet to the left of the main entrance. "That's where the card catalog used to be. The only indication now that the library ever had such a thing are those spots of carpeting near the circulation desk that are *not* faded and worn, showing where the card catalog file cabinets sat for years."

"So everything is now computerized, I assume."

"Right. Most large libraries have either closed or gotten rid of their card catalogs." Brand led Harriet to a bank of computer work stations. "All our collection databases are now accessed solely by computer. We can look for things by title or subject. The search engine we use even allows us to 'browse' through titles that are shelved next to any book we're interested in. Let's start with the topic 'arson.'"

Brand pulled up a chair to his work station and entered his name and password. Then he entered his PIN number. The screen displayed a menu offering several options. He chose "Search," and another menu appeared. The search program would accept Boolean statements as key words, so Brand entered *arson and incendiary devices*. After an interval of about ten seconds, a screen appeared listing a dozen titles. Brand scrolled down the list, stopping on several and opening additional screens for those items that gave the publisher, date of publication, and whether the book was checked out or available on the shelves. One of the books dealt with the cost of arson to insurance companies. Another discussed the psychology of the arsonist.

Brand next tried *incendiary devices* alone. This list included a dozen books, several of which would be useful in chemical engineering studies. He tried other search words, and from each screen wrote down the names of those titles he thought a potential arsonist might choose, noting in each case which books were not checked out but were available on the shelves. Brand knew his methodology was crude, but at the moment he could think of nothing else. He would print out a list of items in the library that a would-be arsonist might find of interest. If any of the items were checked out, finding out who had the books would not be easy. He knew that librarians guarded the privacy of borrowers with an ideological commitment that bordered on paranoia. That was one reason he wanted Strong with him.

After working for five minutes, Brand had a list of ten titles that were possibilities for someone interested in using the resources of the library to learn how to burn down someone's house. According to the library's data base, all of these titles were currently on the shelves. This fact, in itself, did not tell much since the user could have checked out the materials, read them and returned them to the library.

Brand decided that what he now needed was the circulation record on each of the ten titles on his list. This is the kind of information that the circulation librarians could derive from the database, but it was not available to users like Brand. He knew that by going to the director of the library such information might be made available to him, but Brand did not want to have to reveal why he was seeking the information, at least not yet.

Before trying to find out who had been reading these books—if he could get such information—it would make sense first to find out which of these books had been recently checked out of the library. Brand knew that he could find out such information without asking for the aid of the professional librarians; all it would take would be a little time on his part. He would go to the stacks, look in the back of the book for the date due, and then make additional inquiries about the titles that recently were used. Like many university libraries, Calloway State had automated its circulation procedures. Bar codes and laser readers made having a card in the back of the book obsolete. A user presented a library card. The circulation assistant ran the card through a swipe reader, then entered the book's number from a bar code using a pen reader. But the date due was still stamped in the back of the book on a small sheet affixed to it for that purpose. Some things were better done by hand than by computer.

It was still two hours until his class, so Brand proposed to Strong that the two of them do a review of the books immediately. Most were shelved in stacks on the third and fourth floors of the library, so he took the elevator to level four and started working his way through his list. Brand gave Strong a brief explanation of the Library of Congress numbering system and divided the list with her. When Brand looked for the first title, it was not on the shelf. Brand thought that maybe the book was misshelved, so he went to the second title. Also not on the shelf. The third title was on the shelf, but checking in the back revealed it had not circulated in more than a year. Brand continued through his list of five books.

By the time Brand had finished his list, Harriet came back with only one book in hand. "Most of the books on this list are not on the shelves, Jeremy. I found only this one." Brand looked in the back and found that it, too, has not been checked out in over a year.

"This is strange. Eight of the ten are not on the shelves. That's more than we can attribute to misshelving, especially since these books are on such an unusual subject. If someone used library resources to learn how to build bombs, the books on our lists could provide the information. But where are the books?"

"Maybe someone stole them from the library," Strong said. "I've read of several crimes of that sort. There was some guy in Columbus, Ohio, who stole all kinds of stuff from Ohio State before they caught him."

"It's possible that someone took the books from the library, though it would be difficult. Each book spine contains a strip that sets off a detector at the exit and sounds an alarm if the strip hasn't been deactivated at the circulation desk. We also have student monitors who inspect every book bag, backpack and briefcase leaving the library. My bet is that the books are still somewhere in the library. The question is, where? We're going to need the help of the library director. Let's go see if he's in."

Brand and Strong had barely entered the director's office suite when Richard Ellis, library director, saw Jeremy and came out to meet him.

"Hey, Jeremy. A pleasant surprise. What brings you here?"

Brand introduced the chief and started talking about their request as they entered the director's office. "Richard, the chief may need your help with the investigation he is doing of Clem McKenzie's death."

"Anything you need, Chief. Just ask."

Brand told the director about the voice mail message he received with its instructions to look in the library. He detailed how he searched the library's holdings for books that might be of interest to a potential arsonist and had discovered that most of the books he had identified were not in circulation but were supposedly still on the shelves. Yet when he went to inspect them, the books were missing.

"We're hoping, Richard, that you could run the circulation records for us and tell us who has been reading these books."

"Sorry, Jeremy. That's one thing I can't do. Our rules forbid disclosure of borrowers' records."

"I can always return with a court order, Dr. Ellis," Strong said. "But I was hoping that it wouldn't come to that."

"I'm afraid that is precisely what you'll have to do, Chief. Only if you lay a court order on my desk will I divulge that information. But tell me more about your search. You say the books show up on our data base as available, yet they aren't on the shelves?"

"Exactly," Brand said.

"I tell you what I'll do, and this doesn't violate any of our professional standards. Give me the LC numbers, and I will see when these books last circulated. I won't tell you who checked them out, but I will tell you when they last left the library."

Ellis called his administrative assistant and told her the information he wanted. Brand and Strong talked generalities until the assistant came in with a printout, which she handed to Ellis."

"Hmm. None of these books has circulated in the last year. Sounds to me like someone has squirreled them away someplace," the director said. "You wouldn't believe how big a problem that is for us, especially for students and faculty with carrels. It's just easier for them to take the books from the shelves into the carrel without checking them out. The books show up missing from our shelves, and we have no idea where they are."

"Do you make periodic inspections of the carrels to see what's been left in them?"

"Yep. Sure do. We make it a condition of carrel assignment that we will inspect them at least twice a year for books that have not been properly checked out."

"How can you tell?" Strong asked.

"We look in the back of the book. If the due date isn't a future one, we know either that the book has been taken off the shelves without being checked out at all, or that the book is overdue. In any event we retrieve the books and reshelve them."

"When is the next inspection?" Brand asked.

"Not for a couple of months. We do, however, also include in our agreement with users of carrels that we have a right to make unannounced inspections. We could do that right away if it's important."

"It's important," Strong said. "We've already had two murders on campus. I hope we can prevent others."

"That settles it, then," Ellis said. "We'll make an unannounced check of carrel and study rooms beginning tomorrow. But please don't be disappointed if we don't turn up anything. There is always the possibility that the books were stolen. Our defenses against theft are not absolute."

"I realize that," Brand said. "And if the books were stolen…well, that will be the end of this trail. It may be a dead-end in any event, but I thought we should at least try to see if we can find the books in the library."

"I agree," the director said. "I'll personally keep on top of this and let you know if we discover anything."

As Brand walked toward his office to spend a few minutes in preparation for his class, he heard someone calling his name and turned to see Sally Turner running toward him. She closed the distance between them and then matched his stride step for step. "Professor Brand, I wonder if I could talk to you again."

"I saw your earlier piece in the paper, Sally. Why do you need anything more at this point?"

"I wonder if you have any comments on recent developments in the investigation of the deaths of Dean McKenzie and Professor Giles."

"I am not the investigating office on this, Sally. I suggest that you call Chief Strong for an answer to your questions."

"I plan to, but I wanted your comments, too. My journalism professor says we need three quotes for every article, and my editor insists that we follow that standard. So I need a quote from you for my story, even if you don't have any new information."

"Why are you writing another story if there are no recent developments?"

"These two deaths are an ongoing story for the paper. We have to write something about them every day."

"You mean you have to write something, even if there's no new information or nothing new has happened?"

"Yeah, more or less. I have to have six inches of copy on my editor's desk by seven o'clock. President Coles is out of his office, so I can't get a quote from him. Since you're doing the investigation, I was hoping you could give me something."

Brand could see that he would be cited in the story no matter what he said. Even if he said nothing, he would be mentioned as having "no comment," which would make it appear that he had something to hide. If the reporter felt particularly offended, she could even say, "Prof. Brand refused to comment." It was like an ascending hierarchy of disrepute. The lowest level was that so and so "could not be reached for comment." The next level was "no comment," and finally the implication of guilt was strong in saying that the person being interviewed "refused to comment." Student reporters especially failed to see the ethical implications of this—that they could damn a source who simply preferred not to be a part of the conversation. Reporters liked to recite the First Amendment guarantee of freedom of speech as a mantra, not realizing that there is a corresponding freedom of silence. They can ask, but no one has to answer.

Brand knew, however, that the student reporter would fill her six inches, one way or another, and hoped for the best.

"Let me repeat again, Sally, that I am not conducting an investigation. The official investigation of these two deaths is being conducted by the local police. My role is strictly unofficial and advisory in the investigation of these tragic events."

Deaths at University tragic events, professor says. A good headline, Sally thought. Her lead sentence was already forming in her mind: *Prof. Jeremy Brand calls the death of Dean McKenzie and Prof. Sarah Giles "tragic events."*

"Do you think Professor Giles was responsible for the fire at the dean's house, as her suicide note said?"

"At this point I have no more information than has been made public. You'll have to direct that question to the police."

"I have heard that Professor Giles was angry at the dean for denying her tenure. Has your investigation confirmed that?"

"I have heard the same rumors, Sally, but I can't vouch for their truthfulness. What I do know is that no formal decision had been made by the dean's office on Professor Giles's tenure recommendation, so in a technical sense the dean had not denied her tenure."

Brand says Dean McKenzie's office had not denied Prof. Giles tenure.

"Do you think it is right for one person to be able to deny tenure to a professor?"

"Now you are going beyond the story about Professor Giles's death and asking a question about policy."

"So, what do you think?"

"To answer that question I need to mention two ideals: that of collegial governance and shared authority."

"What's 'collegial governance?'"

"In a university, decisions are made by individuals who consider themselves colleagues. The university is not hierarchical with a boss at the top of a pyramid of power. Important decisions like tenure begin with the department where a committee of the faculty make a recommendation. That recommendation goes to the dean whose responsibility is to review it."

"OK. So what do you mean by 'shared authority'?"

"That the dean shares the decision with the faculty. If the faculty do not recommend to the dean that someone be tenured, the dean cannot take unilateral action and grant tenure. When the faculty do make a positive recommendation the dean is responsible for reviewing that decision. The dean may or may not agree with it. The decision to grant tenure is therefore shared between dean and faculty."

"So you think it's OK for a dean to have that kind of power," Sally said.

"In our system of shared governance, that is the way it works."

Dean shares in the making of decisions about tenure, but has a larger share.

"So, why did Professor Giles think she wasn't going to get tenure if the dean hadn't made a decision yet?"

"I can't speak for Professor Giles's state of mind. I only said I have heard the same rumors you have."

Prof. Brand confirmed that he has heard rumors to the effect that dean was going to deny tenure to Prof. Giles, and that is the reason she allegedly set fire to his house.

"If Professor Giles was not responsible for the dean's death, do you think one of the faculty might have set fire to his house? I've heard that Dean McKenzie was unpopular with the faculty."

"As I said before, Sally, I don't have any new information to share with you. Right now all that I know is also public knowledge. Anything more at this point would be pure speculation."

Professor calls alternative theories about the murder of Dean McKenzie "pure speculation."

"Thanks, Professor Brand. You've been a great help with my story. I'll call you back if I have any more questions."

As Brand continued his walk home, he shook his head in disbelief. If this is the kind of journalism we are teaching here at Calloway State, he thought, then no wonder some news organizations prefer to hire English majors.

At six o'clock Strong arrived at Brand's house, and the two adjourned to the cellar. The cellar was arranged so that Brand's trestle table and four chairs were placed in the center. The table was always covered with a white cloth, and thanks to Mrs. Écoles, sitting on it was always a supply of Riedel wine glasses. Light for that corner of the cellar was supplied by a strip of small halogen lamps that provided ample light for inspecting the wine's color. Brand furnished the wine for this tasting, a bottle of Châteauneuf-du-Pape from a small vineyard whose wine neither had tasted before. The bottle was slightly larger than a standard Bordeaux bottle and heavier, thick enough to display in bas relief the identifying marks of this appellation: bishop's miter and St. Peter's keys of the kingdom, a reference to the Pope and his châteauneuf or "new château" in Avignon near the source of this wine.

After both glasses were half-filled with the ruby liquid, Harriet was the first to speak. "I never asked you how you came to be interested in wine."

"For the first part of my life, my sense of wine was shaped by the inexpensive jug wines that found their way to the table in my parents' home. It was on my first trip to France, when I was a graduate student in Paris that I came into contact with the first great wine I had ever tasted. It was a cabernet from one of the first-growth châteaux. I never knew anything could be so complex and yet so approachable. From that point on I was hooked."

"You certainly started with the expensive ones."

"Back then, even the best Bordeaux wines were not that expensive. It's only in the last couple of decades that many French wines have escalated in price."

"Caused by what?"

"A couple of things. One is that the rest of the world has also discovered French wine. The Bordeaux producers also discovered that they could market their wines more effectively if they bottled them at their own châteaux rather than selling their wine to négociants, who bottled it under their own label. The biggest and best châteaux are now owned by national or even multinational corporations. Wine has become big business."

"Then there are the Burgundies. Expensive for different reasons."

"Right. There's just so little of it to supply the huge demand. Most Burgundy holdings are small and the production is limited. That's why their prices are so high."

"But like you, I have turned more and more to California wines," Strong said. "I think French wines have become too expensive and California wines are better values."

Brand took another sip from his glass. "Not only do California wines offer good value, they also are of high quality and are getting better every year. From a handful of wineries in the state not that many years ago, California now has more than eight hundred, some of which turn out an exceptional product."

Harriet set her glass down on the table and reached for the bottle. "I read about a recent restaging of the famous 1976 tasting in Paris of French and American wines, when the American wines outscored everything. The tasting used the same vintages, and the American wines still were excellent."

"Good news for American wines," Brand said. "It means they're aging well."

"I'm not going to age very well if I don't solve the two murders on campus," Strong said. "Right now I am out of suspects, as I mentioned this morning. What we need is someone with information to come forward. You wouldn't believe how many crimes are solved by inside tips. If it weren't for informants, our success rate would be small."

They talked more about the report from George Helms about Hockney's outburst, and both agreed it had not added much to their knowledge. "If I locked up everybody who lost their temper at one time or another," Strong said, "half of College Falls would be in jail."

"I have to admit that Hockney's intensity bothers me," Brand said. "He seems to be a angry young man, but I can't see a strong enough motive for him to do harm to the dean. He was upset at losing his fellowship, but every year several graduate students find themselves in the same situation.

"Like I said, I am better at eliminating suspects than I am in finding them."

The intercom buzzer sounded, and Brand reached over and picked up the phone.

"Professor, sorry to bother you, but Dr. Ellis, the library director, is on the phone, and he says it is urgent."

Brand thanked Écoles and then pushed the button on the wall-mounted phone to connect with the outside line, and he also put the call on the speaker so Strong could hear.

"Richard, glad you called. Do you have any information for me?"

"Sorry to bother you at home, Jeremy, but I thought you would like to know the result of our search. I put several librarians on it. We didn't find all the titles on your list, but we found most of them. As I suspected, they hadn't been checked out but were stashed in a carrel."

"Really? Whose?"

"It's a carrel assigned to a graduate student. Let's see, I looked in our files just a few minutes ago to find out who had that carrel. I laid the note around here someplace."

Brand could hear the rustling of papers as the director rooted around on his desk. In some ways Ellis was more like a professor than an administrator. His desk was crowded with folders and papers, and he was always unable to find things on short notice.

"Yes, here it is. The carrel was assigned to a graduate student in the management department. His name is Gary Hockney."

Chapter 23

POLICE CHIEF STRONG ASKED GARY HOCKNEY to come to the station. She also invited Brand and the library director to be there with him. The interview took place in Strong's office, not in one of the station's interview rooms. The effect was to remind everyone that the chief was in charge.

"Mr. Hockney, you are not under arrest and are free to go at any time, but we would like to ask you some questions about the death of Dean McKenzie."

"Why me?" Hockney asked.

"In its search of the library for materials not properly checked out, the librarians found several books in your carrel dealing with bombs and incendiary devices. How do you explain that?" Strong reached into an attaché case and brought out seven books, which she laid on her desk. "Dr. Ellis can certify that these are the books found in your carrel, isn't that right, Dr. Ellis."

"Yes, it is. We were inspecting all the carrels, and we didn't even know whose carrel we found these in until we looked it up on our records."

Hockney looked sullen. "What are you suggesting? That I had something to do with the dean's death just because you found some books in my carrel? I can read anything I damn well please."

"We're not making any accusations at this point," the chief said. "And you aren't being accused of any crime. We just need to know how these books came to be in your possession. Are they books you are using in your class work?"

"For your information," Hockney said, "I never saw those books before in my life. I have no idea how they got into my carrel. And, no, I'm not using them for my class. But I could have."

"How so?" Strong asked.

"Well, I could be doing a study of how disgruntled employees might strike back at an employer by conducting various sabotage activities, 'going postal,' that sort of thing. It's quite common when there's labor strife in an industry. But, as I said, I never saw those books before in my life."

"How do you explain their presence in your study carrel?" the chief asked.

"As I said, I have no idea. But it is a fairly simple problem to figure out. If I didn't put them in my carrel, then somebody else did. Duh!"

Strong put her hands behind her back and walked in slow circles behind Hockney. "So, you claim that someone else put these in your carrel. Do you have any idea who?"

"None at all."

"Tell me, Dr. Ellis, who has keys to these carrels?"

Ellis, in his sputtering way, began to fidget with the keys in his pocket. "Well, the person to whom the carrel is assigned has a key. The library office has a key, though I don't keep them personally, you understand. The associate director for facilities management handles that. Then the janitors have keys, and Campus Security has a master key that will open all the locks in the library. That's about it."

"Could a student who used that carrel last year have kept a copy of the key?"

"In theory, perhaps," Ellis said. "But it's unlikely. We charge students a twenty-dollar key deposit. If they want their money back, they have to return the key. For a graduate student twenty dollars is a lot. We get almost all the keys back. When we fail to do so, we use the deposit to re-key the lock."

"Could a student have a copy of the key made?"

"That would be difficult. The university uses a keying system from a company that doesn't supply blanks to the usual key-making sources. Also, each university key is stamped with a warning not to duplicate. Local locksmiths would not have the key blanks required to make a duplicate, and even if they did, they probably wouldn't because it's a violation of state law. They wouldn't take the risk."

"Describe these carrels for me," Strong said.

"Well, each is a small cubicle about six feet by six feet with a door that locks. The walls don't go up to the ceiling in order to allow for proper air circulation. However, the space between the top of the wall and the ceiling is not great enough for anybody to get into the carrel that way."

"Why are you making such a big deal out of the books?" Hockney asked. "First of all, I didn't kill the dean. Second, I had no motive for wanting him dead."

"Professor Brand reports that you made some injudicious comments about the dean shortly after you found out he had not renewed your fellowship," Strong said.

Hockney looked at Brand. "So that's what this is about. You think I killed the dean and got your girlfriend the police chief here to haul me in for questioning."

Brand decided to ignore the "girlfriend" crack. He looked directly at Hockney. "Gary, nobody has accused you of a crime, but your name does keep coming up in this investigation. It's been reported to me that you called on the dean at home several times and his wife overheard you yelling at him. We also know about the outburst in the dean's office and the broken table and lamp. Then there is the report that you had an altercation in class with another student and that a professor had to separate you from the student to prevent a fight. You seem to have difficulty keeping your temper under control, and that leads you to do and say intemperate things."

Hockney put his hands on the arms of the chair and started lifting himself up. "Those are lies. Damn lies."

The chief put her hand on Hockney's shoulder and eased him back into the chair. "So you're saying you never called the dean and made belligerent statements or that you nearly got into a fight with another student in class."

"I went to the dean's home because he wouldn't take my calls in his office. I may have yelled at him once or twice, but I didn't threaten him. He always came off in public like sweetness and reason, but let me tell you, behind that exterior was an evil man. He liked making people squirm. He enjoyed seeing my life come apart."

"So you deny threatening the dean. What about the fight in class?" Strong asked.

"Never happened. I don't know who told you that, but they lied. Sure I participate in class discussion, and it sometimes gets pretty hot. But that's the way it is supposed to be. We get credit for class participation. My professors like for us to defend our point of view. They say it's the way the real world is. But I never threatened or hit anyone in class. Never. Whoever said I did lied."

Strong could see that she had taken this interview as far as it was going to go without additional evidence. "Thank you, Mr. Hockney, for talking with us. You are free to go, but please don't leave town."

Hockney got up and pushed his chair back with a loud scraping noise in the process. He said not a word as he turned and went out the door.

"I appreciate your help also, Dr. Ellis. If you come up with any additional information on this, please let us know."

"I certainly will," Ellis said. "Glad we could be of some assistance."

Brand and Strong left the office together soon afterwards. On their way out the door of the station, Strong was the first to speak. "Well, Jeremy, what do you think?"

"The same think you thought after Sarah's suicide. Too pat, too convenient."

"I agree. But we do have the evidence of the books."

"That's pretty thin," Brand said. "It wouldn't be too hard to plant something in any carrel. I could do it myself. They offer privacy but not total security. I think a good defense attorney would rip that evidence of the books to shreds in short order."

"You're right. We're back to square one," Strong said.

"Afraid so, except the more I think about it, I am drawn to the conclusion that we are looking for a single killer who had ties both to the dean and to Sarah Giles. That's another reason I don't suspect Gary Hockney. We know of no links to Sarah. Even his motive for doing harm to the dean is minimal.

"So what do you plan to do next?" Strong asked.

"I intend to poke around the dean's office some more. George Helms won't move into the dean's office until I give the go-ahead, and before I do I want to look at some more of Clem's computer files. I also want to spend some more time working through his hard copy files. Maybe that will turn up something."

As Brand walked from police station across campus, he sensed the cool autumn evening as a harbinger of the cold winter weather to come. The leaves from the trees formed amber-, ochre- and-rust-colored coverings on the yards he passed as he entered the university campus through the alumni gate. His nose caught a whiff of burning leaves somewhere in the distance, a sharp and penetrating smell reminiscent of Latakia tobacco. The sodium-vapor street lights had come on and cast their beams through the now nearly bare limbs of the trees that ringed the central green.

He hadn't intended to, but as Brand passed by Bucks Hall, he had the sudden impulse to stop in the dean's office and pick up some of the other day files. He wanted to give them a careful examination and decided that could be done better in his home office over a nice glass of claret. He knew all the files Beals gave him were still sitting behind the desk on the credenza, so finding a couple he had not yet reviewed should not be a problem.

Brand had the dean's key, which opened both the door to the outer office—the one Naomi Beals used—and the dean's office proper. It wasn't necessary to use the key to open Bucks Hall, since there were classes there in the evening, though mostly on the upper floors, not on the ground floor where the dean's office was located.

Brand turned down the hallway to the dean's office. The other offices were now empty, their users having finished their work day. The echo of his footsteps was the only sound Brand heard. Even the janitors were not yet in the building. They usually timed their work, beginning first with the offices, so that they would be ready to clean the classrooms when the last class let out around 9:30.

Brand let himself into the dean's suite and reached behind the coat rack to flip on the light in Beals's office. Then he inserted his key into the lock of the dean's office and turned the knob. Enough of the ambient light from the secretary's office filtered into the dean's office that Brand could make his way over to the desk where he switched on the lamp sitting next to the computer.

He laid his briefcase down and turned to the credenza behind the desk, where he saw the day files. He picked up two and slipped them into his briefcase. As he did so saw the familiar pattern of the computer's screen saver. That's funny, he thought. Why was the dean's computer on? Naomi must have been using it to check on something. He knew that in some offices the practice was to turn on computers and leave them on throughout the entire week, the theory being that it is less damaging to the machines for them to run continuously than to have them undergo the strains of powering on and off.

Brand hit the Enter key, and the screen saver's password box came on the screen. Brand entered the password that Beals had given him, and the pattern of flying logos disappeared. In its place was a page of text. Must be a memo or something that the secretary needed to read, and she just forgot to turn off the computer. But why would she need to read something on the dean's computer? Brand made a mental note to ask her about that tomorrow.

Chapter 24

THE NEXT DAY BRAND stopped by Beals's office before going to his own. She greeted him with a cup of coffee for him in her hand. "How's your report for the president coming along, Professor Brand?"

"I'm making some progress, but there are still a lot of unanswered questions. One that you can help me with concerns the dean's computer." He told her about stopping by the office the previous evening and finding the dean's computer turned on. "Did you by chance use the dean's computer and forget to turn it off?"

Beals assured him that she had not, that there was no reason for her to use the dean's computer since she could access most anything she needed from her own computer using the shared drive.

Brand pulled a chair up to the side of her desk and took a notebook from his briefcase. "I would like for you to review office procedures with me. I'll make some notes as you talk."

"Of course, Dr. Brand. Anything I can do to help."

"First, let's review who has keys to the dean's office."

"I have one, and so did the dean. The janitor, of course, Campus Security, the associate dean's office. That's about it."

"Why does the associate dean's office have a key?"

"Well, as you can see, I am the only secretary the dean has, or perhaps I should say had. I just can't get used to speaking of him in the past tense. Well, anyway, there is more work in this office than a single secretary could possibly do, what with answering the phone, answering questions from people who walk in and everything. So a lot of secretarial work for the dean's office is done by the associate dean's staff."

"Why is that?"

"Dean McKenzie thought it would look bad to the faculty if he had a lot of secretarial support, and he preferred to have just one secretary. The associate dean's office handles a lot of student matters, so extra secretarial staff there wouldn't arouse as much resentment among the faculty. At least that's what the dean thought."

"So the associate dean's office had keys both to this outer office and to the dean's office proper?"

"No, just to my office. Some keys will open both offices—this one will, for example." She took a key from under her blotter. "I always keep a key here under my blotter. All any of the secretaries in Dr. Helms's office need to do is to come into my office, using their key that opens only the outer office door. Then they can get into the dean's office using this key."

"Why would they need to do that?"

"Sometimes the dean dictated so much that the secretaries in the associate dean's office had to stay after hours to finish. They could let themselves into my office, get the dean's office key, and then be able to place the finished materials on his desk where he would see them the next morning."

As Beals lifted up her desk blotter to replace the key there, Brand noticed several note cards on which were written various things.

"What are those other items under your blotter, Ms. Beals?"

"Oh, just odds and ends. I make notes to myself about various things and keep them handy here. For example, here is the dean's computer password." She handed Brand a card.

"The dean's password! You keep it under your blotter?" As he blurted out the words, Brand hoped his tone would not frighten Naomi into silence. "I mean, isn't that a little risky? Couldn't anybody look under your blotter, get the key to the dean's office, use his password and read his computer files?"

"Maybe. I suppose that could happen, but they would have to get into my office first. Our computer system requires all users to enter a new password every six months. If I didn't write them down somewhere, I might forget the current one, and then where would I be? Couldn't get a thing done. Besides, I haven't written on these cards what these words are for. Nobody but me—and now you—knows that this is the password to the dean's computer. I also keep mine here too, but I don't identify them, so anybody just looking here wouldn't know what they were seeing."

"So, when you gave me the dean's password the first time I was in the office, this is where you got it? From the card under your desk?"

"Yes. I hadn't memorized it then, so I had to look it up. Dean McKenzie had just changed it the week before."

"Tell me about your office routines. Are you here all day?"

"Basically, yes. Of course there are times that I have to go to the powder room, and then the office is empty. But I'm not gone from the office long."

"Do you lock the door behind you during those times?"

"Not usually. But I'm not away from the office for more than ten minutes at the most."

"Other than trips to the powder room, are there other times when the office is unoccupied?"

Beals paused and thought a minute. "There are the times when I make the coffee first thing in the morning, and then clean up the dirty cups just before quitting time. We don't have a sink here in the outer office, so I have to use either the dean's restroom or go down the hall to the janitor's closet. I usually go to the janitor's closet because the sink is so much bigger there."

"So the office is unattended on those occasions when you visit the powder room or are tending to the coffee chores at the beginning and end of each day."

"Sometimes during the day, too. If we've had lots of meetings, I may have to make another pot of coffee or two during the day."

"All this is very helpful. I'm sure your office routines are not much different from those of other offices. We all extend a lot of trust to our co-workers. Do you remember anything special about day before yesterday?"

"Nothing that I can think of. It was a pretty routine day. Since the dean hasn't been using the office, I've been making only one pot of coffee for the entire day. Other than that, everything was normal."

Brand next asked her about the dean's computer. No, she did not turn it on the day before yesterday. She had not turned it on at all since the dean's death. Anything she needed was on the shared drive, and she always used her own computer for routine office matters. And she had no idea why someone would be in the dean's office using his computer after hours, or how the person got into the office. She did unlock the dean's office every day so she could get access to his paper files when necessary, but she always locked it up when she left at five.

Brand walked over to the door and examined the lock. The lock was solid brass and heavy. On the edge of the door Brand saw two buttons.

"Do these buttons control whether the door automatically locks when you close it?"

"Yes, and I always make sure the top button, which locks the door, is pushed in when I leave."

"So when the janitors come in, they don't need to reset the buttons, right?"

"That's right. Their key—my key, too, for that matter—lets them in but doesn't unlock the door. If I want it to remain unlocked, I have to push in the bottom button. If I don't, I could lock myself out of the office. I've done it more than once, I'm sorry to admit."

"So, let me create a hypothetical scenario. Someone wants to get in and rifle through the dean's computer files. That someone could wait until the janitor unlocks the door to clean the office, and then when the janitor is otherwise occupied, our hypothetical intruder could reset the locking mechanism. When the janitor is finished with the cleaning, he shuts the door, not knowing that it had been unlocked. Of course, the janitor could always recheck the door, but that might not happen if the door was locked in the first place, which is the way you say you leave it. Any problem with this so far?"

"No, that sounds possible. But who would want to do such a thing?"

"I don't know, but I just want to make sure that there would be a way someone could get into your office. Then, the intruder looks up the dean's current password from the note underneath your blotter, and everything on the dean's computer is then available. Our hypothetical intruder wouldn't have to hide in the closet but could arrange to get back in after the janitors leave. Any flaw with this that you can see?"

Beals agreed, though reluctantly, that the scenario Brand had sketched out was possible. "I guess I will have to tell the janitors to check the door every time they finish cleaning the office from now on."

Brand left Beals to her daily tasks and entered the dean's office, where he turned on the computer and checked the e-mail files. He sorted them by date and saw that nothing had been changed since the dean had last used the computer. He then exited to the system level and checked the document files in the word processor, looking at the dates to see if any had been changed since the dean's death. Brand knew that computers are scrupulous in date stamping files, and any change to a file, no matter how small, results in a new date for that file. Nothing struck Brand as strange.

He returned to the e-mail program and looked again at the messages. There was no way he could tell by looking whether anyone had read the files; so long as no changes are made, the dates remain unchanged. He then looked at the deleted file directory. Again, he could not tell if anyone had deleted messages, since he had not printed out the contents of the deleted file directory the last time he looked at it. If the intruder hadn't changed any files, then the purpose for the nocturnal visit was either to read files or delete selected ones. If the former, there was no way Brand would ever know which files caught the intruder's interest.

With e-mail becoming more and more the medium of communication on campus, Brand wished there were some way he could find out what Sarah—or whoever—erased from her office computer. Everything had been deleted. Brand knew that his knowledge of computers was insufficient to allow him to retrieve any deleted material, but the Computer Services Center might be able to send someone out with the proper utility program to reconstruct the missing e-mail files, even on a reformatted hard drive. He and the director of CSC, Alice Miller, were social friends, and Brand decided to go to the top for help. He picked up the phone and dialed Miller's number. Her secretary informed him that Miller was out of the office but would get back to him the minute she returned. Brand gave the secretary both his office and home numbers.

With the time required for researching the report for President Coles added to his normal schedule of class preparation and writing, Brand had to squeeze in time to prepare for attending the upcoming wine auction. He attended only the commercial auctions in New York City or Chicago where good values sometimes were to be found, and not the charity auctions, whose purpose was to encourage participants to overpay in order to support the featured cause.

Always found at wine auctions were the collectors whose judgment was clouded by the scarcity of certain vintages, leading them to be willing to pay exorbitant prices for a rare claret or Burgundy. These were the prices that found their way into accounts of the event in wine journals, and the less expensive offerings went unreported. Brand could never understand the mindset of wine collectors who bought wine not to drink but to accumulate. Some wine collectors he had met did not even like wine. Brand's interest in wine was both as a hobby and as a hobby-business. As fashions in wines changed, he would pull from his cellar varietals and vintages that were currently in demand and place them at auction. When he attended auctions he looked for possible values among wines that were currently out of favor but had the potential for appreciating in value after a few years in his cellar.

Among Paul Ruskin's duties was reviewing auction catalogs and noting lots he thought Brand might find interesting. Ruskin and Brand spent several hours before each auction doing their homework. Pointing in the catalog to a listing for a case of 1989 Pauillac, Ruskin highlighted the entry and remarked, "This might be a good value. At the last auction a case of this went for twenty percent below its index value."

"Good, Paul. I'll watch for it at the auction."

Brand also made an entry in his palmtop computer, where he kept notes on the current auction and a database with current prices of the wines he followed. This allowed him to participate in the bidding in a way that insured he would make only offers that reflected good values.

"How did you ever do this before the days of computers?" Ruskin asked.

"I used three-by-five note cards. Almost as effective, but less convenient than a small computer. The one disadvantage was keeping track of index prices, but even with that limitation I rarely overbid."

"I'm always surprised by how some bidders get carried away with the auction process and send prices spiraling upward. At least that is the only explanation I can find for some of the prices I read about in the auction reports."

"The key is to set yourself a bid limit and not exceed it," Brand said. "I shouldn't say 'never.' Occasionally I'll overbid for a special bottle that someone has asked me to locate for a birthday or anniversary—a twenty- or thirty-year-old bottle of wine to mark the occasion. But even then it's important not to get carried away with the bidding process."

Auctions always left Brand exhausted. It was due to several things: the travel itself, the stress of functioning in a large city (small-town living made so many routine things simple, and visiting a large city made that clear) and the psychic energy expended in the bidding itself. Brand was pleased with the results of this auction. Everything he had placed sold well beyond the index amounts, and he had purchased several cases of vintages that he was sure would, in time, appreciate. He also had acquired a 1965 Bordeaux for a friend's anniversary and a vertical of a California wine that was already pressing the best French wines for honors in international competitions.

Getting to New York from College Falls was not easy. There was no direct flight, and even when he took the commuter airline from College Falls and interconnected with a national carrier, he still had to change in the airline's hub. Brand resented the fact that the airlines learned quickly from the overnight package delivery services that the most cost-effective way of routing passengers was to bring them to a central hub, sort them out FedEx fashion, put them on other flights, and take them on to their final destination. It was efficient for the airlines, and in these days of deregulation, cost-cutting of this sort was the only way to stem the flow of red ink that had destroyed several venerable carriers, forced consolidation of others and led still others into employee ownership. But the inconvenience to the traveler was aggravating, all the more since the Sunday flight on which Brand was booked was delayed, forcing him to miss the flight he had scheduled on the commuter airline back to College Falls. The rescheduling of his itinerary meant that he would have to wait two more hours before the next flight. So he sat in the terminal surrounded by several newspapers to pass the time. He now wished he had driven the hour and a half from College Falls to the airport; at least he would be on his way home now rather than sitting here waiting for the next stump-jumper.

A group was deplaning at a nearby gate. Brand was not paying particular attention to the milling crowd of people who were waiting for passengers coming through the gate. Something caught his attention, however, and he looked up just as Archie Scott passed through the door in the boarding area.

Scott was not looking Brand's way and did not see him sitting in the waiting area. Scott turned left and proceeded down the concourse, passing directly in front of Brand, who thought it only polite to speak.

"Archie." No response, so Brand spoke louder: "Archibald Scott."

Scott turned and looked directly at Brand. But instead of the flicker of recognition of an acquaintance, he had a look of surprise mixed with alarm on his face.

"Jeremy. Didn't expect to see you here."

"I wish I weren't here," Brand said. "I'm coming back from a wine auction in New York, and my plane was delayed. I had to be re-routed, so here I sit. And you? What brings you out and about this weekend?"

There was a pause before Scott spoke. "I...I was visiting a friend."

"Oh, where about?

"In...Chicago. Yes, my old college chum now lives in Chicago, and he just got out of the hospital and asked me to come up for a visit."

"Is he OK?"

"Yeah. He's fine. Well, got to go. See you back on campus."

Brand watched as Scott turned and walked down the concourse. He looks distracted, Brand thought, like he didn't want to talk. And if Archie doesn't have to wait for the next flight back to College Falls, that means he must have driven his car. Funny that he didn't offer a ride. Brand looked back at the posting board near the gate which announced the arriving flight. It had not come from Chicago. Brand wondered why Archie had lied to him. What could he be hiding?

The next day Brand returned to the dean's office to give the computer files one final inspection. The flutter of the intercom sounded, and Brand pressed the button. Beals was always succinct with her messages. "Professor Brand, Chief Strong is holding for you."

Brand picked up the phone again and punched the blinking light. "Hi Harri. What's up.?"

"Glad I found you, Jeremy. I've been doing some more thinking about Hockney. I agree with your conclusion that he's probably not our man, but I can't drop my investigation of him until I 'm sure. We know he had a motive to do harm to the dean, but so far we haven't discovered any relationship with Professor Giles."

"I know, Harri. I've also been racking my brain trying to figure out what connection the two might have. If Hockney were in an academic graduate program rather than a professional one, he would have to produce a thesis, and that would require a faculty advisor. But Gary's degree program doesn't require a thesis, so that possible connection is ruled out."

"I still have the Giles house sealed as a crime scene. Her mother and sisters are after me to remove the restriction and give them access. I've held them off but will have to agree to their request sooner or later. Before I do, though, I want to make one last inspection of the place. Maybe there is something there that would point to a connection between Giles and Hockney and we missed it earlier because we weren't looking for it."

"Sounds like a good idea. Will you let me know if you find anything?"

"I'll do one better than that. I was headed over there now. Wanna come?"

Brand's answer was that he would meet Strong at the Giles house as soon as he could get there. He grabbed his coat, and as he exited through the secretary's office, Beals had just completed a brief conversation on the phone and was holding the handset out toward Brand. "Alice Miller is on the line, Dr. Brand. You can take the call here if you want."

Brand thanked her and reached for the handset. "Hi, Alice. Say, I've got a problem maybe you can help me with." He explained the deleted files on Sarah Giles's computers. "I know there are utilities that can recreate erased files. What I don't know if they would work on e-mail files that have been deleted."

He listened to the other end of the conversation. "Really! Hmmm. I understand. You can? That would be great. When you have the materials, please give me a call either at my home number or at the office and I will arrange to have the files picked up. Thanks again, Alice. You're wonderful."

Brand gave the handset back to Beals. "Well, that's certainly a good turn of events. Alice informs me that the Computer Center routinely backs up all files on any LAN they are responsible for maintaining, and that includes Sarah Giles's office computer. She will check to see if any of Sarah's files were backed up. Alice also said some of Sarah's e-mail may still be on the central server, and she is going to check on that for me, too."

"I didn't know the Computer Center backed up files like that. We have our own backup system built right into our computers." Beals held up a small tape cassette. "We routinely back up all our office computers every Friday before we leave the office. I wonder why they do it, too?"

"She said they do it as a fail-safe procedure. I would assume that not every office is as efficient as yours. If some new person or an inexperienced computer operator mistakenly erased all the files on the computer, they can recreate them if the computer is on a Local Area Network, which I gather all the computers in this building are."

"I wonder why that isn't more widely known," Beals said.

"Alice said they don't want all the users to assume that they can ignore standard backup procedures in the expectation that the Computer Center will always do it for them. By the way, if Alice should call here, though I don't think she will, just leave a message on my answering machine at home." Brand wasn't sure Beals heard him. "Naomi, did you hear what I just said?"

"Oh, yes. Sorry. I let my mind wander. If she calls here, I'll certainly let you know."

When Brand arrived at the Giles house, Strong was waiting for him in the driveway. Harriet let them both in and began looking through papers on the desk in Sarah's study. Brand wandered through the living room, then the dining room, then back to the study. While Strong continued to examine Giles's personal records, Brand did what any academic would do: he looked at her books. Even though she taught in a different field, he found it interesting to see what his colleagues in other departments were reading. Sticking out between two textbooks near Sarah's desk were several brochures, obviously college promotional materials. He thumbed through them and saw that they were from Middletown College. This must be some of the material Lester Forrest mentioned that he had sent in his attempt to attract Giles to come to Middletown.

Brand removed the admissions material from the shelf. "Middletown College: Where Excellence Meets Experience." The brochure pictured an idyllic college campus setting: oak trees, brick sidewalks, an interesting mixture of architectural styles for the buildings. In line with the theme announced on the cover, the brochure touted the technology that permeated the campus: Ethernet connections in the dorms, every student supplied a computer, classrooms wired for multimedia. He turned the page and read the caption at the top: "Technology and Tradition are Partners at Middletown." The text claimed that students at Middletown had access to the latest teaching technologies without the payment of an additional fee. Pictured were various computer labs and media centers. On the facing page was a photo of the college's business education lab filled with students at work. A professor was shown leaning down to help one of the students. The picture caption said, "In the program's problem-based learning, teachers are more like coaches than traditional lecturers. Here Professor Harrison Scott helps a student." There was no possibility for a mistake, even though the photo offered a three-quarters view of the instructor's face and it was partially obscured by a shadow. Brand was looking at a photo of Archie Scott.

Chapter 25

THE DISCOVERY OF SCOTT'S PICTURE in the Middletown recruitment brochure produced a hurricane of responses. Brand called President Coles with the information, and the president immediately contacted his counterpart at Middletown College. It was as it appeared to be. Archie Scott, AKA Harrison Scott, was simultaneously serving as a full-time faculty member at two institutions.

Brand knew Scott's duplicity would create a public relations problem for Middletown College, but for Calloway State University, it would be a political disaster. The state legislature was already pressuring the universities to increase faculty work loads. The mood in the capital was now likely to turn ugly. Most legislators held the view that faculty were overpaid and under-worked. When it became public knowledge that a Calloway State University faculty member held two full-time positions at separate institutions, the legislature might be capable of anything. Knowing all this, Brand made sure his first call was to President Coles. Presidents don't like to be the last to know, especially if the news is bad.

The president had been on the road so much of late that Brand had not been able to brief him on the progress of his report. When Brand called with the information about Archie Scott, the news was so jarring that Coles never even asked about the status of Brand's report on the deaths of Dean McKenzie and Professor Giles.

"We've got to move on this quickly, Jeremy," Coles said. "I'll convene an emergency meeting of a small group at four o'clock. I'd like you to be there."

Brand answered that of course he would be there, and offered to help in any other way he could.

When Brand entered the president's office a few minutes before four, he saw that the vice president for external relations, the university's general counsel and the special assistant to the president were already there. A few moments later, the president entered the room.

"I've spoken to each of you individually and briefly about the problem Professor Scott has forced on us. I have talked to the president of Middletown College, and he is as concerned about it as I am. I've also met with Professor Scott, and he has no plausible defense for his actions. Since Professor Brand was the one who discovered this state of affairs, he'll tell you how he came to know about it."

Brand reviewed briefly the string of events that led to his discovery that Scott was teaching at Middletown College as well as Calloway State. He related the conversation with Sarah Giles's former husband and how a casual remark from him led Brand to take a second look at the recruitment brochure in Sarah's house and how it was there that Scott's double life was documented. Brand then related how his first call was to the president.

The vice president for external relations counseled a rapid response and complete candor. "The public will respect us if they see us acting with speed and finality. They will not respect us, and probably never forgive us, if they think we're trying to cover up a scandal of this proportion."

The university's general counsel argued for a quick termination. Even though Scott was tenured, his offense gave grounds for dismissal. The announcement and letter would need to come from the president. There would be subsequent hearings by a committee of senior faculty members on the merits of the case, according to standard AAUP rules. The American Association of University Professors, he pointed out, had succeeded in getting most colleges and universities in the country to adopt their guidelines. These called not only for a full hearing on the offense, but if the faculty committee recommended that the president's action be upheld, the affected faculty member would also receive a full year's salary as severance.

"That's going to be tough to explain to the legislature," the president said. "We find a faculty member violating the expectations of his employment here—that he will give us full-time service—and I fire him and have to give him a year's salary to boot!"

The general counsel went on to explain that it was an *additional* year's salary. The university would be obligated to honor Scott's current contract through the remainder of the present academic year and then give him one more year's salary.

The vice president for external relations was taking copious notes. "Are there no conditions where we could avoid the extra year's salary?" he asked. The general counsel explained that AAUP rules called for no additional salary only in cases of moral turpitude, and that Scott's actions probably would not fall under that designation. "His action was unethical but not to the extent of moral turpitude."

"What would quality for that label?" the VP asked.

"An offense like child pornography. The charge of moral turpitude arises so rarely, however, that there isn't much of a history of how the term is defined in current practice."

Coles decided to hold a news conference and asked his assistant to set it up. He thanked everyone for coming and asked that only his office and the office of the vice president for external relations be the official source of statements on the case.

The next morning the results of the news conference provided the top story in the capital city's daily newspaper. Since College Falls was a small town, most of its residents subscribed to the major state newspaper that was published in the capital. They, like Brand, opened the morning paper to see a four-column headline: *Calloway State Prof Fired for Double-Dipping*. The story was the main feature above the fold, accompanied by file photos of Calloway State and a head shot of Scott from the university news service.

The reporter drew heavily from the university's news conference. When the president was asked what rule Professor Scott had broken, he replied that the university requires every faculty member annually to sign a conflict of interest and conflict of commitment documentation form. Such a disclosure form is required by the federal government for any faculty member submitting a grant proposal for research funds from certain federal agencies, he explained. It was Calloway State's policy to require such documentation of all faculty.

The news story reported the president as saying that all full-time faculty members are expected to certify on the form that they are rendering full-time service to the university. If they do any external consulting, or receive payment from any other institution for services, those must be approved in advance by the dean of their college and be reported on the disclosure form.

When asked if it was true that the university allows faculty members a day a week for such consulting, the president replied that such a standard would certainly be the maximum allowed, but it was not an entitlement. If a faculty member could show that external consulting would benefit the department and students, and it was deemed by the dean not to pose any conflicts of interest or commitment, then it could be approved. When asked for an example, the president gave as a hypothetical instance a business professor doing consultation work for the banking industry. Such involvement might be seen as providing state-of-the-art information about banking practices that would better inform the professor's teaching. In general, he pointed out, consulting or external work should have a professional development component. If it did not, he would not approve such activity.

The newspaper reporter did not include any details about the dismissal process, probably because no questions were asked about it at the press conference. Brand thought that the subject of tenure was probably too arcane for them at this point, though discussion of that would doubtless follow in future articles. Reporters had asked whether Scott would be allowed to complete the current semester. The president was quoted as saying that for the sake of the students Scott would complete his current teaching assignment. It would be too disruptive to the students to bring in a new instructor at this point. However, he pointed out, Professor Scott's contract would not be renewed.

The article concluded with a brief report on actions taken by Middletown College, which had also announced that Scott's employment would be terminated. "Professor Scott declined to comment," the reporter noted. The final line of the news story was succinct: "Professor Archibald Scott has gone from having two jobs to having none."

When Brand reached campus, he stopped by his departmental mail box before going to his office. He removed his mail from the box, picked up a copy of *The Mirror* and went to his office. He hung up his coat on a hall tree just inside the door, laid his briefcase on the desk and unfolded the student newspaper. The headline blared: *President Fires Scott.* The story was factual and followed the news conference questions, as had the local morning paper. The lead paragraph, though, gave the spin that Brand had anticipated the student paper would probably place on the incident: "One of Calloway's most popular teachers was fired yesterday by President Coles. The reason for the president's action was the allegation that Professor Archibald Scott was employed at another college while holding a full-time position at Calloway State."

Brand knew that student reaction to the incident, as informed by Harvey Glock, would be found in the paper's editorial. The rant began with a swipe at the administration's emphasis on research. "If Professor Scott had been doing research at another institution, nothing would have happened to him. But he was *teaching* at another institution. That is why he was fired."

Brand noted that the rest of the editorial continued in the same vein.

It is typical of this university to take the kind of punitive action against effective teaching that President Coles has directed at Professor Scott. Has there been any allegation that he failed to render all required service to Calloway State? No. Has anyone successfully accused him of being a bad teacher? No. Is there any evidence that he shirked any of his duties at Calloway State? No. Would this university have taken the same action against him if his "sin" had been additional research that brought in big bucks? No. Is there any difference between what Professor Scott did and the numerous "consulting" jobs done by other faculty in this university? No.

This university's action in summarily dismissing such an outstanding teacher just shows the low priority it places on the classroom. What Professor Scott did may not have been right. He was wrong in taking a full-time job elsewhere. But he should not be fired because of it. Nobody should be treated as Professor Scott has been. Nobody.

What should the administration do? Let him disengage himself from Middletown College and return to the excellent teaching he is known for at Calloway State. The students at our fine university deserve nothing less.

Brand threw the paper into the trash can. "Typical Harvey Glock," he muttered out loud. There would no doubt be saner voices heard on the subject later, but it was regrettable that the student paper's editorial supported Scott's dishonesty.

As Brand contemplated the status of the investigation into the two faculty deaths, he felt a sense of frustration over the lack of progress. When Sarah had emerged early as the prime suspect in the burning of the dean's house, it seemed possible that she might have been the murderer. If so, her intent could only have been to hurt the dean by destroying something that was important to him, not to kill him. No one doubted that he valued his house. As far as Sarah's motive, worse crimes have been committed out of resentment and anger. It was general knowledge that Sarah felt aggrieved by the coming tenure denial. But when she saw the effects of her action—that she had killed him, not just destroyed a favorite possession—she felt an overwhelming sense of guilt. In the aftermath of the deed gone wrong, a pang of conscience led her to take her own life.

Possible but not plausible. Brand shared Strong's sense that Sarah's suicide looked contrived. He was also being drawn to the conclusion that the two deaths were connected somehow. But if that inference were correct, it would cast doubt on Gary Hockney's guilt, unless they could find some connection between Giles and Hockney. So far they had not. And the evidence against Hockney was too circumstantial. He denied any previous knowledge of the incriminating books found in his carrel, and proving that he was lying would be difficult, especially since anyone could have put the books in his carrel. Brand was sure it could be done easily, so sure that he did not even test his hypothesis.

The carrels lined the walls of a study area in the library. He was sure anybody could drag a chair over to the carrel, stand on the chair and drop the books one by one in the corner where they were found. Another method of placing them there, less noisy even, would be to make a sling out of a scarf, a shirt—anything—and lower the books into the carrel. Then, to retrieve the sling, one would only need to let go of one of the ends and pull it free. Hockney might have set fire to the dean's house, but why would he kill Sarah Giles? Brand wondered if he and Strong were wrong in their reasoning that the two murders were connected somehow, but he did not think so.

Now there was Archie Scott. Could he be the murderer? Could the dean have found out about Scott's double life, leading him to kill to protect his secret? Possibly, but would fear of public disgrace be enough to cause Scott to commit murder? So far there was no evidence placing him near the dean's house the night of the fire. And if both the dean and Sarah were killed by the same person, what motive would Archie have for killing Sarah?

When Sarah Giles was first identified as a suspect, the murderer of the dean—assuming it was not Giles—must have thought this was an absolute gift. Then when it became clear that there was not enough evidence to charge her with the dean's death, the murderer could have decided that the gift was too good to walk away from. Since Giles was already a suspect, the murderer—Archie Scott?—might then have determined to remove all doubt by staging the "suicide."

Strong had introduced another variable into the equation by announcing during the radio show "Eavesdropping" that she had doubts about Sarah's Giles's suicide. That must have panicked the murderer. The suicide set-up had failed. In her comments on air Strong had not completely ruled out the death as a suicide, but the mere questioning of it must have caused the murderer to offer up another possible suspect: Gary Hockney. The mysterious phone message on Brand's answering machine gave only an oblique hint. Was it because the murderer had not yet planted the bomb-making books in Gary Hockney's carrel and could not give a more explicit hint until the incriminating evidence was in place?

Brand also wondered who had been poking around in the dean's office. What was the intruder looking for? And did he or she find it? And how many other visits had the nocturnal prowler paid to the dean's office?

This whole series of questions had the feel of a chain of hypothetical propositions in a logic exercise. Since it is possible to reason correctly from faulty premises, thereby reaching an incorrect conclusion, what Brand needed more than anything else was additional evidence.

Brand glanced to his phone and saw the light blinking, indicating the presence of voice mail. His attention had been so directed to thinking about the murders that he had failed to notice the message light before now. He played his messages. There was one: *"Jeremy, I hold you personally responsible for what has happened to me. If you hadn't been poking around in my affairs, I wouldn't have lost my job. I just want you to know you'll be sorry you did this to me."* The caller did not identify himself, but there was no need. The voice was unmistakably that of Archie Scott.

Chapter 26

WHILE BRAND WAS TRYING to decide how to respond to Scott's threat, Chief Strong was having a talk with Scott. Had Strong known about Scott's implied threat to Brand it would have loomed large in the interview, but the conversation centered mainly on relations between the professor and the dean. Scott insisted that his lawyer be present before he agreed to talk with the police. Strong had assigned a detective to the case, and the four—Scott, his lawyer, the detective, and Strong—were sitting in the living room of Scott's house.

The lawyer, Antony Lipcus, was the first to speak.

"I would like to say at the outset that my client, Professor Scott, has agreed to this meeting in the spirit of good citizenship. We have nothing to hide and are willing to cooperate fully with the police."

"We appreciate that, Mr. Lipcus. I only have a few questions that I hope Professor Scott can clear up."

"Go ahead then with your questions. I'll advise my client on whether he should respond."

"We're investigating the murder of Dean McKenzie, as you know, and given the recent revelations about Professor Scott's dual employment, we would like to know if the Dean was aware of this situation."

Lipcus whispered something into Scott's ear. He nodded agreement. "My client would prefer not to answer."

"So the dean *did* know of Professor Scott's situation. What did the dean do? Threaten to fire you? Did he offer you a chance to resign if you would go quietly?"

"My client's desire not to answer your question should not be interpreted by you in any way as an admission that the dean knew about Professor Scott's employment 'situation,' as you put it. Professor Scott's dual employment is a matter for university authorities to deal with, not the police."

"Agreed," Strong said. "But you will have to admit that if the dean knew of the Professor's dual employment and threatened him with termination or public exposure, that would provide a powerful motive to keep him quiet."

"That's preposterous," Scott said, leaping to his feet. "I would never harm another human being. How dare you accuse me of something like that."

Lipcus gently pulled Scott back down to his chair. "As my client has just said, this insinuation of yours is preposterous. If you have evidence that he committed a crime, present it. If not, drop this ridiculous innuendo."

Strong paced back and forth on the living room rug. "Very well, then. What was your relationship with Professor Giles?"

Scott conferred briefly with Lipcus, then spoke. "She and I were colleagues. We had appointments in the same college. I knew her socially, but not well."

The detective placed a document on the coffee table. "This is a copy of your bank statements for the last two months, both checking and savings. I call your attention to the transfer of two thousand dollars from your savings to your checking account." The detective laid another document on the table. "And here is a copy of a check made to 'cash' for two thousand dollars. Why did you need two thousand dollars cash, Professor Scott? What did you use it for?"

"That's none of your goddamn business. What I do with my money is no affair of yours."

"It may be our affair," Strong said. She laid a third document on the table. "Here is a copy of Professor Giles's bank statement. You will note that she deposited two thousand dollars into her account two days after you withdrew the same amount from your account. We know that she was aware of your employment at Middletown College, since we found the materials in her house that revealed your dual life. What was she doing, Professor? Was she blackmailing you? Did you pay her money for her to keep quiet?"

Scott leaped to his feet? "Where did you get those? That is private information. You have no right to go poking around in my financial records."

"You can be sure, Professor Scott, that we did everything legally. So, please answer the question."

"My client prefers not to answer."

"No, I'll answer it. I have nothing to hide."

"Please, Archie. My advice is to say nothing."

"And let them assume the worst? Let me tell them about this so they will drop this ridiculous suspicion." Lipcus bent down and Scott whispered something to him. Lipcus nodded agreement.

"As I said, Sarah was a friend. She was about to lose her job. I knew it. She knew it. Everybody knew it. I agreed to loan her some money until she got resettled. That's all there is to this matter of two thousand dollars."

The detective was the next to speak. "Do you have a promissory note from her? Did you plan to charge her interest?"

"No. We were friends, as I said. We didn't need any formalities like that. And no, I wasn't planning to charge her interest."

"For a business professor, you proceed in a most un-businesslike way," the detective said.

"So you deny that Professor Giles was blackmailing you?" Strong asked.

"Absolutely. As I said, it was a loan."

"But according to her bank records, she wasn't out of money. Her bank balance was over ten thousand dollars. Why did she need a loan?"

"She was thinking about moving from College Falls. Even though the university would have to give her another year's contract after denying her tenure, she told me she didn't want to stay around a place that didn't want her." She needed money to pay for the move."

"Where did she say she was going to move?" Strong asked.

"I don't remember where. She just said she was going to move."

Strong continued her pacing. "Your story is pretty thin, Professor. You say you gave Professor Giles a loan, yet you—a business professor—have created no paper trail. You have no promissory note, you weren't going to charge her interest, and you expect us to believe that you 'loaned' her the money to help her pay for a move that apparently she told only you about."

"But that's the truth. I can't help it if you don't believe me."

"What would you say if I told you that her former husband was trying to convince her to move back in with him—back to Middletown—and she refused? Don't you think if she were going to move somewhere, it would be to a place where there was someone who still loved her and wanted her back?"

Scott said nothing.

"Did she find out about your dual employment from Dr. Forrest at Middletown? Is that how she knew about your double life? Did she then promise not to reveal your secret life so long as you gave her a monthly payment?" As Strong talked she began to move closer and closer to Scott until her face was about a foot from Scott's. "And did you suddenly see your future written in monthly payments to Sarah Giles? Did she also mock you? Did you get so angry at this blood-sucking woman that you killed her?"

"No! It wasn't like that at all. I was making her a loan. I've already told you that. And I didn't kill her. Besides, I thought it was suicide. Tell them, Tony, that I didn't do anything wrong."

Strong didn't let Scott's attorney begin to reply. "You don't consider it wrong to misrepresent your employment situation to this university? You don't consider it wrong to defraud the taxpayers of this state and the students at this university by giving them less than full-time service while taking a full-time paycheck? You don't consider it wrong that you took a job at another college without resigning from this university first? Just what would you consider wrong, Professor Scott?"

Scott glared at Strong. "You wouldn't understand. I gave full service to this university. I am an excellent teacher. Students flock to my courses. I never missed a lecture. I gave full attention to student projects. I wrote copious notes on their papers. You'd be surprised at how many professors give papers back to their students with no notations of any kind. Not me. I take teaching seriously. This university has nothing to complain about. I was on campus as much as those hot-shot researchers who spend all their time writing grants and little time with students. Students, after all, are the reason we're here."

"I'm sure you're quite practiced at rationalizations, Professor. The fact is you lied, cheated, and in a real sense, stole from your employer. If that doesn't qualify as wrongdoing, then maybe your moral compass needs calibrating."

"I wouldn't expect someone like you to understand, Chief. You're just a policewoman. You don't have any grasp of what the life of the intellect is all about."

Lipcus could see that the conversation was deteriorating. "My client is upset by your questioning. I think this conversation has gone on long enough. You're beginning to deal with Professor Scott's employment status, which is no concern of yours. We will deal with the proper university authorities on that. If you have enough evidence to charge him with a crime, then do so. If not, I suggest you and your detective leave immediately."

The detective had already walked to the police car when Strong, who was about to close the front door to the Scott house, turned around and looked directly at Scott. "It's a good thing you're a business professor, not a member of the English faculty, Professor Scott."

"Why is that?"

"Because you're not very good at fiction."

As Strong was finishing up her interview of Scott, the professor's name was about to re-enter Brand's consciousness in a different way. As he left his office at the university to return home after classes, he noticed a group of pickets walking around in front of Old Main, the administration building. Since his route home took him near the building, he decided to walk out of his way and see what the demonstration was all about, for a demonstration it surely was.

As he approached the group, Brand recognized one of the students as Danny Bennett, whose picture had been in *The Mirror* several times in connection with past demonstrations by SES. Though Brand had never met

Bennett, he recognized him immediately and decided to find out first-hand what the issue was that brought together a group of students on a fall day for a public rally.

"What is this, Danny? Another protest by Students for an Egalitarian Society?"

"No. We're a different organization. You're Professor Brand, aren't you?" Bennett asked.

"Yes, that's correct. What is your organization called?"

"We are now Students Protesting Unfair Dismissal, SPUD for short."

Brand looked at the signs the students carried. On one side was the group's acronym arranged vertically:

Students

Protesting

Unfair

Dismissal

On the back of the signs were various other slogans: *Students Need Good Teachers! Down With Research, Up With Teaching! Good Teaching Now! Keep Professor Scott!*

The last sign told Brand the purpose of the demonstration. "I see. You're demonstrating in support of Professor Scott."

"Absolutely. We think the administration is out to get him. It's about time that students stood up for their rights."

"What rights are those, Danny?"

"The right to have good teachers. Here is an excellent teacher being fired. Everybody knows that Professor Scott is a great teacher and has won many teaching awards. Students love him. Now because of a little mistake, he's being canned."

"You call misrepresenting his situation to two employers, falsifying his conflict of commitment report and simultaneously holding down two full-time positions a 'little mistake'?" Brand asked.

"Well, it's not like he *killed* somebody or anything. I mean, give me a break. Students work two jobs all the time. We have to go to school and work one or two jobs just to pay the huge tuition bills this university sends us. Maybe if this university paid its professors more, teachers like Professor Scott wouldn't have to hold two jobs."

"Have you made the connection between instructor's salaries and your tuition bills?"

The students quit their random wandering and began to walk, single file, in a circle. Softly at first, and then gradually, the group began a chant. "*Keep Professor Scott. Keep Professor Scott. Keep Professor Scott.*"

"You mean, if professors were paid more, our tuition would be higher?"

"Since the university has only two sources of income—state support and tuition fees—increases on the expenditure side are only possible if there are increases on the income side."

"Well, I don't know about that," Bennett said. "All I know is that this university is about to lose a great teacher, and we students intend to do something about it. It's about time our voices were heard."

"So what do you want to accomplish by this demonstration?"

"We want to talk with President Coles. His assistant came out and said the president would meet with us. That was an hour ago. We're going to continue to march until he meets with us and hears our demands."

Looking to his left, Brand saw Sally Turner coming up the sidewalk. She greeted him cordially, and then turned her complete attention to the student demonstrators. "Excuse me for interrupting, but I need to get some quotes for my story." She turned to Danny. "Hi. I'm Sally Turner, a reporter for *The Mirror*. I wonder if I could talk to you about this protest."

Happy to have a reporter scribbling down his words, Danny Bennett began his litany of demands. Brand turned and continued his walk across the Green lest he become one of Turner's three quotes for the day.

When Brand walked into his home office, he found taped to his computer screen a note from his housekeeper: "Call Alice Miller at the Computer Center ASAP."

Brand was put through almost immediately to the director, whose first comment to him was an apology.

"I'm sorry, Jeremy, that retrieving Professor Giles's deleted files was delayed, but at long last I have something for you. However, this is one of those good-news, bad-news things."

"Give me the bad news first," Brand said.

"The bad news is that most of her files are not retrievable either from her personal computer or from the central server."

"Explain, please."

"The software we have in place allows the user to download e-mail messages from the central server. Once the user does that, we have no further record of them. We used to backup all files from the server routinely, but there was such an outcry about personal privacy from the faculty that we stopped that practice. We now backup only the official university transactions like course registrations, financial records and other official university documents. Now about e-mail. When e-mail messages are resident on the individual's computer, the user can read them, file them or delete them. The software also allows for removing the deleted messages completely by 'emptying the trash.' When the user empties the trash, then nothing remains of the message. We occasionally are able to reconstruct some of them with a utility program, but it's iffy. It's impossible when the hard drive has been erased."

"What's the good news?"

"We do have some of her e-mail messages on our server. Apparently Professor Giles read her e-mail both on her home computer and on her office computer. This is a guess, mind you, but it seems that she didn't want her e-mail on two different machines. So, when she read her e-mail at home, she didn't always download it onto her personal computer but usually left it resident on the server. That way, when she was back in her office, she didn't have to worry that a message she wanted to answer was only available to her on her home computer."

"I think I'm following all this..."

"Think of it this way. Our central server is like a post office, and the user's individual account is a post-office box. You can go to your post office box and collect your mail and take it home with you—that's like downloading your files to your own computer. Or, you can read your mail at the post office and then return it to your box. That's like reading the messages on the central server. It would appear that Professor Giles usually left her mail on the server when she read it from her home computer. Every once in a while she would delete her messages from the server, but she hadn't done that in a while. It's those messages that I have copied for you. You can pick up the disk I've made for you anytime you want."

"I'll see that it's picked up yet today," Brand said. "Thank you so much for your help."

Brand ended the call and then pushed the intercom button on the receiver. He knew that Ruskin was in the cellar bringing the computerized records up to date. "Paul, there's a package for me in the director's office at the Computer Center. Please pick it up when you're finished with the data entry."

Ruskin said that he was almost done logging in Brand's latest purchases and would pick up the package as soon as he finished.

Brand unfastened the clasp on the envelope from Miller and turned it upside down. Out came a high-density disk.

Brand inserted it into his computer and looked first at the directory of files. He sorted the files by sender. Nothing much interesting there. He then sorted the files by date and scrolled through them until he came to the date of her death. Then he stopped.

There were a large number of messages from the day before Giles died. And they were all interchanges with one person. Brand opened the files one by one and began to read. As he read, an inescapable conclusion forced itself on him. He was reading interchanges between Giles and her murderer. The murderer intended to erase all the e-mail messages, not knowing that some were still resident on the server. Nothing in the messages provided absolute proof. The evidence was circumstantial and by itself would not provide enough evidence even for an indictment, let alone for a conviction. Brand knew he needed more but was not sure how to get it. What he had to figure out was a way to flush out more evidence, to cause the murderer to make a mistake that would remove all doubt.

The beginning of a plan started to form in his mind. He would tell Strong but not until he had put it in motion because she probably wouldn't approve. But the course he needed to take was clear. And it also was obvious to Brand that he, as a private citizen, could take actions that the police could not. What he needed to do was to apply some pressure, make the murderer feel uncertain. Brand picked up the campus directory and called a number he knew would be answered.

Chapter 27

THE PARCEL SERVICE'S DELIVERY PERSON could find her way to the Brand house in the dark, so frequent were deliveries there. The parcels were bulky, due to the shippers' practice of using large polystyrene holders to cradle the wine during shipping. She did not mind the bulkiness; she was just happy that the parcels were not too heavy. With new rules from the company for increased allowable weights, she often found herself having to deliver parcels that weighed as much as she did. Wine packages were mercifully light by comparison. A case of wine weighed under forty pounds.

Since the delivery service considered Brand's neighborhood to be a safe one, the driver routinely left parcels on the porch, her unfailing pattern unless a delivery receipt was required for a parcel, and that was unusual. Today she needed no receipts or signatures, so she left three parcels by the front door. Ringing the bell, she quickly returned to her truck. The company's time-and-effort specialists had her on a tight schedule that allowed a specified time for each delivery, but her return to the truck would have been even speedier had she known that one of the three parcels she just delivered contained not wine but a bomb.

Ruskin's schedule was in overdrive. He had agreed to teach three sections of English composition during the fall semester. It seemed like a good idea at the time, but now with three sets of weekly essays to mark he was beginning to question the sanity of his decision. Like many part-time teachers, his teaching load was as great as—or greater than–the full-time faculty members in the department. This fact was a constant source of irritation among the cadre of part-timers, many of whom were trying to get a toehold on the academic ladder and saw their part-time employment as a temporary expedient while searching for that holy grail of academic life—the tenure-track appointment.

Some were like Ruskin and had given up on an academic career and viewed their part-time teaching as a necessary component of a multifaceted life.

Ruskin did not feel the envy and bitterness that seemed to be an occupational hazard for many of his friends. He had an interesting job working for Brand, one that involved some travel and the opportunity to set his own work schedule and included the perks of a secure roof over his head and a live-in cook. But more than that, he could see clearly the pressures on the full-time faculty—'full-service' faculty was the current jargon—that included the constant pressures of research and publication and the ever-present pull of duties that eroded the time needed for reading and reflection. He also saw the burnout that affected some faculty after twenty years or so of the grinding pace of academic life. The head of his department had said that his problem as an academic administrator was that the usual professorial career was thirty years, but some of his faculty burned out after twenty and he had to keep them usefully occupied for another decade. Ruskin was happy to be able to teach as much or as little as he wanted. Right now he wished he had turned down the chairman's plea for that extra course. Never again, he told himself.

As he climbed the steps to the front porch, he noticed the three boxes waiting there for him. Their presence reminded him that he was already behind in unpacking Brand's wine purchases and entering the new items in the cellar inventory. These three additional ones would have to wait. He opened the door and climbed the stairs to his room, where he left his coat and briefcase. He returned to the porch and started moving the boxes to the cellar. When he picked up the third one, he noticed that it seemed heavier than the others. Must be magnums of wine, he told himself, as he held open the cellar door with his foot and started down the stairs with the last parcel of the morning's delivery.

When Brand's review of Sarah Giles's e-mail led him to an understanding of the killer's identity, he called Strong immediately and invited her for an impromptu "wine chat" in his cellar. The problem with Brand's evidence was that it was circumstantial in the extreme. It offered nothing that would stand up in court under the assault of a determined defense attorney, yet Brand was convinced he knew the identity of the killer. He might have been rash in placing that phone call, but Brand wanted the murderer to know that the crime was no longer undiscovered. He also hoped that his call would stir things up more and cause the perpetrator to make a mistake.

Strong was aghast at what Brand had done.

"You've already been attacked in this house and nearly killed, Jeremy. Assuming your attacker is the same person you're trying to 'stir up,' as you put it, you could be putting yourself in terrible danger."

"I disagree," Brand said. "I'm in less danger because of my knowledge. Knowledge is power, as Francis Bacon put it. Armed with what we now know, we have a mighty lever to pry the murderer out of hiding."

Strong shook her head in disagreement. "I'm still concerned. If you're right in your inferences, you're dealing with a person who has killed twice. My experience with murderers is that they reach a point where another murder to shield their guilt seems logical to them. I want you to be careful."

"But look where we are in our investigation. We've been turning over every stone we could find for days now, and you still haven't made an arrest. Even though I know the identity of the murderer, I don't yet know the murderer's motives. Without a clear understanding of the motive, you won't be able to build a credible case unless we can force the murderer to make a mistake."

"I understand, Jeremy, but just don't get too carried away. We're dealing with someone who is both clever and ruthless."

Ruskin came into the cellar and pulled up a chair to the tasting table. "I'm sorry that I'm so far behind in unpacking and cataloging recent wine shipments, Jeremy. I took on too much teaching this term, but I think I can catch up this weekend."

"No problem," Brand said. "There's plenty of time and no rush." The wine Strong and Brand were sampling was a bottle of rosé from Provence. Strong picked up one of the wine glasses and poured some of the pink-colored liquid into it. "Have a sip of this, Paul. You can almost taste the Mediterranean sun. You'll especially enjoy the plum and cassis notes."

Ruskin took a mouthful and "chewed" it, releasing a flood of opulent flavors to his taste buds.

"Great stuff," Ruskin said. "Where did you get it? And why rosé?"

"I picked up a couple of bottles on my way home from New York. And why a rosé? I intend to write an article on the virtue of rosés for those who have developed a snobbish dislike for blush wines. White zinfandel has given rosé wines a bad name, but as you can tell, there's no comparison between the two."

"Do some of the boxes that arrived today contain rosés?"

"No. I just picked up a couple of these provençal wines and carried them with me on the plane. Provence produces more of this kind of wine than any other variety, but that fact is not widely known outside of France."

"Speaking of today's delivery, I didn't know you had bought some magnums."

"I didn't. Why do you think I did?"

"One of the packages was heavier than the others. And it's a little larger, too. I just assumed it contained magnums."

Strong was on her feet. "Show me the box, Paul."

Ruskin pushed his chair back from the table and walked over to the pile of unpacked boxes. He removed two of them from a stack of three, and pointed to the one remaining on the floor.

"That's the one I thought contains magnums. As you can see, it's slightly larger than the others, and it weighs a bit more too."

Strong reached into her briefcase and took out a small flashlight. She got down on her hands and knees and began inspecting the box, crawling around it and looking at it from every angle.

"What are you doing?" Ruskin asked. "What are you looking for?"

Strong did not reply. She had both hands on the floor and her face turned sideways and was sniffing along the bottom of the box. In about twenty seconds she stood up.

"I don't want you to be unduly alarmed, but we need to evacuate this house immediately. Call Mrs. Écoles on the intercom and tell her to drop whatever she is doing and leave by the kitchen door."

"Why? What did you find?" It was Brand's question.

Strong turned her flashlight back on and directed the beam to the bottom edge of the carton. "See that stain? At first glance you might think it was wine seepage from a dry cork, since sometime bottles are shipped upside down. But it isn't. No wine I've ever tasted has had diesel fuel on the nose."

Chapter 28

As soon as the Brand household was safely outside, Strong called the state police and requested that their bomb squad be sent to remove the package. Brand convinced Strong to proceed in a low-key way and that the bomber had given them a powerful tool to use in forcing things out into the open–assuming, of course, that the bomber and murderer were one and the same, a conclusion both Brand and Strong couldn't prove.

The state police arrived but with no patrol cars with lights flashing and sirens wailing. The two officers drove unmarked pickup truck. They wore protective clothing, Kevlar helmets and Lexan face shields. The officers set up a portable X-ray imaging system so they could take a look inside the package. Strong explained to Brand that the unit was one of the newest on the market and used a digital storage panel instead of X-ray film as was common with the older units. In less than two minutes the officers were looking at a black image on a bright, electroluminescent background. One agent took a photograph of the image. The storage panel—the ISP, Strong called it—would hold the image for about two hours. The photograph provided a permanent record.

After satisfying themselves that the box could be moved without undue danger, the officers carried the package to the reinforced basket in the back of the truck. Removing the bomb caused no public stir, just the way Brand wanted it. Even the neighbors remained ignorant of the events on their block.

Later that evening, Brand, Strong and Ruskin once again had assembled, this time in Brand's office, and not to share a bottle of wine but to hear Strong's report.

"The bomb was made just as I thought: Ammonium nitrate fertilizer and diesel fuel, the same combination that destroyed the Murrah Federal Building in Oklahoma City. The ingredients are easy to get and not traceable. The whole thing was quick, easy and, as we all too well know, effective. The bomb maker was a bit sloppy and got some diesel fuel on the carton, which was what called my attention to it."

"Did you trace the package?" Ruskin asked.

"That's the first thing we did, but we came up with nothing. The delivery service picked up the package from a package drop-off, and the sender used a fictitious address and a stolen credit card number. The address turned out to be a vacant lot."

"I don't understand," Ruskin said.

"Most parcel services that offer speedy delivery allow you to drop off a package at one of their pick-up locations, fill out a form giving delivery instructions and pay for the service by writing a credit card number on the form. The credit card number was stolen, but the owner of the card didn't know it. That fact only would have come to light when the owner got the monthly bill and saw the delivery service charge. Even then it might have escaped the cardholder's notice. How many of us check every item on our monthly statement?"

"But if the owner of the card didn't know it was stolen, how did the sender of the package get access to it?"

"I didn't say the *card* was stolen, Paul. The *number* was stolen. A couple of months ago I attended a law enforcement convention and rented a car at the airport. In the glove compartment I found a charge slip from the previous user's gasoline purchase. The receipt contained the card holder's name, card number and expiration date—everything I would have needed to use the card illegally."

"Wow!" Ruskin said. "I'm going to be a lot more careful from now on in keeping track of my card-card receipts. So, what did you do with the bomb?"

"We took it to the airport and opened it up with a water canon."

"What's that?"

"A fifty-caliber shell that pushes a water slug instead of a lead bullet. It punctures cartons like the one the bomber used without causing the bomb to explode. That way we can see what the bomb was made of and perhaps trace it to its maker. The Brits made extensive use of this procedure when dealing with IRA bombs. They use a variety of disrupters, as they call them. The point is to break open the bomb and disable it, which is what our boys did."

"How powerful a bomb would it have been?"

"Powerful enough to kill anyone in the room and destroy the house."

"If it was like the Oklahoma City bomb, why wouldn't it have done more damage?" Ruskin asked.

"I can probably tell you more about this bomb than you want to know, so stop me if you get bored."

"No way will I get bored," Ruskin said. "Remember, I was the first person to touch the box in this house."

"Well, to begin with, the ingredients for bombs are easy to buy in this country. But ammonium nitrate prills for fertilizer, available from your local hardware or garden shop, are pretty weak stuff. You can do some damage with a bomb made out of it, but remember in Oklahoma City the bomber used a truck full."

"How was the bomb armed?" Ruskin asked.

"Since blasting caps are regulated products and not easy to buy without leaving a paper trail—unless you steal them, of course—the bomber made a detonator. Besides, a blasting cap by itself would not have set off the bomb unless it was supplemented with a high explosive booster. So, the bomber made a detonator using a plastic pen barrel loaded with primer scrapped from rifle reloading supplies and boosted with picric acid. For all we know the bomber stole it from the university's chemistry department supply room. The trigger was a nine-volt battery activated by a spring-loaded switch. These are things easily bought in an electronics shop. One national chain of such shops is the source of so many supplies used by bomb-makers that law enforcement people refer to it as 'Bombs-R-Us.' If you had opened the parcel from the top, Paul, it would have been all over for you."

That unpleasant thought brought Ruskin out of his chair. He paced for a few moments and then leaned on the edge of Brand's desk. "Did you learn anything about the identity of the bomber from your inspection of the device?"

"Not so far. We found no fingerprints, but that's not surprising since we're dealing with a clever person who would know better than to leave usable prints behind."

"What about the materials used in making the bomb? Any chance of tracing them?"

"We'll ask around the local hardware stores and electronic shops, but I don't expect anything much to come of it. If the bomber bought supplies in different stores in widely separated places and paid cash for everything, there would be no way we could ever link up the purchases with the making of a bomb. Remember, all the ingredients are legal and, in most cases, innocent materials. Buying a bag of fertilizer is not against the law and wouldn't arouse any suspicion. The same goes for reloading supplies and electronic items."

"It's a wonder there aren't more bombs made by crazies," Ruskin said.

"There are plenty, probably more than you know about. Somewhere between thirty-five hundred and four thousand bombs and incendiary devices are planted every year—and that's only the domestic numbers. It doesn't include bombs made abroad by people acting against the interests of the United States. The police are able to locate and disarm many of the bombs, so you never hear about them."

Paul uttered a soft whistle. "I had no idea. So, how do bombers learn all this stuff?"

"It's easy. There are still copies around of a book entitled *The Anarchist's Cookbook*. It gives all kinds of 'recipes' for bombs and other techniques for causing mayhem. Some booksellers refuse to stock it, the contents are so explosive, pardon the pun."

Ruskin groaned.

"There are other sources of information. The Internet, for one. It's amazing the kind of stuff that's out there in cyberspace. You can even order the *Anarchist's Cookbook* to be downloaded onto your computer. Then too, maybe the perpetrator had some contact with militia groups. They know all about making bombs out of materials you can obtain from local sources. It's scary stuff. Using the mail and parcel delivery services for sending bombs is easier than you might think—as the Unabomber made abundantly clear."

Brand had said nothing during Strong's explanation to Ruskin. He swiveled his desk chair and faced her.

"You were right, Harri. I did a foolish thing in making the phone call, and my action put several people at risk. But at least we're seeing some movement. Thanks to your quick thinking, and Paul's being so busy that he was behind in his unpacking duties, we averted a tragedy. But now we can turn it to our advantage. In fact, the bomber's action has provided grounds for several new inferences."

"Like what?" Ruskin asked.

"For one, the bomber sees me as a threat, and Harri was correct in warning me. I was too blasé about my situation. The person who did this knows some things about me—for example, my interest in wine and the fact that I frequently receive shipments of wine here at the house. What the person didn't know is who opens the packages or where. The assumption probably was that I unpack them. It could easily have been the case, though, that Paul would have unpacked the contents of the latest shipment some time when I was not even in the house, but the bomber didn't know that. I think, the package was meant for me."

"Makes sense," Strong said.

"That means I am right on target in my suspicions. I do know who the murderer is and I now think I have figured out a way to force things to a conclusion."

"How?" Ruskin asked.

"If this were a mystery story by Agatha Christie, all the suspects would be gathered together in a resort hotel, or in a country manor owned by some earl, or in the ballroom of a cruise ship where Hercule Poirot or Miss Marple would reveal all. And if we were characters in a story by Rex Stout, we would assemble with all the suspects in Nero Wolfe's office where he, in his usual grumpy fashion, would solve the crime in full view of everybody."

"So, what are you suggesting?" Strong asked. "Get all the suspects in a room and force the guilty party to confess?"

"Something like that. Though I think we can be a bit more subtle than Nero Wolfe would have been. The strategy of using group dynamics to our advantage is a good one. The difficulty is concocting a reason for gathering everyone together in a way that doesn't arouse suspicion ahead of time. I think the perfect cover story for such an event would be a wine tasting."

"You mean, create the country-manor environment but do it in the guise of a wine tasting?" Ruskin asked.

"Exactly. We haven't had a wine tasting for awhile, so we're overdue. I understand that invitations to my tastings are popular. We should have no trouble getting the group that we want all together in the same room. When they're all here, some of them may be suspicious, but by then it will be too late for anyone to back out."

"I wouldn't want you to take unusual chances," Strong said. "We now know the lengths to which this person will go. I don't want you to put yourself at risk."

"You can have some of your officers waiting elsewhere in the house should we run into trouble, Harri. The point of all this is to put pressure on the murderer in a way that will force things to a conclusion. I have a couple of ideas for other strategies, too. We not only have the aid of group dynamics, we also have the wine itself."

"The wine?" Ruskin asked. "How so?"

"You know the old saying, *in vino veritas*. 'In wine there is truth.' We will test that saying at our tasting. It will be a grand tasting indeed."

Chapter 29

BRAND MADE PREPARATIONS for the wine tasting as carefully as any general preparing for battle. He instructed Écoles to put the white linen cloth on the dining room table and arrange twelve stations for the tasting. At each station she placed two sparkling clean wine glasses, one for whites and one for reds. When washing the glasses she was careful to avoid any residue of detergent that might alter the taste of the wines.

At opposite ends of the table she set two candles whose flames would help tasters judge the color of the wines. At strategic locations she also placed pitchers for water, silver trays for small slices of crusty French bread and cheese cubes, and vessels for spitting. At tastings some guests thought spitting was crude and felt compelled to swallow every taste. The veterans, though, knew that the point of the evening was the tasting itself and saved their drinking for the end of the tasting when they could finish off the remaining wines, with special attention to the best ones.

Because of the need for haste, Brand and Ruskin had divided up the list and telephoned each guest with a personal invitation to the tasting. No one had turned them down. Innate curiosity and the reputation of Brand's tastings was enough to produce unanimous acceptance of the invitation—even from Archie Scott, angry as he was at Brand.

In fact Scott was the first to arrive. Even though he had become *persona non grata* in some circles on campus, to those who enjoyed seeing the administration publicly embarrassed, Scott had become something of a hero. Even though he was facing possible unemployment, he went about his duties as though nothing was amiss in his life. Some of the faculty said that he was too dumb to know what a pariah he had become. Others said his behavior was an example of his extreme cleverness. Inviting Scott, though necessary, was difficult for Brand, given Archie's unfailing denseness about all things relating to wine. That was a bigger concern for Brand than the threatening phone call Scott had made.

Tabitha McKenzie was the next to arrive. With the weather turning nippy in the evening hours, she was glad for an excuse to wear her fur coat. She arrived at the front door of Brand's house clad in mink from the tip of her turned-up collar to the tops of her Ferragamo shoes. Ruskin greeted her in the foyer and helped her remove her coat. Melanie Carter was standing by to assist. As she carried the luxurious fur to the hall closet, Carter could not stifle the impulse to run her fingers through the thick fur. She glanced at Ruskin and gave him an expression that combined the raised eyebrow and upward rolling of eyes. Tabitha McKenzie had her back to Carter and could not see the expression that conveyed both envy and disapproval of such a display of conspicuous consumption.

Carter led the dean's widow into the dining room and made small talk with her and Scott while waiting for additional guests. Ruskin remained on duty by the door.

Miles Newlin and Gary Hockney, dressed in the casual style of the graduate students they were, came up the stairs together. Strong followed behind, and all three entered the foyer at the same time and shed their coats into Ruskin's waiting arms. He directed them to the dining room where Carter made sure the conversational circle was widened.

Danny Bennett appeared at the door dressed as though he just stepped from an Ingmar Bergman film: black leather jeans, black turtleneck sweater, black boots, black coat. He said scarcely a word while handing his jacket to Ruskin. He looked into the dining room, and if he felt out of place being the only undergraduate student in the group, he did nothing to show it. He strode into the dining room and found an unoccupied corner where he stood with what he fancied was a James Dean slouch. Carter caught sight of him from the corner of her eye and walked over to him, determined to draw him into conversation. Bennett's sullen demeanor disappeared. It is difficult to remain aloof in the presence of the prettiest woman in the room.

The College of Professional Studies was represented by the now-interim dean George Helms and his secretary, Naomi Beals. They both arrived at the same time. Helms held the door for Beals and then helped her with her coat. They were engaged in an animated conversation as they walked up the sidewalk to the front door, and their entry into the foyer did not interrupt it. Ruskin took their coats and directed them to the dining room.

As Cynthia Lemaster got out of her car, she spied Milton Coles driving up in his Lincoln. This must be a pretty posh affair if the president is coming, she thought to herself. Though she knew that her feminist views did not endear her to the administration, she waited until Coles found a parking place and then walked beside him to the front door. She did not know that the president was there by special arrangement. Before setting the date of the tasting, Brand gave him a full report and disclosed the plan he had developed for forcing the perpetrator out in the open. Coles had to rearrange his schedule but promised to attend.

Lemaster entered the dining room ahead of the president, who was a master of making an entrance. He started greeting everyone he knew and introduced himself to Carter, Hockney and Newlin, whom he had not met before. When he came to Archie Scott, he extended his hand. Scott did nothing in response at first, then reluctantly shook it. To Coles's pleasant "good evening," Scott mumbled an incoherent reply. The president was about to extend his hand and greetings to Danny Bennett when Brand entered the room, closing the door to the living room behind him. The click of the door catch was loud enough to capture everyone's attention. As though on signal they turned to look at Brand.

"Good evening, ladies and gentlemen. Thank you for accepting my invitation to this wine tasting."

Then with the classic statement of the fictional detective he said, "You may wonder why I called all of you here this evening."

The task of selecting the wines to be featured was not an easy one for Brand. Being a teacher, he liked his tastings to be educational as well as enjoyable. He also liked to invite a variety of persons to his tastings—the aficionados as well as the beginners. It was as much a part of the pleasure of the occasion to see a neophyte discover the pleasures of really fine wine as it was to hear the assessments of the veteran tasters with trained palates. He avoided the highly tannic wines which tended to be unapproachable when young. And he also liked to include a variety of wines from different grapes and regions to show off the many possibilities of winemaking. He wanted a proper balance between wines that were interesting and yet approachable to the beginner and those that would pique the interest of the veteran taster.

Sometimes Brand's tastings would be built around a theme—all Bordeaux, all Chardonnays from various regions, a selection of various examples of Chianti, wines from the pinot noir grape made in Burgundy and Oregon. The possibilities were nearly limitless. Tonight, however, the theme would be wines from his latest buying trip. He asked everyone to have a seat and then began his preliminary remarks.

"This is one of the most varied groups I have had at a tasting, and that's what I meant by saying you may wonder why you're here. Some of you may have already figured out the common thread that binds you together, but if you have not, let me explain."

At this Brand paused and reached over to the silver tray that held the five bottles of wine that were to be tasted. He moved it slightly on the table, positioning it directly in front of his place.

"As you all probably know, President Coles asked me to assist the official investigation into the tragic deaths of two of our colleagues, Dean McKenzie and Professor Giles. I say 'assist' because the official investigation is being conducted by the police. I think all of you know Police Chief Harriet Strong here to my left."

All eyes shifted to the chief.

"Each of you has assisted me in my investigation, and I wanted to thank all of you for that assistance and to acknowledge the important part you have had in my inquiries."

Tabitha McKenzie interrupted. "Does that mean you have completed your investigation, Professor Brand? Do the police know who killed my husband?"

"Thank you for asking those questions. The answer is no. Although I will let her speak for herself, neither Chief Strong nor I feel that the investigation is complete. We are still searching for the individual who brought about the two untimely deaths. I will, through the course of the evening, share with you the evidence we've collected during the investigation, but first, let's taste some wine."

Brand selected one of the bottles from the tray and handed it to Ruskin, who began pouring small amounts into the white wine glass at each place setting.

"Those of you who have attended these events before know that I like to build them around a theme. Tonight's theme is paired wines from my recent buying trip to New York. Our little town, though delightful in its own way, is at the bottom of the wine food chain. It's difficult to find many of the finer wines in a small town like College Falls for the simple reason that they tend to go first to the larger wine markets. If you're a producer of a fine California Chardonnay and produce only limited quantities, you want to insure that it is available in the largest markets—New York, Chicago, the large cities in California—because that's where the wine writers and critics are. You'll have the best opportunity to get noticed there by wine reviewers."

Ruskin had reached Brand's place and had poured a bit of the straw-colored liquid into his glass.

"If you're a wine distributor and have worked long and hard to get your restaurant clients to upgrade their wine lists, you're not going to disappoint them by telling them that the premium wine they agreed to list on their menu is no longer available to them because you had to send some to College Falls."

Brand continued talking as he swirled the wine in his glass. He paused to take a good whiff of the wine's nose.

"So if one wants to purchase premium wines, it is almost always necessary to go to major cities to look for them. This Chardonnay you are about to taste is an excellent example of how far California producers have come. It's not overly oaked, and you'll find the nose to be delicate yet almost perfumey."

"Pretty durn good," Scott said, as he downed his allotment in a single swallow. Other guests were murmuring their approval of the wine and noting the clarity of its color.

"When you've finished tasting this one, rinse out your glasses using the water from the pitchers on the table. You can dump the rinse water into one of the silver buckets on the table. They can also be used for spitting, by the way. Paul will then give you a taste of an excellent white Burgundy, made from the same grape as this California Chardonnay. I'd be interested in your evaluation of the two wines."

As Brand was giving these instructions, Strong was still "chewing" the wine and then leaned over to one of the buckets and spit it out.

Danny Bennett looked at the police chief with wide-eyed astonishment. Never having been to a tasting before, Bennett was shocked to see someone spit in such a formal environment. Miles Newlin, sitting next to Danny, savored his wine a sip at a time.

"On a graduate student's budget, I never get to enjoy wine of this quality," he said. "I'm not going to spit out a drop, even if I have to call a taxi to drive me home."

Brand continued. "I now want you to compare the two wines. They are made from the same grape but come from different regions, have a different *terroir*, as the French put it. You will notice the milder sense of oak, due to the different ways of aging the wine and the use of French oak barrels instead of American oak."

"The nose is so delicate," President Coles said. "It has interesting overtones of pear and grapefruit."

"You can smell all that?" Bennett asked, astonished.

"That and more. It's a matter of experience. The more wines you taste, the larger your catalog of aromas becomes."

"Which one cost the most?" Scott asked? "I would assume the French wine did."

Brand emptied the remnants of his wine into the tasting bucket before he answered Scott. "I really don't want to tell you at this point, Archie. I don't want considerations of price to affect your judgment. Sometimes people think the most expensive wine has to taste the best, but that's not always the case.

"While you're savoring your white Burgundy, let me return to the notion of paired wines," Brand said. "These wines are similar and different, yet they are related. As I got further into my investigation of the two deaths on campus, I discovered the same kind of similarity and difference. The two deaths are both murders. They probably were committed by the same person. Yet what are the differences? Was the death of Dean McKenzie deliberate or intentional? It's fairly obvious that Professor Giles's death was a deliberate act of murder, but could the dean's death have been an accident? Did the perpetrator intend only to destroy the house and unwittingly commit a murder in the process? Those are the kinds of questions I've been wrestling with these past few weeks."

"Are we here to taste wine or to hear your theories about the two deaths?" Lemaster asked. "If I'd known you were going to carry on with your theories about the death of the dean and my friend, Sarah, I wouldn't have come."

"Why not?" Brand asked. "Since Sarah was your friend, I would assume you are as anxious to find the murderer as I am—maybe more so."

"I didn't mean that....I just thought—"

"Let me continue," Brand said. "Just as these two wines are similar by being from the same grape, so the two deaths are similar in being by the same hand. But just as you can discover different nuances in each wine, so each murder has its own subtleties. While I go on, I'll ask Paul to pour the next wine, an excellent example of a Bordeaux-style red wine from California, a 1992 vintage, a wine that the critic Robert Parker says is near perfection."

Ruskin began the process of moving from one person to the next, pouring the rich garnet-colored liquid into the red wine glass.

"So what is the connection between the two murders? Danny, your student group had a very public and nasty quarrel with the dean. I assume it was you, or one of your group, who wrote 'Death to the Dean' on the side of Bucks Hall. We know that your group placed a flaming object on his lawn the very night his house was torched. Did you or someone in your group get carried away and think it would be great fun to see the dean's house go up in flames, never intending to kill him, but just to take revenge for your public humiliation?"

"Now, just a minute. I never killed anybody. I didn't set fire to the dean's house. Nobody in my organization did either. Sure, we wrote the graffiti on the side of Bucks Hall, but what harm did that do? Students have free speech too. It was a common tactic during the student protests of the '60s. We were just trying to get the feel for what those demonstrations were like. You could almost say it was a class project."

"I'm not accusing you of the crime, Danny. I'm merely pointing out that you had both means and opportunity, maybe even motive. At least for the death of the dean. I haven't been able to find out any connection you might have had with Sarah Giles."

"You can't pin this on me," Danny said, with a demeanor that suggested he had been watching too many film noir classics. "I didn't do anything."

"No, I don't think you did," Brand said. "But your public and nasty rhetoric set up a climate in which someone brought death to the dean. I see everyone has the California meritage now; take a sip and tell me what you think."

"Pretty durn good," Scott said. "I like it even better than the white wine."

"Highly complex on the palate," President Coles said. Other comments came from around the table indicating that even the inexperienced tasters found this to be an exceptional wine.

"Cynthia, you were one of Sarah's closest associates, and you were at the dean's reception. You also had reason to be angry at him for his behavior at the tenure review committee meeting. You could have come back to the dean's house after taking Professor Giles home and set fire to it after everyone left."

"Now, just a minute. I didn't come here to be accused like this—"

"But like Danny," Brand continued, "I can see no motive for you to take Sarah's life. There could have been professional rivalries I know nothing about, jealousies perhaps, but I didn't seriously consider you as a suspect."

Lemaster sat back down in her chair and with an excessive flourish finished off the wine in her glass.

"Now I'll ask Paul to pour a first-growth Bordeaux for you. Tell me which of the two wines you find more satisfactory. After you've tasted each, I'll tell you the price of these and the Chardonnays we just tasted—since Archie is interested in price—to see if your taste matches the cost of the wines. Be sure to rinse out your glass before Paul reaches your place."

While Ruskin made the rounds again, Brand continued.

"Archie, you have reasons for wanting both Clem and Sarah dead."

"Now, hold on there. I don't have to sit here and listen to this. I thought we came here to taste some wine, not to be insulted."

"Hear me out, Archie. Everybody now knows that you were holding two full-time positions, but did the dean find out about this before you were able to disentangle yourself from one of them? And did you then kill him to keep the information from becoming public too soon?"

"No...no, I did nothing of the kind. And how dare you accuse me in front of everyone like this."

"You could have returned from Middletown and waited until an opportune moment to set fire to the dean's house, knowing full well that he would probably not rouse himself from his alcohol-induced stupor. You picked a time when his wife was out of the house so you wouldn't compound your crime by killing two persons."

"I'll admit that I haven't shed any tears over the dean's death, but I didn't kill him."

"And then there was Sarah. Did you kill her because she knew that you had set fire to the dean's house? Or because she knew about your dual life? Chief Strong discovered an unaccounted-for deposit in her account of two thousand dollars. He also found that you removed the same amount from your savings account and later converted it to cash. She was blackmailing you, wasn't she? She was demanding payment to keep quiet about your double life, a situation she discovered because her ex-husband is on the staff of Middletown College. Don't bother to deny it. I've already talked to Dr. Forrest, her former husband."

Scott pushed his chair back from the table with such vigor that it crashed to the floor. He stood up and took several steps away from the table.

"I'm not listening to another word of this. I'm leaving right now."

"If you leave now, Archie, we might think you are admitting that you're the murderer. Do you really want us to think that?"

Scott took a deep breath and held it like a deep sea diver getting ready to plunge into the ocean. Then he picked up his chair and sat down. "OK, she was blackmailing me, but I hadn't paid her anything yet. I wrote out a check for her, and she laughed at me. Said she wanted cash. I got the cash ready, but she died before I got the chance to give it to her. But I didn't kill her. And I didn't kill the dean, either. You've got to believe me."

"So if you didn't kill her, what were you prepared to do? Keep paying her two thousand dollars a month forever? Is that what you expect us to believe?"

"I was planning to resign from Middletown by the end of the year. If I could just keep her quiet until then, I figured I'd be OK. By the time I quit paying her, I would no longer have two positions, and if she talked about my situation then, I'd make public that she'd been blackmailing me."

"In other words, you were going to blackmail the blackmailer?"

"I wouldn't put it like that. I offered to help her in the transition—colleague to colleague, you know—but she became strident. She made fun of me. But I didn't kill her."

"How did you get her into the car? You drugged her, didn't you? If Chief Strong gets a search warrant for your house, will she find some sleeping pills there? Or have you disposed of them by now? We can check with your physician to see if you had a prescription for barbiturates. You removed some of them from your prescription bottle and put them into an empty aspirin bottle, which you relabeled, so everyone would think that Sarah had gotten these from a friend. And the suicide note. You desperately wanted us to accept Sarah as the dean's killer so we'd quit looking for the real killer."

At this, Tabitha McKenzie began to sob softly. She reached into her purse and removed a handkerchief which she used to dab at her eyes. "Archie, I never dreamed it was you—"

"It wasn't!" Scott shouted. "I didn't kill anybody. You've got it all wrong."

Brand picked up the last bottle of wine from the table.

"Let's pour this last bottle of wine. I'm not going to tell you what it is yet. After you've sampled it, I'll reveal its source."

Ruskin again made the rounds of all the tasting stations. Scott pushed his glass away and refused to take any of the wine.

"As I said when we first began the tasting, the theme tonight is paired wines. I have another little twist on the last pairing for you. As I said earlier, I just returned from an auction and buying trip to New York City. Most of the wines I purchased there have arrived, but we haven't yet had time to unpack them all. I thought it might be interesting to bring one of the cartons to the table and let you choose from its contents the best wine to complement the one Paul has just poured in your glass. Frankly, I've forgotten exactly what this box contains, so it will be as much a challenge for me as for you. Paul, would you please get the carton?"

The box that Ruskin brought to the table was identical to the one that had contained the bomb. Before the original carton was destroyed, Strong took photographs and wrote down a complete description. For this evening's events Brand recreated the original down to the stolen credit card number on the shipping label. Ruskin carried the package around the entire table like a pastor carrying a newly baptized infant before the congregation.

"Who wants to help open the box?" Brand asked.

From around the table there were stares following Ruskin as he moved around the room with the box. No one spoke, yet the unasked questions were evident on everyone's face.

At Brand's signal, he placed the box directly in front of Archie Scott.

"Archie," Brand said. "I wonder if you would do us the honor of opening this box. Paul has a utility knife for you to use. We'll also let you choose the wine to pair with the one just poured, though you will have to reconsider and let Paul give you some to accomplish the task correctly."

Ruskin handed the knife to Scott.

"Sure. I don't know what's going on, but why not. Go ahead, Paul. Pour me some of that wine."

Scott gripped the box with his left hand and poised the utility knife along one edge of the top. But before Scott could cut through the sealing tape,

George Helms and Naomi Beals bolted for the door. So quick was their exit that neither said a word. They rushed headlong through the French doors separating the dining room from the hall and directly into the arms of two uniformed police officers.

"Don't worry," Brand called to them. "This is just a box of wine. What did you think it contained?"

Two police officers escorted Helms and Beals back into the dining room. Nearly everyone was standing now, and all were talking at once.

"If everybody will sit down, I will explain what just happened."

The police, directed by Chief Strong, placed handcuffs on both Beals and Helms and sat them apart from the table on chairs placed against the wall.

"What you have just witnessed, ladies and gentlemen, is a confession. Both Naomi and George thought there was a bomb in this box. It was intended for me, but thanks to Chief Strong's quick thinking, it harmed no one."

Turning to the two, Brand continued. "Were you both in on the murders, or did Naomi get dragged into this affair later? Do you want to tell us how everything transpired, or should I?"

"You don't understand," Beals said. "We're in love. We're going to get married—"

"Shut up, you idiot," Helms said. "Don't say a word. They can't prove a thing. We want a lawyer."

"All in due course," Brand said. Allow me to explain to this puzzled crowd what all this means."

Brand stood up and began to pace the floor in his typical lecturing style.

"We felt that the two deaths were related. Due to the Chief's quick analysis, it became clear that Professor Giles's death was a staged event, that it wasn't suicide at all but that she was murdered. We then began to look at every possible suspect; and forgive me, but all of you at one time or another had to be considered. Yes, even you, Tabitha."

At that, she gave a gasp and began to sob again. Strong picked up the conversation at this point.

"The sad fact is," she said, "that most murders are committed by a member of the family or someone the victim knows. We always start with the family. It became clear to us, though, that Mrs. McKenzie was not involved with her husband's death. And we could find nothing that linked her to Professor Giles in any way."

"So that brought us back to professional colleagues," Brand said. "The puzzling thing was how hard someone was working to make us believe that Gary Hockney was the culprit—the anonymous phone call, the books on bombs and incendiary devices in his carrel. Even your comment, Tabitha, about his loud exchanges with your husband pointed toward Gary Hockney."

"I had nothing to do with any of this," Hockney said. "I shoot off my mouth a lot, but I would never kill anybody."

"And no one thinks you did," Brand said. "But someone wanted us to believe you did. When I met with George Helms as part of my investigation, I noticed how he suddenly became interested in you when I told him what I knew about your background—your Army service and all. By the way, Gary, you should work on ways of better controlling your anger. Shooting off your mouth, as you put it, may get you into deep trouble one of these days."

Hockney said nothing and kept his eyes focused on a minute inspection of his shoelaces.

"After the police proved that the dean's death was due to arson, we needed to find out who set the fire bomb. The murderer probably took it as a gift that suspicion was directed to Sarah Giles. It was just her bad luck to be carrying around two empty gasoline cans in her car."

"What about Sarah's death?" Cynthia Lemaster asked. "Was it suicide, or was she murdered?"

"Oh, it was murder, all right," Brand said. "Chief Strong was quick to see too many inconsistencies with a genuine suicide. And when she discovered the cash deposit of two thousand dollars into Sarah's bank account, the possibility of blackmail was the obvious explanation."

"Getting rid of a blackmailer is not an unusual motive for murder," Strong said. "People have been killed for a lot less."

"So, whom was Sarah blackmailing?" Brand asked rhetorically. "Through a chance conversation with her former husband, I discovered in her study a copy of a brochure from Middletown College that revealed Archie's double life. She knew about it, and the police later found what appeared to be a transfer of money from Archie to Sarah. That made Archie a suspect. But the evidence at that point was entirely circumstantial."

"I didn't kill her," Scott said. "You can't make me out to be the killer."

Brand ignored the outburst and continued. "What revealed the killer was Professor Giles's e-mail records. After putting an unconscious Sarah Giles into her car and directing the exhaust through the window, the killer came back to her computer and wrote a suicide note. But then he reformatted her hard drive to destroy all her e-mail messages. Most of them were innocuous, but some were veiled references to the fact that Sarah was using information she had just uncovered as leverage. Namely, she knew that 'Doctor' Helms doesn't have a doctorate degree."

"They know, George," Naomi said. "They know."

"Shut up, you fool. Don't say a word."

"I can prove that you never completed your Ph.D. degree," Brand said. "I did the same thing Sarah Giles must have done: I called your graduate school and talked to one of the senior members of the department. They'd lost track of you over the years, but the professor did confirm that you never completed your dissertation. They didn't know that you've been passing yourself off as having the degree."

George Helms said not a word. The tight pucker of his lips reflected his resolve to say nothing.

"At this point I am extrapolating," Brand said, "but here is how I think it played out. Sarah Giles found out about your lack of a doctorate. She approached you with a proposition: she would keep quiet about what she knew if you would approve her for tenure. You refused and offered her money from your own bank account instead. She took the money but later on still pressured you for tenure. You feared there would be no end to the payments, even if you granted her tenure. So you killed her. It was probably at that point that you enlisted the aid of Naomi Beals. You probably sent her to see Sarah with some phony message about her tenure. Did you instruct her to tell Sarah that you had decided to award her tenure? Probably. I haven't figure out how you got Naomi to drug her. This is just a guess, but maybe Naomi dropped sleeping pills into her beverage. It wouldn't be far fetched to think that Sarah, being a good hostess, offered something to drink, especially if Naomi had just told here she was going to be awarded tenure. Maybe they were celebrating with a bottle of Champagne."

Beals was weeping quietly. "Tell them, George. They know. Let's get it over with."

"Shut up, for God's sake."

"What you didn't know was that some of Sarah's e-mail messages were still on the central server. You thought you had deleted everything, but you had not. I could tell by the intensity of your exchanges with Sarah that you felt under pressure, even though your communications with her were indirect."

"You can't prove anything."

"I can prove enough," Brand said. "And I suspect that Naomi is going to help us put this matter to rest."

"I didn't know he was going to kill her. I just thought he wanted her to be unconscious so he could erase some of her computer files."

"Shut up, woman. Don't say a word."

"Whether you knew his intentions or not, you're an accessory to a murder, Naomi. I hope you'll make a full confession to the police. To continue the scenario, after Sarah was unconscious, George dragged her to the garage where he completed the deed."

Chief Strong gave a motion with her head, and the two uniformed police led Helms and Beals to the door.

"I think we're finished here for the moment," Strong said. "If all of you will excuse us."

"I think we're finished with the wine tasting as well," Brand said. "After all this sad business is finished, perhaps we can all reassemble for another tasting…without the overtones of murder."

Chapter 30

BRAND AND STRONG WERE REVIEWING the essential elements of the case when Paul Ruskin and Melanie Carter came in the front door. Brand invited them to join him in the study.

"Harri and I were just filling each other in," Brand said. "Why don't you join us?"

Paul placed his briefcase by the foot of the staircase and followed Melanie into the study.

"It's all wrapped up," Harriet said. "Naomi Beals made a complete statement that amounts to a full confession. She didn't have the stomach for continuing the deception."

"I still don't get it," Melanie said. "How did Ms. Beals get dragged into this mess in the first place?"

Harriet answered. "It's the oldest story in the world. She did it for love. But she got involved only after the fire at the dean's house."

"So why did Helms set fire to the dean's house?" Paul asked.

"He felt that McKenzie had not supported his efforts to seek a deanship elsewhere. Naomi Beals claims that Helms's sense of things was correct, that the dean didn't provide much support for his desire to find a job elsewhere. The resentment Helms felt toward McKenzie was real, but the clincher was that the dean discovered that Helms didn't have a doctorate and threatened to expose him if he didn't resign. The dean wanted Helms not only to resign his administrative position but to leave higher education as well. All this is in Beals's statement."

At this point Brand broke in. "Helms accomplished two things by killing the dean. He protected his secret, and he also felt that his chances for a deanship would be enhanced if he could be interim dean here at Calloway. To accomplish that meant getting the dean out of the way. That's the reason he destroyed the dean's house. He waited until Tabitha was gone, since his target was the dean alone. The faculty reception provided the perfect opportunity for him. The dean had drunk so much that he would not likely wake up during the fire. It was a deliberate act of murder."

"Beals had nothing to do with the arson," Harriet said. "At least that's what she claims. She says she didn't even know that Helms had torched the dean's house. She got involved only when Professor Giles started blackmailing Helms about his lack of a degree and agreed to help him drug her so he could erase her computer files. That's pretty naive, however, since the only way for him to protect his secret was to kill Sarah. George and Naomi had been lovers for over a year, though nobody knew about it. He brought her into his plans for Professor Giles because he needed an accomplice. He took her to the professor's house thinking that the presence of a woman would not be threatening. It was Beals who put the sleeping pills into Professor Giles's drink. And it was champagne, just as I suspected."

"I find it incredible that someone could have gone as far in academic life as George Helms did while hiding the fact that he hadn't completed his graduate work," Paul said. "Why didn't someone check him out much earlier in his career?"

"There's a lot of trust in academia," Brand said. "We tend to believe what people tell us. You can bet, though, that this university is going to check out everything from now on."

"I think I'm following all this," Melanie said. "Helms doesn't have a doctorate, a fact that Dean McKenzie found out. The dean threatened him with exposure unless Helms left higher education. By killing McKenzie, Helms took care of that problem and also set up himself up to be interim dean, an appointment he thought would help him get a deanship elsewhere. But wouldn't his lack of a degree be found out when he applied for another position?"

"As incredible as it sounds," Brand said, "applicants for these senior administrative positions are often taken at face value. A friend of mine who's with an executive search firm told me that fully one-fourth of the candidates they screen misrepresent their credentials in some way, though lying about a doctorate is extreme. Most hiring schools do not even ask for a transcript. One of the roles of a search firm is to check all applicants thoroughly in order to discover things like this."

"So the dean's death created a vacancy. How did Helms know he would be named interim dean?"

"It wasn't a sure thing," Brand said. "There was always the possibility that the president would name someone else, but it's not uncommon for an associate dean to be named interim, and that was what George was counting on."

"What made Professor Giles look into his background and discover that he didn't have a doctorate?" Melanie asked.

Brand was quick with an answer. "Remember that she desperately wanted tenure. When George Helms was named interim dean, she thought there might be something in his background that would help her put some pressure on him to grant her tenure. Sarah probably couldn't believe her luck when she found out his big secret. She then used that knowledge to pressure George into granting her tenure. George suspected that tenure would just be the beginning of her demands. George saw a way to get rid of her when she emerged as a suspect in the dean's death. He contrived the suicide and the note to make her appear to be the murderer. If he had succeeded, he would have done two things: given us the murderer of the dean, thereby removing any possibility of his being suspected, and also getting rid of the problem Sarah had become. When Harri didn't buy Sarah's death as a suicide, Helms tried to give us another suspect in the form of Gary Hockney."

"In fact, Helms may have decided to kill Professor Giles even before I announced on the radio show that she was no longer a suspect," Strong said. "That just moved his timetable up some."

Melanie broke in with a question. "So Professor Giles was blackmailing two people? Scott for money and Helms for tenure? But at the tasting Professor Scott said he hadn't paid her any money."

"He lied about that," Brand said. "Not surprising, since his whole life had become one big lie."

"So who attacked you in the cellar?" Paul asked.

"It was Helms," Strong said. "He was afraid that I'd found something on Clem's computer that would point to him as the murderer. I hadn't, but George didn't know that."

"What made it clear to you that Helms was the murderer?"

"Sarah's e-mail files, just as Helms feared. George and Sarah had exchanged several messages about his situation. The wording was discreet, but Helms knew that if someone read the e-mail his secret would be out. So he deleted every exchange he and Sarah had. If his lack of a doctorate were to become known, he would have been out as interim dean and his prospects for a permanent deanship ruined."

"You mean he didn't know about the e-mail messages still on the server?" Paul asked.

"Apparently not," Brand said. "Few persons on campus understand all the intricacies of networks and servers. When I saw the content of the deleted messages between Sarah and George, I suspected that he was hiding a huge professional secret and would probably do anything to keep it from coming out. It wasn't difficult for me to construct the supposed scenario, but proving it would be difficult. So I called him and told him I knew he killed Sarah and Clem. My reason was to provoke him into an action that would allow us to prove his guilt."

"But you didn't count on the bomb," Harriet said. "You provoked him into action, all right. You almost got yourself killed."

Brand shifted in his sheet and continued. "By the time George decided to send me the bomb, he had grown nearly immune to murder, so killing me was the only way he could see to protect himself from being charged with killing the dean and Sarah. He still thought that Clem must have had something on his computer that would implicate him, so he kept going back to be sure. It was Helms who was in the office when I stopped by one evening and found the computer turned on, though I didn't see him. It was lucky for me that I didn't, for by then he was becoming desperate. He also got into Sarah's office and erased her hard drive."

"Why didn't he just give Professor Giles tenure and be done with it?" Paul asked.

"It's the classic case of one murder leading to another," Brand said. "Once George committed one murder, he felt he had to kill a second person to hide his crime and his professional secret. He would've killed me too had Harri not discovered the bomb. By telling Naomi about the bomb, George got her even more deeply involved in his crime, thereby helping to insure her silence."

Turning to Brand, Paul said, "This would make a really good story. I could write it and be Boswell to your Dr. Johnson, or Dr. Watson to your Sherlock Holmes, or Archie Goodwin to your Nero Wolfe."

"Go for it," Brand said. "though you may not have anything else to write about that is quite as exciting as these events have been. At least I hope you don't. I've had quite enough threats on my life."

Brand got up from behind his desk, moved next to Harriet on the couch and took both of her hands into his. "Harri, these attacks have made me realize that I need to put my grieving behind me and get on with my life. What do you say about our going somewhere where the sea is blue, the beaches sandy, the sky clear, and the water warm?"

"Who's going to call the travel agent?" she replied. "You or me?"

Epilogue

Jeremy Brand remains at Calloway State and is making plans to travel to California for the grape harvest to gather additional information for another book on wine.

Archie Scott became dean of the business program at a proprietary college that receives state funding to train former welfare recipients for meaningful employment.

Tabitha McKenzie used the insurance settlement to open a successful catering business. She is in great demand for catering the best parties in College Falls.

Gary Hockney abandoned his interest in a business degree and moved to Maui, where he owns and runs a surf shop.

Miles Newlin completed his doctorate and is an assistant professor of humanities at a university in the Midwest.

Lewis Thomas was denied promotion from his colleagues in the political science department and currently heads a movement to unionize the faculty at Calloway State.

Danny Bennett went to law school but did not graduate and now works in a brokerage firm in their arbitrage department.

Milton Coles left the university presidency and became head of a charitable foundation in New York City.

Cynthia Lemaster wrote a women's studies textbook and filed an EEOC complaint against the university for unfair treatment of women in hiring and promotion.

Harvey Glock left the university and bought a upstate weekly newspaper that is fighting the county commissioners over tax abatements used to attract industries.

Sally Turner took a job at a supermarket tabloid where her latest story deals with mutant sea turtles that are terrorizing south Florida.

George Helms and **Naomi Beals** are guests of the state. Helms is working on his dissertation. Beals offered to type it for him, if the warden of her prison will allow it.

Paul Ruskin continues to work for Jeremy Brand but has limited his teaching at Calloway to one course per quarter. He is completing his second book.

Melanie Carter completed her doctorate and works for a bank offering wholesale banking services. She and Ruskin continue to see each other, mainly on weekends.

Acknowledgments

Many people have helped me in writing this book, and I here acknowledge their assistance with thanks. Elsa Kramer for her editing assistance, David Bruce for his proofreading skills; Chuck Emrick for suggesting the project in the first place; Robert Gall for his sharp pencil and insightful comments; Paul Gandel for sharing his knowledge of computers; George Jackson for help with various technical matters involving explosives; Gene Mikel for getting me in touch with technical experts; Ron Stefanski for his unflagging support and for sharing his knowledge of book selling; and my wife, Audrey—my researcher, first reader and best critic. To them all I express sincere thanks and free them from any responsibility for inadequacies the book exhibits.

0-595-33334-6

Made in the USA
Lexington, KY
15 September 2019